VENDETTA VICE

THE MEDICI SQUADRON

Jacquelyne Morison

Medici Publishing
Cheltenham

ISBN 978-0-9929973-7-3

Published by Medici Publishing in 2021

Revised and reprinted in 2022

Cover design by GermanCreative

Contents

PART I
SKATING ON THIN ICE

ROUCHUKA'S DISILLUSION

The screaming, the yelling and the wailing had all ceased at long last. The lights had been dimmed several times after six encores. The adulating fans were wending their way homeward eventually.

It was the final concert of an eight-week run at the Scullen Stadium in the north of England and Rouchuka was so relieved that rehearsals and performances were all over now for a couple of weeks. She began to breathe again.

The stage had been cleared and swept clean of its debris. The detritus had included some shoes and someone's shirt. Did that someone think that the band could not afford to buy their own or that they wanted someone else's cast-offs? Bracelets, an earring, some exotic necklaces and a purple wig had also found their way on to the stage somehow as well. A pair of soggy knickers had even been hurled on to the stage! Perhaps the ex-owner of the pants would be chilly where it hurts on the way home as a punishment. Was this an example of humanity these days? For fuck's sake! Not exactly unusual, however, for an audience gripped by mass hysteria. And certainly not the first time that this sort of thing had happened. Rouchuka still shuddered with disgust at the thought of such incidents.

Several bouquets of flowers from her dressing room had already been taken along to the nearest hospice – unwanted by the band and impractical to transport home anyway – but gratefully received by the hospital staff and patients. The expensive chocolates sent to Rouchuka from persons unknown had been greedily scoffed by the stage technicians and by the front of house staff. But they had certainly earned this treat several times over. Rouchuka did not have the chocolate-eating tendency.

Harriet Chantry – known to the rest of the world by her stage-name of Rouchuka – felt nothing but sheer relief at this moment now that the show and the whole run in the north was over. The reprieve had been long awaited. A storm cloud had dispersed suddenly and the sun was now shining through at last for Rouchuka.

While Rouchuka loved it when onstage, she had snatched herself a moment of respite in her dressing room after the final close of the show. The delightful Greta, Rouchuka's personal assistant, had handed her a glass of sparkling mineral water mixed with apple juice before making a rapid exit from Rouchuka's dressing room. Rouchuka did not indulge in the champers which some others were gurgling down at lightning speed in one of the other dressing rooms, perhaps accompanied by a dollop or two of speed too.

When possible Rouchuka always insisted on a dressing room away from the rest of the boys in the band and, on most occasions these days, she was granted her wish. The only so-called invader at this time was Greta who was quiet, patient and unassuming and who understood and respected her employer's needs.

The luxury of a separate dressing room was not as a result of any modesty but simply because Rouchuka had little in common with her workmates. She was a self-confessed loner. Someone who relished her own space and felt apart from the general hubbub of showbiz life.

Coming off the stage, she had kicked off her high heels, had handed her dress to Greta and had simply lounged back on the couch in her dressing room. Greta quietly hung up Rouchuka's dress lovingly and then unobtrusively left her alone. Rouchuka had worn a silver panelled sequined dress with long flowing scarves for the show. This outfit had been made specially for her by Jaffeta Clarkson of Paris in order to reveal most of her body without being embarrassing or obscene while simultaneously allowing for maximum dance-movement ability.

Rouchuka reflected on where she was now and how she had got there. She had achieved worldwide fame in just eight years. She had metamorphosed from an ambitious and excitable teenager into a superstar. She had felt that stardom was the epitome of her wildest dreams in the past and her mind and body were constantly electrified as she climbed the ladder swiftly to worldwide success. She had achieved this meteoric rise to fame from just one unbelievable talent contest which she had won in her late teens. From this accolade had stemmed the opportunity to form a band with five similarly talented boys. The band had been manufactured by their agent, now their business manager, Gerry Paxton, and their Mr-Fix-It producer, Henry Sissingford.

But Rouchuka's dreams had, over the course of her career, turned into a nightmare. Now that she was on top, the excitement had waned and the tours had become a ceaselessly tiring and somewhat mundane experience. Most of the boys did not find this so but she did. Perhaps Rouchuka's ambition was only a teenage fantasy which had dispersed abruptly because she had grown up equally rapidly in the process? Disillusion had set in steadfastly. Rouchuka no longer relished her work to the extent that she felt she ought to have done. Basically she was rudderless.

Rouchuka also now felt that her life was not her own. She knew she was being used by most of the world. People were gushing only for what they could get out of her.

Gerry especially was really only interested in money when it came down to brass tacks and thus he extracted it from her both cruelling and cynically. Gerry, indeed, made more dosh than she did.

Most of the boys were interested only in the fizz and glitter of world fame, the money they earned, the adoration of the populace and the drugs which they could consume before and after the show. The high life gave them a reason for their existence and they got high on the high life. Rouchuka, of course, had never been tempted by drugs because she had her own natural woman-made supplies of adrenaline which achieved a similar effect.

The glitzy lifestyle, therefore, was beginning to drag Rouchuka down into despair but she dared not reveal her true feelings to anyone – not even to Greta who was, of course, on Henry's payroll. Even the shrewd and ever-charming Gerry was not fully aware of her deepest thoughts. No one would want to listen. No one would be interested in her wishes. She would only get stick from those who had a vested interest in her career if she were even to consider abandoning it now.

Rouchuka wondered what the alternative to this life would be like and whether a change of career would be possible. Of course, Rouchuka did not, in fact, need to take up any new occupation for monetary gain. She had merely to resign from her current lifestyle. After all she had earned enough money in the last eight years to see her through the next twenty-seven lifetimes. She did not need to earn another penny in order to maintain the kind of lifestyle for which most people would give their eye teeth.

Rouchuka had actually been sensible with money during her career. She had not blown all her considerable earnings on luxuries, inessentials and frivolity. She had purchased several properties, both at home and abroad, as an investment portfolio and she could certainly live in one of these assets quite comfortably.

Rouchuka would have liked, for instance, to live in her chateau in southern France which was currently being restored and to help in the management of the vineyard which brought in profits both for herself and her profit-sharing workers. Rouchuka had, furthermore, purchased a restaurant in London and one in the provinces which brought in a tidy little sum for day-to-day expenses of a sumptuous nature.

A financial wizard had also respected her level-headed inclinations and had steered Rouchuka in the right direction in terms of other financial market investments. And so Rouchuka wanted for nothing financially and she never would.

Rouchuka compared herself with some of the boys who poured most of their pay down their own throats or wined and dined more than willing women and/or men in exotic locations around the world. Rouchuka despised these tactics but the boys, she knew, in turn, sneered at her for being a wet blanket and not a party animal.

The final reckoning left Rouchuka feeling that she must get out of her current position and settle down with the not inconsiderable dregs of her profits over the last several years. But she was contracted for months, if not years, to come and withdrawal would exact a heavy penalty which might be extremely unwise, although not impossible.

ROCKER'S INDULGENCE

Rocker Blaize, whose real name was Dave Wellington, was prodigiously talented, devastatingly handsome and monstrously over-sexed. Some kind of genetic aberration obviously. He was a human sexual electromagnet for both women and men. And he knew it, unfortunately. There was obviously no hope for Rocker. Poor sod!

Rocker had an olive skin and a ruddy complexion with blond hair which was unusually wavy at the roots and curly at the edges. His dark brown eyes mesmerised and transfixed his doting public and his prospective bedfellows. He tanned easily and was, therefore, well bronzed for most of the year because of his frequent trips to sunnier climes. Rocker was, in other words, an attractive specimen of humanity.

Rocker was a man whom no woman would kick out bed because of his body. A girl might kick him out of bed, however, because of his mind but that was a different story entirely. Pulling the birds, consequently, required no effort on Rocker's part and most fans would not have declined an hour of passion with him even though reason might have advised his victims otherwise.

He infinitely preferred women as sexual partners but he was not at all averse to the odd dalliance and a bit of over-the-top experimentation with a bloke if the mood took him when he needed more excitement in his life. Rocker lived for kicks as part of his need for a constant adrenaline rush.

Living the high life as the band's bass guitarist and chief songwriter, Rocker could relish the excitement and the opportunity which after-show parties could afford him. And this included non-stop sex, drugs and drink. He was thus the first to arrive at every post-show rave-up so that he could indulge his whims to ludicrous excesses.

Rocker wrote most of the stuff which Vendetta produced and he was generally the leading light who drove the bus. Rocker had, furthermore, been instrumental in getting the band together, with Gerry Paxton's help, of course, and keeping it together. Rocker had accordingly earned Gerry's respect and he, Gerry, may have been a little afraid of Rocker if truth be told. Certainly Gerry thought twice before trying to manipulate or to push Rocker around as he often did, albeit subtly, with the other members of Vendetta.

Rocker was fully alive even after the show, having psyched himself up on spliffs and speed beforehand. And because Rocker had slept until 2 pm that day with his latest conquest, he was still raring to go. He had easily endured a three-hour pre-show rehearsal and a three-hour-long show at high energy levels. Rocker was, consequently, more than ready to start the night – or, at least, what was left of it – with high-octane vigour. For Rocker the night had not yet begun and he was unlikely to tire for several hours yet.

The Vendetta Ice band was all that Rocker had ever wanted in life and he gloried in everything it could provide in order to satisfy his cravings, his sexual lust, his need for self-aggrandisement and his hunger for fame and everything which these commodities brought in their wake. Rocker's needs and his tastes were, hence, simple. Rocker was, after all, beneath the floss, just plain Dave Wellington from downtown nowhere.

Rocker had led a humdrum existence in childhood with two very unambitious parents who had run a small corner shop in the north of England where it was always raining and snowing. Rocker had reacted against this regime and so he had propelled himself towards world fame and fortune in order to uplift himself from his drab existence. Lucky bugger! Well, maybe?

Rocker had worked his way up the career ladder by dint of sheer determination and hard work. He had appeared at every audition or public profile opportunity until he finally got noticed by Gerry Paxton and a few others. Rocker believed that this was something of a momentous achievement and, in essence, he was correct in his estimation but, in truth, it was really his parents whom he was attempting to impress. But had he actually achieved this ultimate ambition?

When the money started rolling in, Rocker had been able to purchase for his parents a fine detached house on the south coast where the weather was a bit better and he had then provided them with enough money on which to live for the rest of their days. Rocker now felt that he had proved his worth to his Mum and Dad. But he also felt that his small-minded parents still hankered after the simple life of their little corner shop in the colder part of the country. Gratitude or praise did not seem to be readily forthcoming from Rocker's parents. But he tried hard to ignore this patently obvious fact in order to spare himself any distress. Poor sod!

His brother, Jonathan, had set himself up in business as a plumber near where his parents lived and Rocker secretly felt that his Mum and Dad were prouder of Jonathan's meagre achievements than they were of his own. And it rankled.

Rocker did not, surprisingly, actually despise his brother for his elevated position in the family but he merely ignored him most of the time, claiming that he was too busy working. Jonathan, however, just got on with his own work on a daily basis and tried to forget that he had a famous brother. Rocker, of course, did not actually realise that these facts were his problem and that they unconsciously dictated his life. Rocker really needed some counselling but he had not even heard of the word. And so that was not an option or a solution.

The final post-show knees-up, which marked the end of the exceptionally long run, was to be held in one of the suites of their hotel. Thirty bottles of champagne had been ordered beforehand and Gerry and Henry had furnished the troops with enough food to feed the starving multiple millions of the world. Although the bubbly was on a sale-or-return basis, Gerry doubted that much would be returned before the night and morning were over. Drugs were, of course, supplied by the band-members themselves and all, except the prissy Rouchuka, the sober-socks Kicker and the boring Bluey, and their respective entourages, partook copiously.

The boys together with most of Vendetta's bodyguard team were driven back to the out-of-town Hotel Splendora in the minibus whose chauffeur was John Dawson, their road manager and stage manager. John and Rocker had had a brief dalliance when the couple first met but, these days, they were just good friends and their brief encountered was virtually forgotten.

The excitement, tension and anticipation of a night of indulgence was shared by most of the boys but Rocker was the chief protagonist in this respect.

Rouchuka stayed behind at the venue having a quiet nap in her dressing room and she would follow later. Rouchuka had asked Greta to tell the boys that she would arrive in due course because she wanted to rest and gather up her things after the show. Rocker regarded this as a lame excuse from Rouchuka but he was used to her being a wimp and, while admiring her talent and energy as a performer, he secretly despised her as a spoilsport. Rocker's secret was, however, known to most of the band – including Rouchuka herself and, of course, the astute Gerry – but, otherwise, his contempt for his lead singer-dancer when off the stage was not public knowledge for reasons of professional integrity.

VENDETTA'S LIBERATION

Gerry and Henry had been working hard on the preparations for the end-of-run celebration. Henry's attention to detail was immaculate and Gerry's timing was perfection itself.

When the Vendetta boys burst into the Majestic Banqueting Suite at the Hotel Splendora, the party officially began and the room became instantly alive. Rocker, Max and Myra were the first to crash through the swing-doors which triggered Gerry to signal the start of proceedings. The bunch burst into the hotel suite as if they owned the place and they certainly could have done with the money they earned. But they were tolerated by all the hotel staff who were anticipating hefty monetary rewards from Vendetta's coffers after the party.

Max had quickly showered at the venue beforehand and Myra had done likewise at the hotel and then dressed in his favourite costume for the occasion. Rocker, however, went to his room but did not bother with a shower. He had then simply launched himself on the assembled company at the party confident that everyone was merely hanging around expectantly for his arrival. He entered the room as if he were the only person on the planet for whom it was at all worth waiting. To an extent he was correct, of course, in the eyes of his fans.

The evening ensued with much jollity, celebration and congratulations. The overgrown kids were now officially on the rampage. The lights blazed and strobed, balloons fell from the heavens, streamers scudded across the room and champagne corks popped as if all were orchestrated by a timebomb. A whole cacophony of shouts, applause, cheers and screams filled the room. This routine was followed by hugs and kisses all round by way of mutual congratulation. Rocker and Max, in particular, adored this form of adoration while the rest found it somewhat monotonous and predictable.

Rouchuka, Bluey and Kicker had not yet arrived but no one was really that concerned. Everyone's interest was either in themselves or directed at Rocker, Myra and Max who lapped it all up even though the end-of-season formulaic routine had been enacted numerous times before.

Rouchuka had a slept in her dressing room for a while before hailing a taxi which took her and Greta to the Hotel Splendora. She then took her time in having a leisurely shower and dressing for the party. Greta, who occupied a room in Rouchuka's hotel suite, did likewise.

Kicker and Jenny similarly freshened up as did Bluey and Wanda in their respective rooms before joining the gathering. This group of friends attended these after-show shindigs principally because they were hungry after the show but not really because they were the wild-party types.

Gerry, and his two sidekicks, Tad Green and Eve Rushford, lost no time in rushing forward in order to greet the brat-pack boys when they arrived.

Rocker's greeting to Eve was the warmest because he really wanted to spend the night with her sometime but Gerry had obviously instructed her to keep him at arm's length if she valued her employment. And she did. Rocker thought that he would one day have to get this matter sorted with Gerry but now was not the time to do battle. And besides there were several other females in the room from whom Rocker could selected his prize.

The bodyguard team were customarily detailed to round up a number of attractive girls in order to please Rocker and Max at the after-show party. Men and boys were similarly assembled for Myra's benefit. The bodyguards did not believe that this activity was really part of their employment remit but they knew it was either accede to these requests or be out of a very well-paid job.

Rocker surveyed the totty at the party and his eye caught on a blond standing with a group of others who were all looking at him with sheep's eyes and promise. I'll screw her tonight, thought Rocker, but first I must eat and drink and party. Rocker accordingly earmarked the blond for when the feast was over. He instructed John Dawson to line her up as a guest in his hotel bedroom.

When he was desperate, Rocker sometimes actually had sex at the party in a quiet corner while most of the other guests simply turned a blind eye. Those who were really offended by Rocker's behaviour, of course, merely left the party in disgust. But, for this particular dame, Rocker wanted to have the comfort of a bed on which to cavort.

He was not sure which of the others he would go for after his first foray into sexual adventure with the blond but he decided that he would worry about that later. John soon reported back to Rocker that he simply had to say the word and the blond, Diana by name, would be willing. Rocker couldn't care less what her name was, for heaven's sake.

Rocker decided to take his time in summoning the blond, however, as he was still enjoying his other indulgencies at the bash. He would wait until he was a high and a little more raring to go before he eventually beckoned Diana to his room in order to give her the time of her life. Rocker would even have a shower, he decided, in preparation for this seduction which was a true compliment to the girl.

When Rouchuka, Bluey and Kicker with their respective companions did eventually arrive, the party was in full swing. This group discreetly took tables near to the side of the room and then merely watched the antics of the others with a mixture of curiosity and revulsion. Rouchuka and Bluey, in particular, found all the over-the-top showing off rather distasteful while the affable Kicker merely smiled indulgently.

Rocker, Max and Myra were universally known as the brat-pack by everyone while Rouchuka, Bluey and Kicker were regarded by all as lacking any spine. But the two factions jogged along genially together which was fortunate because their fortunes depended on it. Gerry, of course, played the role of peacemaker and go-between when necessity demanded.

GERRY'S PERCEPTION

Gerry was an out-and-out business tycoon. He had all the attributes for being an ace business manager for Vendetta Ice. He was steeped in charm and business acumen. He was shrewd and canny. He was intelligent and wise. He was single-minded and determined. He was the ambitious go-getter of all time.

Gerry was also fairly good looking for his advancing years because he was quite distinguished with his grey hair and his eye-colouring to match. He also had a presence which could have been useful had he wanted to be a performer but this vocation had never been his heart-felt desire.

Gerry had started life as a runner for a theatre company and he had made many useful contacts in that way. He had then worked for a while as an assistant in a talent agency and ultimately he had learned everything which he needed to know in order to set up on his own. A bank loan had helped him to establish Gerry's talent-booking agency and he had flourished from then on. Gerry had finally decided that the real money could be had in managing a rock band and eventually Vendetta opened this door for him. And the rest, as they say, is history.

Gerry had been in the entertainment management business for several years now and, therefore, he not only knew the ropes but he was also unshockable at the behaviour of the band. Nothing which the brat-pack ever did would, in fact, cause Gerry even to blink. Gerry was not even fazed by the reticence of the quieter members of the troop, namely Rouchuka, Bluey and Kicker Sax.

But, most important of all, Gerry's chief accomplishment was that he understood how people ticked. He detected people's moods and motivations. This was his chief asset by far. He could predict behaviour and reactions. He knew precisely what pleased his fellow creatures and what rattled, niggled or angered them. And, even more important still, Gerry understood each and every member of Vendetta as if he had known these individuals all their lives. He was intuitive even to the point of being clairvoyant and telepathic. Gerry made light of this talent but he could effortlessly read each one of the Vendetta clan like an open book.

Gerry's strength and survival lay solely in his ability to notice everything and to subtly manipulate, pander, curb and influence everyone while pulling the marionette's strings from behind the curtain. Here was Gerry's salvation together with the hold which he tenaciously maintained over the Vendetta flock without anyone ever realising what was happening. Clever sod! Lucky bugger!

He understood, for instance, Rouchuka's need for seclusion and solitude. Alive to the point of infinite exhilaration without drugs when on the stage, she craved peace and quiet like a hermit after the show and in her private life. Gerry acknowledged and respected this trait and went out of his way in order to ensure that she obtained her prize. He and Henry had recruited the loyal and gentle Greta in order to ensure that Rouchuka had the kind of companion who would never intrude or interfere with Rouchuka's much needed quiet moments.

Gerry appreciated, therefore, that Rouchuka was really a gentle soul and that, after she had delivered the goods so superbly in performance, she was entitled to be rewarded in whatever way she deemed appropriate. So if she craved seclusion, he would guarantee that she got it. This evening, therefore, at the end of the long run, Gerry had carefully ensured that

Rouchuka was left alone for as long as she wanted to be and that Geta was put on sentry-duty in order to ensure that the status quo was not disturbed.

Rouchuka was also kindly as well as a great asset to the band and she was in no way part of the brat-pack. She had had a happy childhood and she still maintained a good relationship with her kin. And so she did not need to display any neurotic tendencies when off stage as the brat-pack did.

Gerry also realised that Rocker Blaize (or just plain Dave Wellington) and King Max (alias Bob Pollard), both of whom took an active part in the song-writing and were, therefore, the life-blood of the outfit, needed constant stimulation and 24/7 excitement.

Rocker complemented Max's personality both on and off stage. Rocker's bass guitar spoke worlds to Max's keyboard, guitar and clarinet renderings. Max was possibly the most talented, and certainly the most versatile instrumentalist, in Vendetta. And so he needed to be respected as such even though the limelight usually fell publicly on Rouchuka, Rocker and Myra in particular.

Gerry endeavoured to cater for the whims of both Rocker and Max, therefore, while, simultaneously, ensuring that they did not display too much in the way of wild-child tendencies. He had to be very subtle in this respect in order to allow the two to believe that they were in control when, in fact, Gerry actually held the pin of the grenade. This was the kind of tightrope-walking which Gerry achieved effortlessly with his left hand because it was in his own interests so to do.

Myra (in reality Nigel Dulse) was Vendetta's lead guitarist and occasional singer who was known for his unashamed cross-dressing and his preference for men and boys. Now he was a slightly different proposition and so sometimes Gerry struggled to ply his trade where Myra was concerned. But Gerry still managed it. If persuasion or manipulation did not do the trick, then Gerry would resort to threats and punishment. Myra was prone to temper tantrums and, on these occasions, Gerry simply had to act like a controlling parent because this strategy usually worked satisfactorily.

Bluey (that is Pete Jenkins), Vendetta's drummer, was a different kettle of fish altogether from the rest of the troop. Bluey was basically a boring git whom the band tolerated because of his talent rather than his faceless personality. Bluey would make a rainy day look interesting by comparison. He was like a dead worm who had suffered from anaemia during its lifetime and was, therefore, of no interest to anyone, except, of course, a helminthologist (worm scientist, to you). Bluey, for instance, really did not want to adopt a stage-name because he was so lacking in imagination. Gerry, therefore, had to engineer things surreptitiously so that Rocker and Max had insisted that Pete be called Bluey whether he liked it or not. And he didn't really. But Bluey was eventually stuck with his stage-name for publicity purposes. Bluey did, however, have a largish fan-club which grew only because no one outside the clan really knew what he was like.

Kicker Sax (Timothy Aitken), the saxophonist for Vendetta, was amenable, happy-go-lucky and generally loved by all the band and its crew. Kicker was actually Gerry's secret favourite because of his sweet nature which success had not changed in the slightest. Kicker was, therefore, an easy option for Gerry to handle.

Of Vendetta's immediate hangers-on, the principals were Wanda Beck who was Bluey's half-sister and Jenny Lander who was Kicker's long-term girlfriend. Both of these females presented no threat at all to Gerry's wishes and predominance. Wanda and Jenny were co-operative and amenable to the business interests of the Vendetta cavalcade. Gerry, therefore, went out of his way to be nice to Wanda and Jenny in order to secure friends and allies in the camp.

The girls also lent a helping hand willingly when the show was on the road and so Gerry regarded them both as an indispensable part of the team. Wanda and Jenny did not, in fact, get paid but then they were supported financially by those who loved and could easily finance them. Gerry was, of course, aware that, for this reason alone, the girls would usually be amenable to Vendetta's needs and in synch with Gerry's aims. After all their livelihood depended on their being well behaved.

The gentle Greta, moreover, presented no impediment to Gerry's supremacy and, therefore, he was hardly aware of her presence because she could do her job efficiently, she never complained and Rouchuka was obviously delighted with her assistant in every respect. Greta was paid a salary, of course, and, as far as Gerry was concerned, she was worth her weight in gold as Rouchuka's assistant.

Gerry, in essence, thus ruled the roost while others gained the admiration and the accolades. But these prevailing circumstances suited Gerry just fine.

Gerry did, of course, have to keep a watchful eye on Henry, the band's producer, and John, Vendetta's road manager and stage manager. But he felt sure that each of both vital team-members knew his job and did it efficiently. And they presented thus Gerry with very little in the way of headache. If the status quo could be maintained, then Gerry was happy and he regarded himself as being in control of everything which mattered to the continuing health and success of Vendetta Ice.

MAX'S DISINTEGRATION

After a few speeches, thanks and lavish presents for the technical crew and the front-of-house staff, the food was brought out when Gerry signalled that the time was right.

Food consumption might also ensure that some of the drink was mopped up before too much damage was sustained, thought Gerry. Generally the food was greedily consumed but drugs were flung about as if they had been legalised last week and were advocated by the government of the day as a health necessity. Rocker certainly considered drugs to be essential to his life.

The press had been kept at bay by Gerry and Henry who had promised to grant an interview with Vendetta on the morrow. This also gave Gerry an incentive to keep the jollity at the party to a minimum if he could manage it.

The tables of food were arranged in a sort of broken square so that the diners could circulate around the outside while the serving maids stood inside the configuration in order to ladle out the grub. The waitresses were clad in pretty pale blue dresses with traditional white aprons, caps and cuffs but with the addition of a bright pink sash tied around the waist with a large bow at the back. Obviously the pretty dresses looked prettier on some than others.

The catering manager, Kevin Clayburn, stood in attendance but did not savour the prospect of a long night and much in the way of damage to clear up afterwards. His only consolation was the forthcoming income to himself and his long-suffering staff.

The tables housed sections for different types of food from across the globe. The hotel chef was adept at predicting the tastes of his diners and pitching the level of gastronomic sophistication accurately for such an assembly. Not too much in the way of posh nosh but enough gastronomic flair in order to make the punters believe that they had educated palates. This ploy worked a treat with Vendetta. The chef had got them down to a tee. Clever bugger!

The main table served Thai and Indian curry which was very much sought after by the boys. Another table held a seafood paella of questionable derivation, a variation on the theme of sole véronique and a smoked mackerel mousse with olives and cream cheese. Vegetarians were well catered for with an aubergine and pepper lasagne, a veggie version of pasta carbonara and a creamy mixed vegetable chowder.

Starters consisted of smoked salmon roulades, caviar vol-au-vents, venison terrine and mini spinach tartlets.

A variety of salads occupied space on a separate table together with the plates and the cutlery. Several dishes of chips and baked potatoes graced this table for the less discerning palate – cheek by jowl with a selection of nutritious vegetables for the more health conscious.

The champagne for the evening was served from the bar both as an accompaniment to the meal and as a pre-dinner tipple.

One large table was also entirely devoted to decorative displays. The table decoration consisted mostly of flowers, baubles and silver streamers and it had obviously taken many hours of hard work and a great deal of artistic skill in its creation. But again it was a hotel speciality much needed for elaborate banquets such as this one. Candelabra also enhanced this stunning and breath-taking exhibition.

In the centre area of the table complex, the serving wenches comprised five youngish girls who were gaining experience as waitresses prior to going off to university, two slightly more senior staff and one, Cynthia Pringle, who sat somewhere in the middle of the age-range and who was also a trainee manager.

Max wandered into the inner sanctum of the food tables in order to greet the serving staff. He liked venturing where he was really not supposed to be.

Max had come from humble stock but his legally adopted family were far from destitute as farmers who owned their own land. Max had thus begun life by feeding the pigs, milking the cows and driving a tractor around the smallholding. His adoptive father had wanted Max to join the family business but his son had other ideas. Max liked the indoor life rather than the great outdoors, although it had had the positive advantage of giving him an olive skin with a weather-beaten look which resembled his father's cornfields back home.

Max was very keen on music and he had worked unceasingly to master the keyboard, the guitar and the clarinet to a professional standard which had been put to the test and had not been found wanting. His compositional skills had developed organically from his natural musical talent.

Despite his father's slight disappointment that Max had not become a farmer, father Pollard had, nevertheless, supported his son both morally and financially in his chosen career. Max was, in fact, the only member of Vendetta who had actually had some proper musical training. Thanks, Dad! Mr Pollard senior had, therefore, backed a winner and his son has been able to provided him with a handsome return on his investment. From that point on, of course, Max had gone seriously downhill when fame had changed him dramatically for the worst.

Max saw it as his right to hug and kiss all the waiting staff and, in the case of the younger girls, to caress their anatomy below the region of the pink bow of their sashes. The girls did not, however, object too strongly to this invasion of their person by pleading pressure of work but Kevin was more than slightly concerned for their welfare. The younger waitresses, in essence, relished this attention from a world-famous musician but the rest of the females in the room were not that overjoyed.

Cynthia got her fair share of the affection but the two older waitresses were acknowledged with merely a quick hug and then largely neglected. Cynthia tempted Max to some food by way of defusing the potentially difficult situation and as a means of pacifying Kevin. The fans, who had followed Max into this notionally off-limits territory, were also much relieved when the competition was deflected.

The diners at last were encouraged by Kevin to be seated at the various smaller tables which were placed around the room for the purpose of consuming the food in the hope that not too much of it would hit the floor before the drinks and the drunks did.

Max decided to partake of a dish of smoked mackerel mousse and a Thai curry in order to please Cynthia. Max naturally wanted Cynthia to join him but Kevin intervened by explaining that she had work to do. Gerry got ready to intercede here if the situation warranted it in the interests of keeping the hotel management happy. Max, however, decided to behave himself after some subtle pressure from Gerry who had keenly observed his antics. Max, therefore, resolved to put his attentions to the girls on ice for the time being. The night is yet young, he thought.

Rouchuka had slipped unobtrusively into the Majestic Banqueting Suite with Greta in tow as the food was being served. Rouchuka opted for the seafood paella and a green salad. She was also tempted by a small portion of venison terrine which Greta obtained for her so that she did not have to queue with the rabble.

Gerry kept a watchful eye on Rouchuka in order to ensure that she was not unduly pestered by the hangers-on in the room while he sat at a table with Rocker, Myra and Max by way of hoping to keep them in order. Gerry caught a couple of bread rolls which were thrown about but otherwise the three errant overgrown teenagers were so engrossed in their meals that they were inclined to behave.

Bluey and his half-sister Wanda sat with Kicker Sax and his girlfriend Jenny near to Rouchuka's table. They were all great friends and served as a foil against the brat-pack members of Vendetta. The occupants of these tables could always be trusted to behave themselves without supervision.

Towards the end of his meal, Max began to feel a bit jaded. He had downed almost a full bottle of whisky immediately after the show in his dressing room and, together with the champers at the party, this amount of alcohol was beginning to take its toll. Max had, furthermore, been on the go for almost two days now without any sleep – sustained only by drugs – and inevitably he was beginning to feel the strain.

Max lay down on one of the sofas in the room and Gerry saw this action as an early warning portent. Gerry instinctively was up on his feet in an effort to get Max back to his hotel room. Max was amenable to this plan and did not protest too much about leaving the party early as if he were Cinderella. Before actually quitting the Majestic Banqueting Suite, however, Max spoke briefly to John in order to ensure that he was able to obtain Cynthia's telephone number for future reference.

Max could still walk to his room but only just. So Gerry felt it advisable for him to have the assistance of a couple of the bodyguards. Sleep came easily and instantly for Max that night.

Gerry was really thankful that Max would be off the scene from now on before he disgraced himself too much and prior to running the risk of exposing Vendetta to adverse criticism which could escape to the hovering press in the area.

John approached Cynthia with successful results for Max. John pocketed her number with a promise that Max would be calling her in the not-too-distant future for a bit of a friendly chat. Cynthia smiled but was not at all fooled by John's lightness of touch. She knew the score all right.

ROCKER'S DESPERATION

Rocker thought he would have this Diana wench before he continued with the rest of his adoring fans throughout the night and next morning. But he was wrong. Poor sod!

After his shower Rocker expected to show Diana the time of her life in bed but he found, to his astonishment, that he was the one who got bitten in various intimate places. He was spell-bound by his latest conquest.

Diana was one of the best shags he had ever had in his life as far as his memory could recall. And, moreover, she captivated him as a women which had not happened very often before for Rocker. He even deigned to show her respect which had certainly never been Rocker's modus operandi previously.

Diana was fascinating, enchanting and endlessly mysterious. Yes, that was the word, he thought, mysterious. Rocker found her mysterious. He didn't usually care about the personality of his doxies because he was simply interested in getting his rock offs. His stage-name was Rocker after all. But because she was mysterious, he wanted to know more about her in order to get closer to her and to understand her. What was in her mind? How did she tick? What prompted her behaviour? Why did she agree to come to his room? Would she be for keeps? Well, Rocker would probably not go that far.

So Rocker was smitten hook, line and sinker. He could not get this woman out of his thoughts. He watched her every move, drank in her body perfume, revelled in the intonation of her voice and hung on her every word. He noticed the way in which she walked, talked and laughed.

She was also highly intelligent and yet she appeared to be uneducated. Mysterious obviously. The beautiful Diana was apparently an out-of-work, low-grade actress who was working temporarily as a secretary. When employed in the acting profession, she merely did odd bit-parts and extra work which required almost nothing in the way of intelligence or even artistic skill. She was, of course, not without ambition and she claimed that she expected better things of the future in her career. She also did a little modelling and, with her looks, that was not surprising.

How is it, thought Rocker, that she charms me to this extent? How come I am so fully satisfied with her that I have spent the entire night with her and disregarded all the others in the queue? Is she seeking a lucky break with my help perhaps?

But Rocker decided that he was not about to let this one out of his sight for some while yet whatever the consequences. They spent most of the next morning together, therefore, at Rocker's insistence. And he still did not want to let Diana out of his life even after this weekend encounter. Rocker was disturbed by the direction of his thoughts in spite of himself.

"Do you fancy a trip to the Caribbean?" he ventured somewhat tentatively.

"When were you thinking of going? In the summer?" Diana replied with caution.

Rocker then jumped in quickly with, "Next week. Say, leaving Wednesday or Thursday, maybe. I have a couple of weeks off now and I was planning to spend it in my villa in St Lucia."

Rocker thought that he could impress Diana with this information but she still looked doubtful. This was also a first for Rocker because no woman had ever refused this sort of invitation before. No woman could usually resist the combination of his body and the Caribbean simultaneously, surely? Perhaps he would need to try even harder?

"I would pay for everything, of course," Rocker continued.

But she still seemed to hesitate.

"I don't know that I can afford time off work," Diana replied.

"Well, I can give you some money to tide you over the break. But do say you'll come, angel."

Rocker sounded desperate and he did not like this emerging tendency within himself but he seemed powerless to restrain his compulsion.

"I'll think it over and see what arrangements I can make," she replied as if hedging her bets.

Rocker was getting really fraught now and he looked it. But Diana took pity on her poor lapdog.

"I will make some calls tomorrow and see what I can arrange," she agreed tentatively.

"OK."

Rocker started to become more hopeful.

"I shall, of course, need to set off for home soon now in order to get back to London in time for work tomorrow."

Rocker's hope diminished. She was telling him that she would shortly be leaving him, was that it? But he might lose her that way forever. Desperation! He asked for her mobile number which she supplied with a promise to meet him again soon. And another promise to get back to him shortly about the holiday jaunt. Rocker had to be satisfied, therefore, with this small crumb.

After lunch at a nearby restaurant, Diana announced that she would now really need to get to the station in order to catch a train back to London. Rocker tried a bit more pleading and persuasion but finally he had no choice but to accede to her request as she obviously was not going to budge on this resolve. And he didn't want to alienate her with too much high-pressure inducement. Rocker wanted to come back to London with her, for instance, but he dared not even suggest it for fear of another rebuttal. Besides he still had to wind up things at the venue, to attend the mid-afternoon press conference and to settle up at the hotel. There were certain aspects to his professional life which could not be circumvented even in his eminent position.

They walked to the station together with Rocker hoping not to be accosted by more fans or the press who might have got wind of the fact that he was entertaining a female. They kissed passionately yet discreetly before she boarded the train and then waved him goodbye. Rocker's heart sank as she disappeared from his sight but he hoped not from his life.

Back at the hotel, Rocker had to confront Gerry, Henry and the team who were part of the clearing-up operation as well as John who was winding up the gear from the show. Rocker felt dismal at the prospect of the toil of tidying up after the show.

Once on the train, Diana pulled her mobile from her bag and rang Barrington who was delighted to hear from her.

"Maisie, darling," he exclaimed, "are you OK?"

"I've got him, you know. By the knackers well and truly. Hell's bloody tits, I've grabbed him," she announced proudly in her natural cockney accent.

"Well done, darling! But, please assure me that you are not in any danger," Barrington was especially solicitous of his ex-girlfriend, Maisie Clifton, for whom he had a great affection as well as a good working relationship. He did, therefore, have reservations about sending her on such a potentially dangerous mission.

"No danger at all, honey. And he's offered me a trip to the Caribbean next week. But I will keep him on a string for a couple of days yet."

Maisie was a consummate professional.

"Well, that could be really dangerous, darling."

"Relax Bal, I know what I am doing. And I can take care of myself," she concluded convincingly.

Maisie was the only one who ever called him Bal as her token of their affection.

"Well, if anything goes even slightly awry, just take the next flight home. Promise me."

"I will. But I must go now. The train is nearly in London. Give my love to Calendula. I will keep you posted," Maisie promised.

"Happy landings, darling! Bye."

MYRA'S CONSTERNATION

Once Max was off the scene and Rocker's lust had taken him away to his room with a girl in tow, the party started to fizzle out much to Gerry and Henry's relief.

Gerry looked at his watch at shortly after 2 am and then decided that Rocker was not going to need any more females tonight for his personal entertainment and so he, Gerry, could risk dismissing them all now. If Rocker did, in fact, want another woman tonight then Gerry or John might try to bribe one of the young waitresses. But hopefully Rocker would now be asleep and his companion for the night would be similarly slumbering or else she had crept out of the hotel. Problem solved!

The Majestic Banqueting Suite had not actually been totally wrecked and, as it was now quite late, the staff had virtually finished clearing up most of the debris of the meal, had taken out the uneaten food and were cleaning the tables.

Gerry and John circulated among the guests, politely telling everyone that the party would now be winding up for the night.

Kevin, the Catering Manager, noticed the mass exodus of the invitees to the party with some degree of relief. The thirty bottles of bubbly had been consumed long ago and Gerry had used this alcoholic drought as an opportunity to wind up proceedings.

Rouchuka and Greta had made a discreet exit much earlier in the evening and Kicker and Jenny had also eased themselves out of the room unobtrusively. Bluey and Wanda were still up but they both needed little persuasion in order to retire for the night. And John was able to oblige in this respect by reminding them that there was a press conference tomorrow and that they ought to get some beauty sleep in readiness for this important event.

The only problem-child left was Myra and he was less flamboyant without Rocker and Max in front of whom to show off. Myra liked the limelight but once the lights were dimmed, he was less of an unmanageable infant than his two compatriots. Myra liked to party but his thirst for drinks and drugs was not that acute. Also Myra's sex-drive was rather intermittent. Gerry had to be thankful for some small mercies.

While Myra did not appear to be desperate for a bed-warmer for the night, Gerry did notice that he was making overtures to one of the newly-appointed bodyguards who was detailed to be on guard duty with him tonight.

Hal Caxton was built like a tank and had the strength of ten bodyguards but he was really a gentle giant. He was a great one for a regular workout in the gym and he prided himself on his staying power. Hal's choice of career as a bodyguard was an obvious one and he was successful and content with this line of work.

Hal's only immediate problem was Myra. Hal knew that Myra fancied him something rotten because he had made it plain enough in the recent past since Hal had joined the team. Hal, therefore, had to think of numerous ways in which to sidestep Myra's approaches. When Hal noticed Myra sidling up to him with intent, his mind started rapidly to think of ways of avoiding the impending onslaught. Hal actually wanted to tempt Myra for his own reasons but he was not inclined to obliged him in any other way.

"The party's nearly over, Hal," was Myra's opening statement. "Do you want to retire for a snifter? I have drinks and other stimulants in my room. You can take your pick."

"Thank you, but no. I am on duty all night tonight."

"But, as you are only guarding me, then it would make sense to be near me."

Hal felt that he had laid himself open to this obvious rejoinder.

"My instructions are to remain outside your room and to keep a watch on the corridors," countered Hal.

Hal agreed, in principle, however, to come upstairs with Myra. But as the pair headed towards the lift, Hal endeavoured to think of additional ways in which he could deflect Myra's sexual advances.

A straight refusal might do the trick, for instance, Hal thought. Or I could just turn tail and call for Gerry's help, perhaps? On the other hand, a quick drink might not go amiss at the end of the evening. He had, indeed, remained dry throughout the night when more possible danger could have been lurking. Hal was, after all, certainly strong enough to fend Myra off physically if necessary. And, moreover, Hal could pull the you-have-offended-me card as a last resort. He was not that worried about retaining his job because he was employable almost anywhere but he did want to stick around for a while at least.

Myra offered Hal an assortment of drinks and drugs in his room but Hal eventually opted for an orange juice despite being pressed for something stronger. Hal was beginning to worry about the outcome of this foray into unknown territory when a knock came on Myra's bedroom door.

Much to Hal's relief, Gerry entered without waiting for a response or an invitation to enter. Hal didn't even have a chance to get to the door in order to check on this late-night caller as would have been expected of a bodyguard.

"I need to talk to you, Myra," commanded Gerry. "We need to talk business. Urgently. And now!"

Hal seized the opportunity to announce his exit.

"I will wait just outside," said a determinedly retreating Hal.

Neither Myra nor Gerry attempted to detain him. But Myra's consternation and disappointment was patently obvious to all concerned. Gerry felt that Myra was just about to have a temper tantrum now that his pet dolly had been snatched from under his feet. And he was right! But that's tough, thought Gerry. We have business to discuss and no one is going to get in the way. Myra would just have to put up with a bit of interruption and now tow the party line.

Hal waited outside Myra's room, however, with his ear pretty close to the door.

When the waitress and trainee manager, Cynthia, appeared about ten minutes later with some brandy, cigars and chocolates, Hal gave her a wink, exchanged knowing glances with her and then opened Myra's door so that she could enter unimpeded. Cynthia then took a deep breath, smiled beatifically and entered Myra's room with the cigars, brandy and chocolates for the hotel guests.

Gerry's symposium

Gerry took a seat near Myra who was sitting in one of the chairs placed around the oblong coffee table on which Myra was resting his feet. Gerry then patiently waited for the outburst from Myra which was not long in coming.

Myra got up and started to disrobe truculently. He snatched off his pink wig, he tore off his favourite Little Bo-Peep costume and he flung it on to the floor at Gerry's feet as a token of his current mood occasioned by Gerry's interruption. Gerry was interested to noticed this manoeuvre from Myra because he was normally so fastidious about his clothes and his appearance, not to mentioned his extensive collection of wigs. Myra was very proud of his Bo-Peep get-up, for instance, because it complemented his fair curly hair even without a wig, his blue eyes and his pale complexion.

Gerry studiously ignored Myra's eruption and left the dress on the floor. He did not need to pick it up because it was not a part of the band's costume wardrobe and, therefore, was not an asset which might be devalued by Myra's action. Myra then donned a frilly nightdress for the occasion in order to appear decent for once.

"We need to talk urgently about the next consignment, Myra," began Gerry.

Myra seemed to sober up at this remark. But he did not want to stay sober for long and so he picked up the house phone and ordered some brandy, cigars and chocolates to be brought up to his room. This tactic was also designed to make Gerry wait as a further example of Myra displeasure.

"Anything wrong, dearie?" Myra asked casually.

Myra tried valiantly to sound unflustered. Gerry considered that he had failed miserably.

"Nothing's wrong that I am aware of but we need to verify the plan," retorted Gerry as he pulled from his jacket pocket a large map which clearly showed a route across the globe.

The two of them studied the map with its defined route from St Lucia in the Caribbean by sea to Venezuela and then overland to Mexico in South America. From here the route took to the Pacific Ocean across to South Korea. The final lap of the voyage went overland from South Korea through Mongolia, Kazakhstan, Russia, Ukraine, Poland, Germany, France and finally landed in the UK.

"How long is this journey likely to take?" enquired Myra.

"Eight to ten weeks, we believe."

"Won't that be a bloody big risk, darling?" continued Myra. "A couple of months is a hell of a long time."

"No, not at all, the secret lies in the fact that the cargo will change hands more frequently than you usually change your knickers. Besides it is not an established route. The customs people are expecting couriers to fly – not to go overland and by sea and take ages about it. Can you not see the beauty of that?"

Myra wanted to say that he rarely wore knickers and that surely his recent disrobing would have reminded Gerry of this fact even if he had been lamed-brained enough to have forgotten it. But he decided to let the moment pass. Myra considered Gerry's premise about the plan for a moment and then agreed with a reluctant nod of his head.

A knock on the door interrupted any further discussion when Cynthia arrived with the French cognac, the highly priced vintage cigars and the extremely fattening Belgian chocolates. She smiled as she placed the order on the coffee table and asked Myra to sign the bill as proof of his purchase. Cynthia then left the boys to continue their important business discussion and their detailed examination of the interesting route-map.

"Do you think she heard any of that?" asked a nervous Myra.

"Relax, Myra dear. We haven't said anything incriminating. Hotel staff are immune to idle chatter, anyway."

Myra breathed again.

"Everyone will be paid in cash locally and, therefore, we should cover our tracks really well," continued Gerry.

"And, presumably, the goods can be sold locally as well?"

"Exactly!" confirmed Gerry. "It's a foolproof plan! It's an investment."

"Yeah, darling," the other agreed, "most traders want quick returns but we are not in that position, are we?" mused Myra.

"We win all round," concluded Gerry decisively.

"But it's not tried and tested," returned the nervous party in the conversation who was still unconvinced.

Gerry was beginning to get irritated with Myra's wet-blanket reservation.

"That's what's good about it, you fool! We have tested the principle of the scheme on a number of other occasions before and so we know, in essence, that it will work. The fact that it's a new route is actually in our favour because no one will have gotten wise to it."

"OK, I get it!"

"But we do need to get some dosh across to Europe and Asia pretty smartish."

Myra nodded again. "I can get that arranged easily."

Myra knew how to shift money across the globe at lightning speed before anyone who might care had even noticed.

"I will do likewise. And so will Max. But we need it there by Tuesday at the latest. You have the account details, right?"

"Right!"

"Then that's all we need to do," concluded Gerry as he stood up as a precursor to leaving. "Oh, and, by the way, don't even think about trying to take advantage of any bodyguards around here. Got it?"

Myra gave a sulky grimace but he failed to reply to Gerry's edict.

Outside the door, Cynthia and Hal decided that now would be a good time to disperse as the meeting in Myra's room was actually looking as if it would break up at any moment. Hal walked along the corridor so that it appeared that he was patrolling his patch while Cynthia disappeared into one of the other guest rooms as if she were nonchalantly going about her business.

Gerry left Myra's room with a feeling that he had accomplished the most important task of the night and he headed to his room for a good night's kip. This would be the first of many successful meetings, he considered.

Myra still felt apprehensive about the plan but he began to relax when his head hit the pillow. Perhaps he would dream of the delectable and muscle-bound Hal tonight? Poor sod!

Cynthia came out of the bedroom and spoke briefly to Hal before she retired for the night. Hal sat down outside Myra's room with relief that Myra had not started again where he had left off previously. Had Myra taken Gerry's warning to heart maybe? Probably not. But Hal was, at least, spared further pressure on this occasion.

KICKER'S COMPASSION

Kicker Sax loved everyone and he was loved by everyone.

The brat-pack loved him for his sweet and gentle nature, Gerry loved him because he was amenable to his requests, Rouchuka loved him because he was so kind to her and to Greta and Bluey and Wanda loved him as a true friend.

But Kicker loved his Jenny above all others. She was the woman with whom Kicker wanted to spend the rest of his life. And she had agreed with this sentiment which might even include marriage and babies one of these days.

Jenny was beautiful with her reddish hair and her creamy skin. Her eyes always sparkled especially when she looked into Kicker's own. Kicker himself was not that unattractive either with his jet-black shiny hair and his green eyes. But his eyes were reserved only for Jenny.

Kicker had met Jenny at a party when he was in his early twenties and she was in her late teens. It had been love at first sight for both of them. Five years on they were both devoted to each other still. Kicker would have liked to have settled down with Jenny permanently somewhere away from the glare of the limelight and, perhaps, raise a family but, for the present, he was happy with life on the road and their life together. They already owned a house on the Norfolk Broads as well as a pad in Bulgaria both of which were mortgage-free and so when Kicker did eventually retire from the pop-music scene they would be set up for life.

Kicker had learned the saxophone at an early age and was now an accomplished musician. He played both the alto sax in B-flat and the tenor sax in E-flat and, occasionally, he would pick up a soprano instrument. And he often serenaded Jenny with his devotion to playing.

One of the reasons why Kicker was so much liked was because he did not criticise, complain or sit in judgement on anyone. He was a happy-go-lucky guy in essence. He had a loving family who supported him all the way, frequently came to his concerts and ran his fan-club. Jenny's parents were also friends with Kicker's family and so everything in the garden of Jenny and Kicker was rosy. So where's the catch here?

Well, Kicker would have liked to work with Bluey as a duo and not been part of the large and ostentatious cavalcade of Vendetta Ice. Kicker was not really that ambitious. He had found himself caught up in the Vendetta experience – as were Rouchuka and Bluey, he suspected – as if by accident. But being in a gigantic enterprise was not really Kicker's cup of tea. Kicker, in fact, had approached Bluey about branching out on their own as a twosome but Bluey had been rather non-committal about the suggestion. And so the idea had been shelved for the time being.

Kicker and Jenny and Bluey and Wanda, however, remained close friends and spent much time together. At every after-performance party, for instance, they always sat together and ate together and they usually had hotel rooms near each other for the sake of convenience.

One day Jenny asked Kicker if he had had any thoughts about retiring so that they could settle down and start a family. Kicker said he did not think that this would be likely immediately but he certainly had it on the agenda for the future.

"Why, darling, are you discontent with being on the road? I know it must be an awful strain for you," Kicker asked rather concerned.

"I'm not unhappy, of course, but I would like us to look to the future and, perhaps, plan ahead. After all, you would need to state your intention a long time before you actually slung in the towel."

"I don't suppose Gerry would like it for one moment, darling," came Kicker's reply.

Jenny reacted with, "What's it got to do with Gerry?"

They both knew that Gerry, and Rocker for that matter, would be an obstacle to anyone wanting to break away from the clan but they were also aware that they had their own lives to think about.

"I'd just like to feel that we would be settling down some time and starting our family," continued Jenny.

Kicker realised that Jenny was getting broody and this fact worried him slightly. He did not want to lose her and he wanted to settle down himself sometime but now was not really the opportune time. This discussion, however, did not cause any friction between the couple but it did flag up markers for the future.

To this end, therefore, Kicker reminded Bluey of his former suggestion that the two of them might team up as a break-away unit. Bluey, much to Kicker's astonishment on this occasion, did not seem to reject the idea out of hand. Indeed, Kicker got the distinct impression that his close friend would now be more amenable to the notion.

So Kicker and Bluey started jamming together just for fun, of course. Kicker appeared to be the front man with his saxophone while Bluey took his usual back seat at the drum-kit. They could work well together but it seemed that alone the pair did not constitute a viable enterprise. Just a saxophone and a drum-kit were insufficient for them to go it alone, despite the fact that they were currently household names as part of Vendetta Ice.

And so both Kicker and Bluey started to think about their future plans. But they did not actually come up with anything which would constitute a successful strategy. But each kept thinking and looking ahead.

Kicker reported his conversation with Bluey to Jenny as a means of reassuring her that he, Kicker, had her interests at heart. Jenny thus felt optimistic that their future did have a direction which could be pursued at some point sooner rather than later. She told Kicker that if he did not work, then he could still keep his hand in on the sax with Bluey as part of the equation. And then, if they wanted to operate as a professional ensemble, they could easily find, say, a singer, and perhaps a guitarist, as a front-runner.

Jenny felt optimistic at this development because, of course, she knew that deep down Kicker would be lost if there were absolutely no music and no performance opportunities in his life. She also saw the possibility that her beloved Kicker could downscale his work while raising their family and being a more or less full-time and hands-on Dad. She was, in fact, delighted at this prospect and she felt that she could face the immediate future with more enthusiasm than ever before.

So things were looking good for Kicker and Jenny. And Bluey seemed quite sanguine about the future too.

VENDETTA'S EXHIBITIONISM

A despondent Rocker took a taxi from the station after waving farewell to Diana. He returned to the Hotel Splendora for a quick bracing shower and to change into his allotted costume. A shower? Can you believe it? Nevertheless, it's true!

Rocker was obliged to face the press conference in mid-afternoon as one of the group's leading lights and he had somehow managed to sober up in time for this event. All the gang were required to pose for the press photographers. All needed to look sober and not be hungover and so gallons of black coffee had been chucked down their throats during the morning and early afternoon. If the coffee and aspirin did not work, then a cold shower would be the ultimate deterrent.

Obviously Rouchuka, Bluey and Kicker didn't need any such sobering-up devices.

Rocker was slightly late for the photo-call which was held up until he arrived suitably clad and ready to go. He received a dark frown from Gerry when he did eventually appear in the recently spruced up Majestic Banqueting Suite for the press conference and photo-shoot.

Vendetta Ice were all dressed in identical flashy gear — both the men and their crowd-pulling woman. Dressing in costume when facing the press was Gerry's brainchild and Vendetta Ice was noted internationally for this promotional tactic.

The team wore boating-style jackets with vertical stripes in white, green and pink. They all worn boaters with a green hat-band which matched the green stripes in their jackets. White shirts, black bow-ties and full-length white trousers with turn-ups then gave the team an old school look, despite the fact that none of the cohort had ever been educated in a school of any note. And, indeed, most had not really been educated at all. But all the group were talented, intelligent, streetwise and worth millions so what did it matter anyway? Patent black-leather shoes with silver buckles provided the finishing touches and, indeed, complemented the entire theatrical effect of the costume ensemble.

The newsmen and photographers from the nationals were seen in abundance with a few journalists from abroad in order to swell their numbers.

The main protagonists in the band were asked general questions about the way in which the long run at the famous Scullen Stadium had gone for them and how it had been received by the fans. Rocker elected himself as the spokesman and replied in appropriately elaborate terms to this enquiry.

This line of questioning then led to further enquiries about Vendetta's plans for the future in terms of recordings and concert tours. Rocker, Rouchuka and Max fielded these enquiries with an aplomb which was impressive and Gerry was delighted with the result.

Enquiries about what the individual members of the band intended to do during the three-week interlude before the next recording session and the forthcoming tour were skilfully evaded by the respondents. No one, of course, wanted too much prying into their personal and private lives.

Towards the end of the press appearance, Rocker and Max stepped forward in order to allow one or two of the fans, who had been permitted into the banqueting suite for the occasion, to come forward and to kiss their hands. The press photographers got busy at the juncture.

This gesture then sparked more photo-calls during which various choreographed poses were adopted for the benefit of the press. Rocker and Max, for instance, stood back to back with a forefinger on the chin and an arm across the chest together with an expression of surprise. Rouchuka and Rocker then embraced and kissed each other pretentiously, albeit unpassionately, with one eye on the audience in a similarly cutesy pose. Myra, not to be outdone, tweaked his bowtie, winked at the cameramen seductively and blew a kiss to the audience. The cameras flashed but no one in the photography crew was contemplating taking Myra up on his implicit invitation.

Bluey and Kicker were merely onlookers during the event with the audience virtually unaware of their existence beside the main crowd-pulling attractions. These two escaped with just one or two photo-shots of the pair of them together in a pleasing attitude but they were otherwise left alone.

Gerry stepped forward at the end of the show in order to remind the press contingent of Vendetta Ice's imminent recording session and its forthcoming tour of the southern countries which was due to start after the three-week break. He then finally called an end to the proceedings and thanked the press for their visitation. The press gratefully retired to the hotel bar, much to the delight of the hotel management.

Gerry was thrilled with the reception which his band had received both during the run and at the final press meeting. Gerry was laughing all the way to the bank because the run had exceeded even his wildest expectations in terms of box-office receipts. And this fact augured well for the future. Gerry and Henry, therefore, began to heartily congratulate each other immediately after the press conference.

The final part of the clear-up operation ensued whereby the instruments, costumes, stage properties and personal luggage were finally loaded on to the van and a fond farewell was taken of the hotel staff and some fans who had hung around to the bitter end.

The team at last set off for London and the southern counties in the band's minibus, singing most of the way, on the final lap of their journey, at which point each member of the convoy would then go his or her own separate way for a time. While on the journey, each member of the clan contemplated the three-week vacation ahead.

Much to Max's disappointment, Cynthia was not on duty that day in the hotel but, because he had already pocketed her mobile number, he trusted that he could make up for lost time when they eventually met again. Max intended to spend his break with her and a few others if possible.

Rocker fervently hoped that he would be joined in St Lucia by the delectable Diana but he worried that she might not agree.

Myra didn't have a clue about what he wanted to do during his period of respite and, to make matters worse, he was not going to have Hal at his side during this holiday period. Hal had been called to another job, unfortunately, although he would be back on Vendetta duty when the next tour commenced.

Rouchuka was destined to return to splendid isolation during the respite by burying herself in her small chateau in southern France which she was in the process of having restored. The faithful Greta would accompany her for part of the time but she, Greta, would also be enjoying a well-earned rest.

The so-called boring Bluey and his sister Wanda were scheduled to visit their parents in Wales. No one in the band commented on this mundane fact but the band-members were not surprised by these intentions.

Kicker and Jenny had planned a trip to Rome for a romantic interlude before journeying on to their estate in Bulgaria where the quiet life could be guaranteed and where they were loved and welcomed by the locals.

Gerry, Eve and Tad returned to the London office in order to complete the paperwork following the Scullen Stadium visit and to prepare in earnest for the next tour and the impending recording session.

Henry and John would return to the London office shortly.

Gerry also needed to shift some money across the globe for his own personal reasons.

JOHN'S PROFESSION

John Dawson was Vendetta's stage manager and road manager. He had a very responsible job and he was justly remunerated for his part in Vendetta's continuing success. But as John enjoyed his backstage work, the money was a secondary concern. Never in a million years did John even contemplate appearing in front of the footlights but he loved every minute of his time in the wings.

John was responsible for seeing that everything in the way of technical equipment, such as lighting, scenery and stage properties, were available and/or transported to the various venues which were utilised by the group. He also had the responsibility of transporting instruments and luggage wherever the team went. John was, moreover, in charge of directing the work of the technical and backstage staff for each occasion. Staff were permanent fixtures on contract who travelled around with Vendetta in most cases but occasionally temporary assistance was employed locally when necessary.

John had started life in the entertainment business as a lighting technician, although he had in the past undertaken most of the backstage jobs necessary for producing a show in order to gain much needed experience and to make himself more employable. To this end, John's experience and efficiency had promoted him to the level of stage manager. He had worked as a freelance stage manager for a while before securing his current employment with Vendetta Ice as his lucky break.

But the work was tiring and it had elements to which John was not that partial. Keeping the brat-pack in order was, for instance, not a role which he relished, although he was cognisant of the fact that it had to be endured by all members of the company.

John, however, felt that he was not being stretched enough in his management role when working for a pop group in a hermetically sealed unit. John, in fact, hankered after working in situ at a theatre somewhere in the role of stage manager. This would probably mean a drop in salary but, John felt, the sacrifice would be worthwhile and, in any case, he was not that strapped for cash. John liked working in a theatre most because this job would not only offer him more scope but also he would not have to be continually on the road. Having a punishing peripatetic occupation was all right for youngsters but he was getting on a wee bit. Ideally John would have liked to have worked in a large theatre in a city — not necessarily in the capital — in which he could also reside.

John had, in fact, bought himself a house near to the administrative office for Vendetta Ice but, because he was constantly on the road, he had rented his house out on a long-term lease. John, at least, got the income from this rental but it also meant that he had no fixed abode these days. But the extra money allowed him a small nest-egg and he was fine with this idea.

John felt, moreover, that the personalities within Vendetta left a lot to be desired and he was getting sick of the infants on the team. Admittedly when he first joined, John had enjoyed his brief fling with Rocker but he, John, was then a lot younger and less wise in those days.

Now that he had surpassed the big four zero, John had a different opinion of Rocker and an altered view on life generally. While he was not as intolerant of Rocker as many of the other backstage and technical staff, John was a bit fed up with waiting for Rocker to grow up. And he would be waiting for a long time for this maturation to occur, he felt. John did content himself, however, with the knowledge that he had not actually contracted AIDS following his encounter with Rocker which he easily might have done in the circumstances.

As John had known Rocker intimately, he did, of course, realise that Rocker's outrageous promiscuity was only a means of seeking the love which the star had not really obtained from his Mum and Dad. Rocker's brother Jonathan apparently received all the approbation from the parental quarter.

While John was reasonably tolerant of the brat-pack in action, his real admiration was for Rouchuka, in particular, as well as the long-suffering Bluey and Kicker. He knew, for instance, that Rouchuka would have been happier in a theatrical setting, say in musical theatre or in light opera, and so he saw her as a kindred spirit in this respect. John hugely admired Rouchuka's talent and he respected her stage presence but he knew deep down that she was a fish out of water just like himself.

John felt that he worked and jogged along reasonably well with his immediate colleagues, Gerry and Henry, and so there was no friction here in his working relationships.

John knew Gerry to be very efficient as the official business manager for Vendetta who was also adept at handling, and even manipulating, the brat-pack. John, in fact, admired Gerry's skill in this respect. However, John wondered about Gerry's ethics sometimes and he had heard some nasty rumours about shady deals in which Gerry was, at least, involved, if not, instrumental.

John also liked and respected Henry as a friend as well a congenial working companion.

While not exactly being disgruntled, therefore, John had put out a few discreet feelers in order to see if he could in time secure a job in a theatre for himself. He was quite prepared to do the provincial circuit for a while before installing himself in a London venue so that he could reclaim his house in the east end of London or even buy himself another. So far, however, John had not got any nibbles on his fishing line but he lived in hope. It would only be a matter of time, John believed. And so, in the meantime, all he had to do was stay with Vendetta and wait.

In an ideal world, therefore, John would have liked a nice stage management job in a London theatre at a respectable salary and with regular hours, a nice little pad in the suburbs and perhaps a loving live-in partner in order to delight the rest of his days. But this was some way off for John.

John believed, however, that one day the good fairy would grant his dearest wish. And then John could die a contented man. Bless him! But in the meantime, John strove to deliver the goods for Vendetta, to dream wistfully about the future sometimes and to make the best of what he had so far achieved in his chosen career.

HENRY'S SUSPICION

Henry Sissingford was the suspicious type. He suspected everything and everybody of wrongdoing and dereliction of duty. Sometimes his suspicions were genuine and sometimes they were utterly unfounded and neurotic.

Henry had grown up in a dog-eat-dog world because his parents had been in the buying and selling trade and this had left an indelible mark on all their offspring.

Henry's mother had been very wary of her wheeler-dealer husband and her eldest son, who had followed his father into the business, because they both appeared a bit shifty and wily in their business dealings. Henry's father had also kept the cards very close to his chest in that he had played away from home on a couple of occasions. So Henry's initial training and experience of life was very relevant for his current employment.

Henry, for instance, had learned early on how to develop into an entrepreneur because he had run his own public relations company and, from there, he had become so much involved with travelling repertory companies that he had gained a taste for this line of work. It was then a very short step towards sponsoring small music groups and later keeping the profits. And, ultimately, working for larger ensembles, such as Vendetta Ice for whom he now worked full-time. He was, consequently, good at negotiating contracts and at pulling off deals because he was generally so over-cautious of situations and distrustful of people with whom he had business dealings.

Henry's job as Vendetta's resident producer was to raise finances, book venues, negotiate terms, issue contracts and manage the budget for each jaunt. He was also responsible for hiring John's technical staff and his stage management team. Henry, in other words, was the Mr Moneybags for Vendetta and he was responsible for ensuring the financial success of each of their projects from initial inception, throughout rehearsals and up until the final live performance or recording.

Henry's work for Vendetta's jolly at the Scullen Stadium, for instance, had entailed securing the performance and rehearsal venue at the most advantageous rates, organising transport, hiring equipment, recruiting backstage and front-of-house staff and generally keeping an eye on the budget. He could, of course, usually unload most of the recruitment work on to John as stage manager but he, Henry, still needed to control the finances.

With his work for Vendetta, of course, Henry's role was a lot more than just that of a theatrical producer in that he had to pander somewhat to the whims of the household names. In this respect, Henry worked in cahoots with Gerry Paxton.

While Henry admired Gerry's intuitive management of the band, he did not in reality trust him and, in any case, Henry approached people in a very different way from Gerry. Some would say that Henry's handling of the team was complementary to Gerry's approach and, in some ways, more effective.

Gerry, on the one hand, read people in order to control or to manipulate them. Gerry applied his talents not only to the members of the band and the wider team but also to those to whom he sold the services of Vendetta.

Henry, conversely, was more interested in personalities so that he could understand them and detect whether they were genuine or not. Henry studied others hence in order to assess whether he could trust them. Henry thus understood the band and placed its personnel in one of two categories – those whom he admired and he could trust and those whom he did not.

On the plus side, Henry felt admiration and respect for Rouchuka, Bluey and Kicker Sax and he sympathised with their trials of having to put up with the antics of the exhibitionists. And he trusted them, and their various appendages, implicitly. Henry sympathised with Rouchuka, for instance, because he believed that she was really in the wrong job and that she had just been swept along with the tide of rock music but it was not really her metier. Henry felt that she would be much better suited to musical theatre or to light opera.

As for Bluey, the drummer, Henry did not actually think that he was as boring as some of the other members of Vendetta did. He simply felt that Bluey was misunderstood. But he trusted him. Henry also trusted Kicker who was, of course, loved by all and he had no hidden agenda as far as Henry could tell.

Rocker, Max and Myra, on the other hand, had yet to earn Henry's trust. And so Henry kept a careful eye on each of these team-members and he doctored everything which he said in their presence accordingly. He was aware, of course, that the triumvirate were just a bunch of kids with the mental age of a child who had just completed a course in potty-training but had not made the grade. Henry did actually feel sorry for the bunch, however, because fame had taken a heavy toll on their ability to exist.

Rocker allowed his sexual appetite to reach hideous heights, Max felt compelled to be a money-grabbing exhibitionist but he was not really suited to the role and Myra didn't know whether he was on his head or on his heels. Despite pitying these individuals, Henry still did not trust any of them any further than he could throw them.

Henry suspected, for instance, that there was a bit of drug-peddling going on beneath the surface but he had not yet identified who was actually involved and how this business was conducted. Henry had heard one of two questionable comments from certain members of the brat-pack recently or he had noticed the way in which a conversation had instantly dried up the second he had come on to the scene. Very suspicious, Henry thought. Henry also wondered what Gerry knew and whether he turned a blind eye or whether he actually took an active part in the scam.

So Henry remained suspicious of this cluster of personalities and he maintained a watching brief on the situation. He planned in future to keep all his senses employed in discovering the truth. By this means the cautious Henry would be in a position to decide what could be done about the situation and how he would need to act if the position erupted.

Henry, therefore, speculated long and hard. Who might be involved? What are they doing? How long have they been doing it? Who would know the truth? Who would admit to the facts? How can I find out? Who can I recruit to do my investigation? Do I need to take another individual into my confidence about my suspicions? And how will it all affect me personally?

Henry mulled over his thoughts and speculations and decided that he must take some action in order to safeguard his position and, once the true facts were obtained and verified, he would then be able to take the appropriate steps in order ensure his survival accordingly. But he was still undecided about how to proceed and who might assist him.

Perhaps my friend John would be a suitable candidate? At least I can trust him. Henry had a dilemma but his problem was not insurmountable and it was not a situation which he could neglect for much longer. So he invited John out for a drink after work.

MEDICI'S MANOEUVRING

Calendula and Barrington were having a preliminary meeting at the start of their investigation into the misdeeds of Vendetta Ice. Calendula had got wind of some underhand drug-dealing within Vendetta from a private detective friend who had been visiting the Caribbean when following an errant husband on behalf of one of her clients.

"Have we had a report back from Cynthia and Hal yet, poochie?" enquired Calendula.

Barrington stated that he had as yet only received confirmation from the pair that Gerry and Myra were involved in some extra-mural activity but that they had no idea who else might have been involved.

Hal had informed Barrington that he and Cynthia had overheard a meeting taking placed between Myra and Gerry in Myra's hotel bedroom after the final party on Vendetta's northern tour. The gist of the enterprise was plain but so far they had no tangible evidence out of which they could make any capital. Hal mentioned, moreover, that Myra had shown some sexual interest in him and so his position was key as well as potentially dangerous.

Hal had also told Barrington that his services would not be required by Vendetta until the next tour which was not due to start for a couple of weeks yet. Hal, therefore, could not feed any information back to Barrington for some weeks. Barrington also understood from Hal that Cynthia had captured the interest of King Max and so some information might be forthcoming from her depending on circumstances.

All this news had been fed back to the curious and contemplative Calendula at their meeting at Grove Naxton Cross in middle England.

Calendula and Barrington were sitting in the dining room of their house rather than in the garden because the weather was somewhat inclement in mid-April. Barrington, however, gazed many times out of the French windows at his beloved garden which he tended lovingly for most of the year.

"So Hal's contribution could be vital and yet we might need to withdraw him at a moment's notice if things get difficult," decided Barrington.

"And what about Hal's ex-girlfriend?" asked the other.

"Well, apparently Max fancies the pants off Cynthia and has obtained her number."

"But not made any contact yet?"

"Well, they are still on holiday following the long run in the north."

"And when will Vendetta be on the road again?" asked Calendula.

"Starting again in early May apparently when Hal will resume his duties as Myra's on-tour bodyguard."

Calendula, the creative inspiration of the team, then considered the situation.

"I think we ought to have a rapid-exit plan for Hal and another plan for enabling Cynthia to take over from him if necessary," she concluded.

"You think of everything, buttercup. I can easily set that one up. I could even get the bodyguard agency involved in this because they owe me a favour which I can pull at any time," was Barrington's response. "But we may not need to involve Cynthia just yet."

Calendula's mind was, however, still active and silence reigned because of her contemplation.

"And will Cynthia be up for Max's seduction, if necessary?" interrupted Barrington.

"Of course, lion cub," avowed Calendula. "Why do you think I recruited an ex-pole-dancer in the first place?"

Barrington bowed low as his means of acknowledging his partner's intellectual superiority when it came to creative thinking and attention to detail.

"But we still need to find out the nature of the consignment, the route it takes and exactly who is involved," continued Calendula. "We may have trouble nailing this job."

Calendula was playing devil's advocate at this juncture. She often had misgivings at the start of a project.

"That goes without saying. It will take time but we shall get there in the end. We always do!"

Barrington tried to reassure her. But Calendula still did not look too convinced.

"Any news from the press conference after the northern tour?" Calendula's mind was taking yet another about-turn.

"Not a squeak. I have already spoken to my press contacts who covered the melodrama," Barrington concluded.

But was Calendula satisfied? Only time would tell.

"But Maisie has nailed Rocker, no doubt?" enquired Calendula.

"Sure thing! She never fails. She's a good actress."

"One of our best operatives. But you will keep her safe, won't you, darling heart?"

Calendula was always solicitous of the female members of the team whom, she knew, were worth their weight in gold.

"But we need another angle, you know. Have we got someone who could get in by the back door, perhaps? Say, focusing on the lesser bods?" mused Barrington as his means of resolving the impasse.

"Yes, I think we can fix that knotty little problem," came the optimistic reply from Calendula, "and, of course, we still have our key cards to play yet."

Calendula's mind was again active.

"But we definitely need some concrete evidence. Speculation is insufficient. We must make some more phone calls," she decided, "in order to ensure that we can wrap things up nicely."

"And I need to get on to the press boys," contributed Barrington.

"I think we could provide gainful employment to a couple more from the team," concluded Calendula with finality.

"Do you have anyone in mind?"

"Oh, yes! Certainly. My mind is simply teeming and scheming."

Barrington did not need to argue with his partner's mind in this respect. He knew that she could solve all their dilemmas with a bit of creative inspiration. And so he just relaxed and smiled.

The discussion then continued and took a slightly different turn before the meeting came to a close. The meeting of the Board of Directors of the Medici Squadron then broke up and Calendula and Barrington proceeded to go their separate ways before dinner.

Calendula decanted to her art studio in the house while Barrington pottered around the garden gathering produce for supper.

Later they both retired to their ensuite shower room for some interesting activity which was aided by a spray of Rose Garden Mist. Not that either of them actually needed an aphrodisiac for this venture.

PART 2
BREAKING THE ICE

ROCKER'S DEFLATION

Diana's mysteriousness continued to dominate Rocker's daydreams as he assembled his gear after the press conference at the end of the north of England run. But Rocker's thoughts also turned to his holiday villa in St Lucia in an effort to distract himself from any potential disappointment.

St Lucia is a Caribbean island in the West Indies. The island sits between the Caribbean Sea and the Atlantic Ocean. To the immediate north lies Martinique, Dominica and Guadeloupe and to the south is St Vincent and Barbados. South America is not too far distant from St Lucia either. Merely a boat trip away.

The island features the Pitons, a World Heritage Site on its west coast. These two mountains display an impressive volcanic spire in the shape of an upward-pointing spike. St Lucia also boasts volcanic beaches, luxury resorts for the playboys and playgirls of the world and a coastline which attracts keen coral-reef divers in their hordes every year.

Rocker chartered an aircraft in order to ensure that he reached his holiday destination at the earliest opportunity because he was very eager to begin his vacation.

Castle Lucia, Rocker's villa in St Lucia, is a little inland and away from the main thrust of the plebeian resorts and the popular beaches but not too far from the coastal capital of Castries which was built on land reclaimed from the flood plain on the western coast. Rocker had purchased the grounds and the castle ruins some years ago and he had spent millions on having it restored to a ludicrously lavish standard by a local architect-builder. The castle had been the residence of a prince in centuries past and, as Rocker now felt like a prince himself, he wanted to do the property appropriate justice.

A large central misshapen tower was Rocker's main dwelling-place. This eye-catching edifice constitutes the focus of the building complex as it had done in previous centuries. The central tower has three floors with a spiral staircase built within a central tubular section. A few minstrel galleries lead off this principal section to the bedrooms on the upper floors.

Rocker's bedroom, within the central tower, sports a roof-terrace with a private roof-garden and a swimming pool as well as steps which lead down to the main pool and the garden area.

At the very top of the central section is a bell tower whose bell, unfortunately, has been broken and thus it no longer chimes. Rocker had meant to get the bell fixed but he had never got around to it.

The ground floor houses two dining rooms, one for everyday eating while the other much larger room is reserved for sumptuous entertaining. An enormous multi-sectional lounge dominates the ground floor of the property which leads out to the extensive gardens, a large patio, the main swimming pool and a collection of gazebo-style summer houses. The gardens which surround the central tower and the outbuildings constituted something of a rival to Versailles.

Kitchens and bathrooms on all floors are scattered about the place for the convenience of those concerned in living and visiting.

A larger outhouse-type wing off the central tower complex caters for every musician's needs in that it houses a music room, a rehearsal-cum-recording studio, a performance space and an area fully equipped with the latest gear for Rocker's composition, recording and playback. Sometimes the Vendetta band come here for recordings and try-outs when this destination is the nearest to their latest gig.

Several grand pianos are also scattered about the castle, including one In Rocker's triple-aspect bedroom in case he should become inspired during the night to compose yet another hit number.

Max, as Rocker's fellow composer, is obviously a frequent visitor to Castle Lucia when the two of them are composing anything on a large scale. But, during this vacation, they were not intending to work and so Max was somewhere else in the world.

Several outbuildings, which link to the main central structure like the tentacles of an octopus, house the staff accommodation, the main catering kitchens and some storage space.

The architectural design and decor of Castle Lucia has an unmistakeable local flavour as a salute to the Caribbean but, of course, the stamp of the tourist and the international superstar are still in evidence. The atmospheric architecture reflects the centuries of influence from American, African and European tourists and other invaders.

Marie and Léon, a husband-and-wife team, are the resident housekeepers who call on their friends and relatives in order to supplement their activities as necessary – especially when Rocker is in residence. Rocker is very fond of his Creole servants and he is usually careful not to offend them with too much in the way of seduction of the younger members of the wider household team.

Léon, in particular, is very useful to Rocker in many ways. Léon, for instance, has contacts all over the Caribbean islands who can supply him regularly with drugs and women when required. Marie, Rocker suspected, knew little of her husband's assistance here. But he could have been wrong.

Marie and Léon actually take little interest in Rocker's music and are not particularly impressed by his global fame which suits Rocker rather well. He might have been a household name internationally but this did not include Castle Lucia. It seems that in his home in St Lucia, therefore, Rocker can simply remain just plain Dave Wellington from downtown nowhere.

Rocker speaks little French and communication between him and his servants is all conducted in an amusing array of pidgin English, strange un-English catchphrases and hand signals. While English is the official language of the Caribbean islands, the patois of the Creoles is really the principal means of communication among the natives and Rocker respects this tradition while making no obvious attempt to learn very much of it.

Rocker was greeted on arrival at Hewanorra International Airport, in the south of the island, by two local bodyguards, Ernesto and Daniel, whom Léon had engaged for his employer's visit. The minders, who had accompanied Rocker on the plane, handed over their precious cargo to the locals and were thanked, tipped handsomely and discharged from sentry duty. Rocker, of course, knew that his tip would allow his ephemeral guardians to now go out and have a bloody good time.

Initially Rocker did the tourist bit for a few days until he got bored with this familiar routine. He did the bars, the nightclubs, the beaches, the diving experiences, the adventure playgrounds and some sailing, as well as getting his fill of helicopter rides and yachting trips.

Several women and a few men catered for his sexual appetite but, essentially, Rocker was pining for Diana in a mood of deep depression and this state of mind also sapped his musical inspiration. And so no compositional ideas came into Rocker's mind.

Once Rocker had settled into the mundane part of his existence in Castle Lucia and he had concluded that Diana was not actually going to join him, he considered the dismal prospect of a return to the UK. He bordered on becoming clinically depressed as a result of his belief.

After about a week, however, Rocker unexpectedly received a text message which galvanised him into making arrangements for Diana's flight and accommodation. Rocker was now able to start composing again and he was generally jumping for joy.

Marie and Léon both breathed a sigh of relief now that their employer was back in good spirits.

But Léon, of course, was rather sorry that his services as a drug-pusher and a talent-spotter were no longer required by his employer.

ROWAN'S OCCUPATION

Rowan Boyd-Fuller was a professional wastrel. He had originated from a well-to-do family who had taught him, if nothing else, how to be irresponsible. Rowan's parents had high hopes of his taking up law as a career and of earning a good crust in adulthood but, unfortunately, Rowan's upbringing had only taught him how to take unearned income for granted. He certainly did not expect to have to earn money himself in order to survive at any time in his life.

Rowan, consequently, blew it at university and had, from then on, taken a steadily declivitous direction. Rowan, in fact, thought that the world owed him a living but, unfortunately, it had not yet paid up. He bummed around the world after his university fiasco trying unsuccessfully to make ends meet and regularly begging his parents for cash handouts. Rowan did odd jobs here and there but nothing really interested him as a full-time lucrative career.

Skid row was an ever-hovering possibility and Rowan knew it. His earning potential in menial jobs, of course, never really met his outgoings. The discrepancy was rarely made good and his deeply hostile parents did not for a moment believe that they might have been in any way to blame. Eventually, of course, the Bank of Mum and Dad dried up and he was more or less disowned by his disappointed parents when they realised that he had no natural talent for earning copious sums.

After years of globe-trotting and drifting, Rowan finally ended up in the Caribbean and then spent all his spare cash, and the last dregs of Mum and Dad's donations, on a small motor-powered yacht, appropriately named *Ocean Spray*, in which he lived and from which he could derive some income by offering cruises to the tourists. By Rowan's standards this was a wise move and a good investment in a lively market. Rowan, of course, promised Mum and Dad that he would repay his latest loan from them. But he conveniently forgot to keep his promise and he was careful not to put a time-limit on his return of their money or to offer to pay any accrued interest. Wise guy!

Rowan's life, therefore, settled for a while. With the upturn in his fortunes, Rowan could just about manage on his meagre income but he really would have liked to have had a nest-egg or, at least, a safety-net.

Then fate intervened in order to help poor Rowan attain his innermost desires and to fend off the demon of starvation.

When on his pleasure craft one day, Rowan was approached by a man who asked which of the Caribbean islands he, Rowan, regularly visited. Rowan replied that he was a free agent and that, consequently, he travelled liberally and easily between all the islands of the Caribbean.

"And do you do night trips as well as day-time cruises?" asked the stranger.

"I go wherever the customers want me to take them," replied Rowan, eager to oblige this potential new customer.

"And do you transport cargoes as well as people?"

"If the price is right, I will take anything or anybody anywhere, any time."

The stranger smiled. Rowan had obviously given the correct answer.

So eventually Rowan found that he could get a regular income from this stranger who asked him to ship packages in *Ocean Spray* from various Caribbean islands, and St Lucia in particular, to the mainland overnight. Sometimes Rowan delivered parcels to Mexico and sometimes to Venezuela – usually at night when the human boat-trippers were not interested in employing his services. Rowan was careful to ask no questions about the nature of the contents of his consignments. This was also the right attitude to adopt, Rowan realised.

Rowan's regular customer said that his name was Sid but he neglected to provide any surname. Rowan was only really interested in the money which Sid could provide and so he was unconcerned about what a man might be called or what he chose to reveal about himself.

On a number of occasions Sid told Rowan that a diver would fasten one of the packages for transportation to the bottom of his yacht before he left and that another diver would then remove it surreptitiously at its destination. Sid explained that these packages needed to be kept cool in water and Rowan agreed to this arrangement. Again this was the right attitude for Rowan to assume.

Thus these requests then became a regular event and again Rowan still asked no further questions. Rowan began to get a taste for being solvent and he was definitely happy to oblige whenever he was required to do a night voyage. So Sid certainly felt that Rowan was the right man for the job.

Rowan, of course, still continued with his daytime passenger cruises and trips around the various Caribbean islands and he honed his skills in becoming a first class narrator and an excellent tour guide who spoke enthusiastically about the wonderful life in the Caribbean.

One morning a pair of very beautiful legs stepped on to Rowan's boat. He tried desperately to ignore this distraction because he was busy checking the yacht prior to its departure but he failed miserably. Obligingly Rowan held out his hand in order to help the beautiful legs on to the pleasure craft but he then realised that he needed to repeat the process for a couple of old trouts who had followed his prize. Rowan did not normally perform this service for his passengers but he had decided to make an exception in the prevailing circumstances.

Rowan earnestly hoped that the young lady would be doing a full round-trip with him and, on enquiry, he was delighted to learn that she would be with him for the whole day's excursion. Rosemary Devlin apparently wanted to do the full Caribbean cruise and she had chosen Rowan's boat because he had very few other trippers on board.

When he got talking to Rosemary, Rowan discovered that she was a conference organiser who came from New York, although he had gathered that much from her accent. Apparently Rosemary was doing a recce of the islands so that she could organise conferences in various offshore locations and she could identify some extra-mural activities with which to tempt the punters. Rowan speculated about whether his services could be included on Rosemary's schedule of possible attractions. He soon decided, however, that he was too small a fry to hope for this nugget of gold because he could not compete with the big boys.

The round-trip took the fee-paying customers around Martinique and Dominica in the morning with lunch scheduled for midday. Drinks and refreshments were always served on board by the owner but lunch, of necessity, was a stop-off for refuelling and exploration. The afternoon saw the trippers admiring St Vincent and Barbados before, finally, returning to St Lucia where the voyagers had originally boarded Rowan's vessel. This whistle-stop tour seemed to satisfy Rowan's favourite passenger much to his own relief and delight.

Although Rowan had not been able to afford to bother with womanising in the past, mainly due to his impecunious state, he decided to risk asking Rosemary out for a drink after the trip. After all, Rowan had his night trade on which to fall back and the old biddies had kindly elected to pay him in cash and so he could afford to squander a little money on a woman at last. Rowan, therefore, plucked up the courage to ask the lovely Rosemary and

her beautiful legs out for a quick drink once the yacht had moored itself in
St Lucia. Much to Rowan's surprise, she accepted with a seductive smile.

MYRA'S INVESTIGATION

As he found himself at a loose end for a couple of weeks and because he
had reservations about Gerry's so-called foolproof plan for the drug-
shipping operation, Myra decided to engage in a bit of checking up on his
own account. Myra accordingly booked himself on a flight to St Lucia, with
his route-map in hand, without telling either Rocker or Gerry a dicky-birdy
about his intention.

Myra also believed that it would be politic for him to travel as a bloke
rather than to indulge in his usual cross-dressing routine. Myra found, by
this means, that he could remain inconspicuous and he could pass
unrecognised by the public who were not used to seeing him in this unusual
masculine attire. He took with him the minimum force in terms of
bodyguards which Gerry had insisted on at all times for the brood, even
though Myra was proficient at giving these guys the slip or bribing then to
take time off.

Myra decided to ditch his bodyguards with a hefty bribe on arrival in St
Lucia and to find a not-too-posh hotel in which to lie low. If he played the
pauper tourist, then that seemed to be the way forward, he concluded.
Myra's hotel was thus comfortable and unpretentious and, consequently,
away from the main thrust of the wacky tourists. From this base, Myra
found that he could do his snooping around without inviting too many
comments or being asked too many questions. Or being recognised and
accosted by any unwanted fans.

Myra's first port of call was the coastal regions by night where he observed
the comings and goings of small pleasure craft and, more importantly, the
activities of the customs officials. The customs brigade were, in fact, the
key to the success or otherwise of the smuggling trade.

He soon tracked down Sidney Hackett, whom Gerry had mentioned at
their last meeting, as the principal contact in St Lucia. Sid apparently
frequented a shack on the east coast of the island and he often visited this
place at night. Myra could not identify where his mark actually lived because
he appeared to be of no fixed abode. It was to this east coast shack,

therefore, that Myra followed Sid one night and waited outside until his quarry appeared at the door.

Myra showed himself in what he thought was a casual manner but, in actuality, it sounded alarm bells in Sid's brain. Was this stranger a customs fellow? A drug-dealer? A hit-man? He was certainly a nosey bugger!

Myra opened the batting by talking about the weather and the balmy evening as part of his greeting. Sid merely grunted but concluded that this stranger must be British if he talked about the weather.

"You're a stranger here?" asked Sid.

"Yes, I'm just visiting and exploring the island. Would you know if this path leads to any local taverns?"

Stupid question thought Sid but I will play along with the game.

"Just follow that path and you will arrive at a small fishing village," Sid stated. "A small tavern is then in the centre of the village."

"Are you going that way yourself? Would be like to join me?"

Myra felt that he was making inane conversation and Sid came to the same conclusion.

"I may be along in a while," Sid ventured.

But eventually the pair ambled along together, with each desperately trying to assess the motives of the other, but they finally ended up in the nearest tavern.

At first they talked inconsequently and, of course, the topic of the weather came up once more. The talk between the two men turned to drugs after a while and Myra admitted that he would not be in any way averse to buying some. Sid was, however, cautious in his responses and Myra began to think that he was on an uphill climb. But once the two of them were sufficiently well sodden in drink, Myra revealed his identity as a contact of Gerry Paxton. Dressed as a man, of course, Myra was not recognisable as a pop star.

Fortunately for Myra, the mention of Gerry's name opened a few doors while his true identity remained unknown to Sid. A few days later Myra contacted Sid again and, by this time, Sid had verified Myra's bona fide existence by contacting Gerry directly. Myra was not too happy about the fact that Sid had contacted Gerry but there was not much he could do about it now.

Thus it came to pass that Sid confessed to being in a bit of a spot with the customs people and that he wanted to store some goodies overnight before moving the stuff on to its next port of call. Myra then immediately suggested that he could help with this dilemma.

While Sid was not unwilling to entrust the stash to Myra for a short while – during which time the heat could be induced to die down – Sid did not trust his new friend with any more detail than he felt absolutely necessary. And so Sid cut his coat according to his cloth at the time. A plan was, consequently, hatched between the two criminals which had benefits for both parties. Myra felt that he had made great inroads into his surveillance mission and he believed that he could save the day for Sid in return while Sid felt that he had extricated himself from potential trouble with the law.

So Myra departed from his newfound friend with what he thought was much information and Sid left his new associate with what he believed was a good get-out clause. Sid thus gave Myra some stuff to stash overnight and also made arrangements for the gear to be collected later once the customs men had found other chaps with whom to play cops and robbers.

Myra now considered that he had very usefully identified the first stage of the drug-route operation and that the chief contact in St Lucia was a really reliable laddie for whom he had done a great favour and, therefore, he had won for himself a few brownie points.

Even though Sid had obviously revealed Myra's whereabouts to the dictatorial Gerry, Myra still believed that he could square it in that quarter and so he gave the matter no further thought. Gerry could assume that he was in charge but Myra was still a rebel.

Myra then decided to have a look around the hot spots in St Lucia and to become a drunken tourist for a while before entering on the next phase of his journey. Once Myra was well oiled, he then set off for his destination in order to ensure that the stash were kept out of harm's way and away from the prying eyes of the customs bods. Myra accordingly made his way in the direction of Castle Lucia with a small rucksack on his back and a smile on his face. Poor sod!

DIANA'S ENTERTAINMENT

He arrived at the airport with an obscenely large bunch of red roses and white marguerites, as the national flowers of St Lucia, for the occasion. He was heavily disguised with opaque sunglasses and a bizarre sombrero-style sunhat. So as not to look too much of a prat, Rocker took Marie, who was old enough to be his mother, along with him in order to carry the bouquet. Actually Rocker still looked a prat in his latest disguise.

Diana's plane was over an hour late which heightened Rocker's anticipation but he endeavoured to hide his anxieties from Marie by assuming an attitude of carefree hyper-joviality. But she was not fooled. Marie realised that her employer was very smitten with the traveller who was just about to arrive.

Eventually Diana graced Hewanorra's concourse with her presence looking as fresh as one of the marguerites in Marie's arms. Rocker greeted her in an over-the-top fashion even though he was trying to play it cool. He had even had a shower for the occasion.

Marie was brought forward, she curtseyed on cue and she coyly presented the guest with the bouquet while Rocker took Diana's suitcase. Diana was flattered but she appeared somewhat overwhelmed by all this attention and welcome. Yet she calmly walked through the airport with Rocker, heavy suitcase in hand, tagging along behind her like an excited puppy.

When they arrived back at Castle Lucia, Diana was escorted by her attentive lover up to his vast bedroom where she could then shower and relax. They also had a nude dip in Rocker's private pool on the terrace and the pair splashed around like a couple of kids.

Rocker then went into overdrive by offering her drinks and nibbles before a splendid night on the town where he could show off his knowledge of the most expensive restaurants and the most sought-after nightspots as well as his fabulous wealth.

After a long night of bliss, Rocker continued to show Diana the delights of the island. And he began to shower regularly in her honour. It also looked as if Rocker might start to adopt this particular habit permanently. Within a week the couple had done all the tourist haunts, including a trip into the rain forest in order to see the Toraille waterfall and gardens, a boat-trip around the coast, a helicopter tour and a catamaran cruise. They also sampled the various beaches, did some snorkelling and admired a few dolphins. Diana was exhausted after only a few days of this full-on pressure to impress her – not to mention the over-energetic night-time activity.

When the mad pace of their lives was beginning to take its toll and a day of rest at Castle Lucia was indicated, the pair elected to laze by the garden pool after a splendiferous haute cuisine lunch prepared by the resourceful Marie.

Rocker was the first to hear the footsteps approaching and he sat up rapidly in surprise. At the same moment, the internal phone rang in order to announce the arrival of Myra who had, in fact, already arrived. Myra had also managed to evade the attentions of Ernesto and Daniel who were very embarrassed and apologetic for this dereliction of their professional duty. Rocker, however, simply waved the lapse aside as of no consequence. Rocker was really not particularly pleased to see Myra but Diana was grateful for the distraction.

Myra was clad in the St Lucia equivalent of Bermuda shorts. Myra frequently ditched his preferred female attire as he believed himself to be less conspicuous when not in costume and when he needed a touch of extra anonymity. Rocker suppressed his annoyance at Myra's intrusion by offering him a drink which was gratefully accepted. Rocker also proudly introduced Myra to Diana by way of showing her off. Myra could not really remember her from the after-show party but he pretended that he did in order to oblige his host and to avoid any embarrassment.

After exchanging a few pleasantries, a lull in the conversation then began to dominate the scene. Rocker could not decipher the reason why Myra had descended on him unannounced and he was more than a little concerned at this interruption to his holiday.

"I've had some ideas about a new song," announced Myra enigmatically.

Rocker knew this phrase to be a tried-and-tested formula for saying that Myra wanted to see him alone and on private business. Miffed though he was, Rocker led Myra into one of the music rooms so that they could talk uninhibitedly.

"What the fuck are you doing here?" he began.

"Just dropped in to see my dear friend Rocker," came the reply.

"Get to the fucking point, doll-face."

Myra obeyed.

"I want to store some stuff in your bell tower for a while."

"What?" Rocker exploded but then remembered to keep his voice down in case Diana should overhear.

"Just for a few hours. Can't do any harm."

"What is it this time, more coke?"

Myra remained silent.

Rocker became worried.

"You don't mean . . . something stronger?"

Myra remained silent.

"Not in my bell tower you don't, Bo-Peep!"

"Go on. Just for one night only. I'll never ask again. Until the next time, of course."

"Definitely, not, chummy, and close the door behind you as you leave," was Rocker's final word.

Myra still didn't budge.

Rocker then went on patiently to explain – as if to a child – the dangers to himself, to Myra, to the band and the dire consequences of being found out. Myra, of course, like Rocker, was, in truth, still a child.

Myra again remained implacable.

Rocker then began to walk out of the room in disgust when he was arrested by Myra's words.

"I could just leave it on your bedroom floor if you like. But the bell tower would be safer."

Rocker didn't remain silent in reply but instead grabbed Myra by the throat, snarled at him menacingly and was about to throttle him when the phone rang again. It was Marie again stating that a friend of Myra's had arrived with a parcel for him. Rocker nearly did kill Myra now but he had no alternative but to accept the parcel, to dismiss the so-called friend with an expletive and to take Myra with his bloody parcel up to the bell tower.

Maisie, meanwhile, just sipped her drink by the poolside, although she did send a text message to Barrington.

After Myra had left and Rocker had rejoined Diana, it was Diana's mobile phone now which interrupted their afternoon rest.

"That's wonderful news! I'll return immediately," affirmed Diana much to Rocker's alarm.

Diana literally jumped for joy once her phone call had terminated. She announced that she would have to return home on the next flight because she had, at last, secured the career-break for which she had been waiting for many years. No degree of hysterics, pleading, bribes, cajoling or even threats on Rocker's part would alter Diana from her course. She gathered up her things which were scattered about Castle Lucia and she caught the night-flight home to London.

Rocker kissed her goodbye with tears in his eyes and a fervent hope that they would meet again soon. But, essentially, he was now a broken man quite who was stunned by her premature departure from his life.

WANDA'S ADDICTION

After about week of staying with their parents in Wales, Bluey and Wanda simply couldn't wait to get away.

Whenever Bluey and Wanda returned home to Wales, it seemed obligatory that the siblings should be inspected by the whole village and then paraded around the nearby villages as if they were prize exhibits in a wax-works museum. Bluey had even dismissed their trusted bodyguards because they would both be surrounded by so many others in Wales.

Wanda always drew people's notice because she was a tall chestnut brunette but she did not, in fact, relish this attention. The whole point of having a three-week break between tours was so that the members of Vendetta could get away from the limelight and from the attention of the fans in order recuperate. The cattle market was not, therefore, Bluey and Wanda's idea of a good rest.

Wanda consequently decided to spell out the facts in no uncertain terms to her mother as the organiser of the puppet-show but it really had no lasting effect. As Pete and Wanda were half-siblings, they both shared their

Mum in common. But Wanda, as the younger sibling, had been born to Mum's current husband and as such she commanded fractionally more favour than her first-born child who had been the result of her former and disastrous first marriage. Wanda was accordingly elected by the pair to be the primary spokeswoman with her brother merely hovering in the background.

But no advantage was gained and Mum continued to plan their schedule of presentation to all and sundry who might be impressed by Bluey's fame. And so Bluey and Wanda finally chose, in desperation, to return to their house in the suburbs of London. Here they could relax and just be themselves, far away from the glaring eyes of autograph-hunters and nosey-parkers.

As almost ten days of the three-week vacation had elapsed in wasteful pursuits, it seemed sensible to just stay put at home and to shell out. Bluey was able to go ten-pin bowling and to play a bit of squash while Wanda wandered around the shops, both locally and in the west end of London, and read endless crime fiction.

One day when Wanda had leisurely visited her local library and the charity shops in order to acquire more detective novels for her enviable collection, she noticed that a fellow addict was also on a similar hunt for new material. Wanda realised that she kept bumping into this girl who was so avidly in search of fodder in order to feed her habit that she hardly noticed anyone else. Wanda saw in this female a glimpse of herself and she was curious to note her behaviour.

Wanda smiled as she watched while the girl visit every charity shop in town and she searched the appropriate sections for detective fiction. She even entered a bookshop in her quest for new material where she squandered some cash by paying full price for some works which were not available either for free at the library or at a reduced price when second-hand in the charity shops.

This girl had obviously read and re-read Agatha Christie, Phyllis Dorothy James and Dorothy Leigh Sayers from the Golden Age of crime fiction as, of course, Wanda had done. But Wanda was curious to discover what else the stranger might be able to introduce her to for her own prize collection. Wanda's thirst was insatiable and she was so fascinated by this insight into her own life via the antics of another that she decided to approach the stranger. Eventually she spoke to her doppelganger in one of the bookshops.

"I see you are a detective fiction addict, like me," said Wanda as her opening gambit.

The girl removed her glasses and looked at Wanda.

"I have noticed you in all the charity shops and the library," Wanda added.

"Yes," replied the bookworm.

"I am a bit of an addict myself actually and so we have been following the same trail."

Wanda was beginning to feel that she was intruding into the stranger's personal space and so she smiled and endeavoured to move away, slightly embarrassed by her rashness in approaching an unknown individual. The stranger then elected to come to life and she enthusiastically took up the scent.

"I find that detective novels serve a very useful function in keeping me occupied. I am out of work for a while just now and reading stops me worrying about it."

"I am sorry to hear that you are unemployed but I can understand why crime fiction is so useful for you at the moment," replied Wanda.

The other smiled.

"Yes, crime fiction is my salvation right now especially," asserted the girl.

"It has always been mine," continued Wanda. "I can't get enough of it. I have long periods of idleness in my work and it fills the gaps beautifully. I have probably read all the Golden Age stuff."

Wanda was beginning to feel that she was going on a bit because her correspondent looked shy and retiring.

"Me too," the girl replied, "but I am trying to find some of the more recent stuff like Clare Frances, Caroline Graham, Simon Brett and R. D. Wingfield."

Wanda had found a kindred spirit.

"Oh, what have you found this morning then?"

The girl showed Wanda her impressive acquisitions for that day and explained that she was hoping to get a full collection of all her favourite authors before long.

"Have you got time for a chat and a coffee," asked Wanda tentatively while expecting to be refused. "We could compare notes and perhaps arrange to swop some books."

"I can spare a lot of time at the moment," replied the dejected girl with a dry laugh.

The two women then sought out the nearest coffee shop in order to avidly discuss their addictive passion at length and they agreed to exchange some books.

Then the conversation took on a very different turn. It transpired that both Wanda and her new acquaintance, in fact, had more in common than just an addiction for detective mysteries.

"What kind of work do you do, Janice?"

"Well, I took a degree in Technical Theatre Studies and did, for a while, become an assistant stage manager for a repertory company but, when the troop disbanded, I lost my job and have been applying for others ever since but without any success."

"Well, I may be able to help you out a bit if you would be prepared to travel abroad."

"I certainly would," replied Janice who had suddenly perked up and was interested in what her companion had to offer.

Wanda knew that John required some additional backstage help and it seemed an ideal opportunity to assist Vendetta, on the one hand, and to solve Janice's problem in one fell swoop, on the other. Wanda also felt that to have a fellow addict in the Vendetta team would be a very good move on her part. The conversation now took on a new level of excitement as each party saw many possibilities for the future.

CYNTHIA'S ASPIRATION

Cynthia Pringle had spent most of her young life dancing and she had finally turned professional in her late teens immediately after she had left dance school. She was, as a child, put through her paces in classical ballet but, in teenage years, she had turned to jazz and modern dancing. It was in modern dance that she had started her not-very-successful professional career.

Cynthia had danced with a troop who toured the country as disco-cabaret dancers in pubs and clubs and at occasions for celebration, such as significant birthday parties and weddings. The troop then, unfortunately for Cynthia, disbanded due to internal squabbles and dissention in the ranks which did not involve Cynthia but which certainly affected her.

She thence drifted from nightclub to nightclub and she ended up at rock bottom as a pole-dancer. As a pole-dancer, Cynthia's income was reasonable but she still needed to supplement her pay in ways which she found distasteful and which were possibly illegal.

Then Cynthia had met Hal Caxton, who was a bouncer at one of the nightclubs in which she had worked, and he became her bodyguard both literally and metaphorically. Their relationship had been short-lived but their friendship had endured over the years. Hal was a really nice guy. Hal, moreover, had introduced Cynthia to Calendula Fortescue-Bligh who had changed her life and who had boosted her income substantially. Cynthia, therefore, had no need to increase her income in unwelcomed ways.

Cynthia finally decided to go straight and to get a proper job. She had decided to ditch the dancing and to offer entertainment of a very different kind in the guise of hotel catering. Accordingly Cynthia had taken a diploma course in hospitality management and she had then secured her present employment with the Hotel Splendora. Cynthia initially found herself being a glorified waitress at the Splendora. But as her direct line manager, Kevin Clayburn, was due to retire at the end of the year, she was confidently hoping for promotion into his role as catering manager for the hotel.

Cynthia was currently able to live rent-free in a one bedroom cottage in the staff quarters of the hotel but, if her promotion materialised, she would then be asked to move out or to pay rent for the dwelling. Cynthia felt, however, that if she were promoted, it would be worth moving out into a place of her own perhaps with a mortgage attached. If she were bypassed for the promotion, however, Cynthia had already decided that she could easily find employment elsewhere with her current qualifications and her accumulated experience.

For a bit of pin-money, however, Cynthia was still not averse to working for Calendula by being a well-paid snoop, particularly while Hal was around in order to keep an eye on her welfare. The money which Cynthia earned from the Medici Squadron could then be put towards the deposit on her future residence.

When she had entered Myra's room, after Vendetta's farewell party, therefore, she had kept her ears pinned back in order to hear the essence of Myra's conversation with Gerry while appearing to be invisible in the background – an essential qualification for all hospitality staff.

Cynthia, of course, knew that if things got difficult while she was serving these distinguished guests with brandy, cigars and chocolates, she would only have to raise her voice in order to summon assistance from Hal.

Her dilemma now was simply evading the approaches of King Max who had asked for her telephone number. Cynthia, however, decided to keep him on a string for a while and so she did not immediately answer his calls or reply to his voice messages on her mobile phone. Max had rung her several times and he had left inviting messages but she had deliberately chosen to ignore him for the present. Does playing hard to get make the admirer keener, would you say?

Max, meanwhile, had taken himself off for his vacation but he was anxious for the delectable Cynthia to join him. He was slightly perturbed that she had not yet responded to his calls but Max felt that he could not go on pestering her indefinitely.

After about a week into his holiday, Max was relaxing by the pool one evening when his mobile phone vibrated and, to his astonishment, the elusive Cynthia was at the other end of the line. Max then proceeded to tempt her with the delights of his body and his villa in Greece but she protested that she could not get time off from work at present.

Max was, of course, disappointed because he had a strong penchant for the slightly older woman. Youngsters were creatures with whom he got easily tired and bored. Max was looking for a mother substitute, perhaps? But he was another of the brat-pack who had never heard of the notion of counselling.

Max's own dilemma was now to decide whether he should curtail his holiday and go chasing after Cynthia or whether he should simply ignore her completely for the present and enjoy his holiday alone. Poor sod!

But Max did have an idle streak and so he decided that he would relax still further at the poolside in order to recharge his batteries in readiness for the coming onslaught of more hard work. Besides, Max concluded, there was enough local and willing talent hanging around for him to be entertained just now.

But he resolved to track Cynthia down in the near future. Perhaps she could join me at some stage during the next tour? Or I could escape from the tour and catch up with her if I get some free time? Some hope!

Max then lazily fell asleep on his sun-lounger even though it was only mid-afternoon.

Serves you right, Cynthia. You've missed your opportunity for a whirlwind romance with me! You could be sorry! Was Max right? Or was he wrong? You judge for yourself! And now read on.

MAISIE'S REINSTATEMENT

"Maisie, my darling, I am so relieved to hear from you."

"Relax, Bal, I can take care of myself. I've already told you."

"I'd never forgive myself if anything happened to you."

"You fret too much, honey. How's Calendula?"

"She's fine but how did you get on with the bizarre Blaize?"

"I discovered, in fact, that Rocker is not really at the centre of things but Myra certainly is."

"I see," commented Barrington.

Barrington found this piece of information very interesting because it was unusual and not what he was expecting to hear at all.

"They made plans to stow some heroine, I think, in the bell tower at Castle Lucia, Rocker's residence in St Lucia. God, what an eyeful I got of that place! Hell's knackers, it's out of this world. Oh, and I had great fun there at his expense."

"No doubt, he got his money's worth too."

"Yeah, I am shagged out totally."

"Literally and metaphorically."

"I was and I am," Maisie concluded.

"Sorry about that, darling."

"Oh, it was fun while it lasted. All good experience. When he's killed himself, I can tell all my friends that I once had a ding-dong with the mighty Rocker Blaize. But am I done now?"

"Certainly! Diana can disappear forever probably and Maisie can return to being a brunette again."

Maisie then went on to explain how she had obtained her information about Myra bringing some stuff into Castle Lucia and then bamboozling Rocker into storing the gear temporarily in his redundant bell tower.

"Oh, and by the way, I managed to plant a few bugs in the place just as you instructed. And that allowed me to learn what I was prevented from overhearing. I will send them on to you via courier for a listen."

"Wonderful news," concluded Barrington before the business ended.

The conversation then concluded with the usual round of thanks and best wishes as well as a promise from Barrington to pay Maisie her remittance for services rendered.

Barrington then reported progress back to Calendula who was delighted by their scheme.

Maisie thankfully now intended to let her dyed blond hair grow its way out naturally. She had worried, in fact, that the roots were beginning to show somewhat in St Lucia but, as her trip had come to an abrupt halt, she did not need to seek out a hairdresser over there.

Maisie was, however, quite accustomed to changing the colour of her hair and appearing unrecognisable to those who might have actually known her quite well. She had originally trained as an actress who had specialised in character parts and so she thought nothing of switching personalities at the flick of a switch. In addition to altering her hair-colouring, Maisie could also enhanced her disguise with an extensive array of accents and dialects from both home and abroad and, furthermore, she possessed an enviable supply of alternative attire in her costume wardrobe. These talents, of course, came in extremely useful during her work for Calendula and Barrington of the Medici Squadron.

Meanwhile, back in St Lucia, Rocker pined restlessly for some days for his lost love but eventually he managed to console himself with some local crumpet for a couple of nights and then he finally found an American tourist who could replace Diana for the remainder of his vacation.

Myra's gear was stashed for a very short period in the bell tower at Castle Lucia but Rocker was very much relieved when it was collected and sent speedily on its journey. Rocker considered the implications of Myra's nefarious dealings and he decided that he would need to have a quiet word with Gerry very soon with a view to keeping Myra in order in future.

When Rocker rang Gerry, however, his business manager seemed rather evasive and non-committal. This reaction also got Rocker thinking but he did not come to any tangible conclusion and he did not dwell on his thoughts for too long. Gerry did, however, agree to speak to Myra in order to pacify Rocker but, behind Rocker's back, Gerry did not wish to do so in the terms which Rocker had specified. Rocker now felt that the matter would be finally and satisfactorily dealt with by passing the buck to Gerry. He was wrong actually. Poor sod!

Marie and Léon were much relieved when their master finally went home. The fuss was all over and their life could now return to a lazy degree of normality once more.

Their pet Labrador, Timeo, who was not normally allowed in the main part of Castle Lucia, especially when the master was in residence, was, at last, able to roam the grounds, to swim in the pool and to obtain his fair share of attention from his owners.

When Gerry did eventually ring Myra it was to excoriate him severely for involving Rocker in St Lucia.

"What the hell were you thinking of Myra, dearie?" began Gerry.

"Well, there was a bit of a panic when the customs guys were sniffing around, once the gear had arrived but could not be sent on, and so I had no choice," protested the suitably admonished Myra.

"You could collapse the whole operation like a pack of cards, you fucking idiot!"

"Well, I had no choice," Myra repeated petulantly yet ineffectually.

"Never, never do that again! Or I'll kill you, buster."

Myra merely grunted and shrugged.

"And don't go snooping around to check up on me ever again. Do you hear me, sweetie? Or the consequences for you will be astronomical. Understand?" continued the angry Gerry.

Myra reluctantly promised to behave in future, although he was quite certain that Rocker had not suspected what the stash actually was and, therefore, Rocker would have notion of the scope of the entire operation. Myra was another one who was wrong. Poor bugger!

Gerry checked up on progress generally of the consignment of stuff and he then returned to put the finishing touches to his planning of Vendetta's next tour.

REGGIE'S MACHINATION

Reginald Trevelyan sat at his desk in the offices of the Benefice Charity Trust. This outfit was a charity for whom Reggie was the Chief Executive.

The Benefice Charity Trust raised funds for worthy and deserving causes and it had obtained government sponsorship in order to keep the show on the road. Various hopeful organisations then applied for donations which were granted or declined accordingly following a monthly meeting of the Board of Governors of the charity.

Reggie had single-handedly built up the trust from its inception and he was proud of his altruistic and benevolent expertise. Reggie was an ex-corporate accountant but he had been able to turn his hand to promotional activities while the Benefice Charity Trust was being launched. But after the successful launch and establishment of the trust, Reggie had handed over the task of marketing to Patterson Promotions – a switched-on marketing agency in the west end of London with offices nationwide. Reggie and the owner and founder of Patterson Promotions, one Donald Patterson, were great chums and drinking buddies.

Although Reggie was munificent by trade, he was, however, corrupt by nature. For this reason, Reggie had devised a means of forming a bogus company which then promptly applied for the trust's own charitable funds. The said bogus company was later dissolved but the grant received was conveniently pocketed by the Chief Executive of the Benefice Charity Trust. Reggie had, somehow, managed to claim bankruptcy for his duplicitous corporations for any number of reasons, such as stock thefts, market nosedives, pandemics and staff shortages, when his companies were sadly dissolved.

The fruits of Reggie's disreputable activity, of course, kept him in clover and he had become accustomed to his elevated financial status. Reggie had repeated this scam quite a few times and he had not yet been detected. Shame!

The process resembled an incestuous loop which never got broken. On each occasion when Reggie managed to pull off one of his swindles, he then promised himself never to repeat the deception not only because his conscience got the better of him but also because he was nervous about being detected. Reggie's promises to himself, of course, were invariably broken. And so the wheel of fortune was in perpetual motion for Reggie Trevelyan.

Reggie was shuffling some papers on his desk one day in early spring. He was assembling the latest crop of applications which were begging for a handout from the trust. The trust's official application form adopted a standard format in order to enquire why the applicant needed a handout, what the gift would be used for and how it could benefit the wider community. A profit and loss account and a balance sheet from the contender also needed to accompany the application form in order to expose the financial position of the organisation concerned.

Because Reggie was in charge of filtering each set of applications which the trust received and he was responsible for assessing each applicant's financial prospects from the accounts submitted, he was easily able to slip his own fraudulent bid into the batch which would be presented to the governors and then duly considered at the next board meeting.

Accordingly Reggie included his own contribution from the counterfeit company of Marshbrook Theatricals. This Marshbrook Theatricals venture purported to be set up in order to offer live theatre to small villages, the inhabitants of which could not afford to go into the main towns for their entertainment. Or so the grant candidate claimed. The application of Marshbrook Theatricals was for a modest sum – a mere £30K – by comparison with some of the other scams which Reggie had managed to pull off.

Reggie had formulated the bright idea of putting in a humble request occasionally in order to deflect interest away from himself by way of a double-bluff. If Reggie supported a modest cause at the meeting of the Board of Governors, then no one would suspect any skulduggery. But were his fellow committee members actually deceived?

Donald Patterson, who served as an honorary member of the board, and who knew Reggie quite well, had his suspicions but he had nothing definite on which to base them. For the time being, therefore, Donald elected to push his thoughts about Reggie under the carpet because it was in his own business interests so to do. Donald's misgivings, however, did trouble him somewhat, especially at night when he was trying to get some much-needed rest.

Reggie's secretary and the trust's administrative officer, Madeleine Pearson, moreover, was the intuitive type who seemed to observe all — both Reggie's furtive evasion and Donald's troubled brow. She noticed, for instance, that she had no record of the application from Marshbrook Theatricals. And she would normally record the receipt of all grant applications which had arrived in the post each day as part of her daily routine.

So Madeleine wondered how this proposal from Marshbrook Theatricals had suddenly appeared on Reggie's desk. And she also remembered other occasions when a fresh application had appeared mysteriously from out of nowhere and yet she had had no previous record of it.

Strange that, she thought. And it has happened before, she remembered. Funny that. How could these things slip through the net? It could only come from the direction of my boss, Reginald Trevelyan. Is there a distinct pattern here, I wonder?

The scheduled date for the meeting of the governors soon arrived and Reggie was glad that the day had at long last been reached. The meeting was attended by Reggie, in the chair, and Madeleine as the official secretary of the Board of Governors. The other committee members were Philip Cowan, Anita Banks and Lionel McNaughton as well as the honorary member Donald Patterson. There were no apologies for absence because all were present at the meeting.

Discussion quickly ensued about the latest batch of applications received by the trust for grants of their funds. The vast majority of applications were rejected for numerous reasons, mainly concerned with company ethos when community interests were not adequately served as well as general financial incompetency due to mismanagement.

As it happened Marshbrook Theatricals ticked all the boxes splendidly at the meeting and thus this organisation was granted its tax-free gift of £30K which went straight into an offshore account in order to await its fate. When sadly the business folded unexpectedly and unannounced some months later, no one was at all concerned with the exception of Reggie who was rubbing his hands with glee. Surprise! Surprise!

Reggie knew that the Benefice Charity Trust never checked up on the progress and the activities of the organisations to whom they dispensed the trust's money like tea from a tea-urn. Interesting!

Only Madeleine was aware of the closure and the bankruptcy of Marshbrook Theatricals but she kept this secret encased within her bosom in readiness for a rainy day. But she could now detect the pattern clearly.

MAX'S ENTERPRISE

Max had retired to his place in Greece in the Peloponnese foothills for the duration of the holiday. He had previously purchased a plot of land here and had detailed one of the local architects to take charge of constructing for him an impressive domain in record time.

Max had visited several times since the completion of the dwelling and it was to this location that he had attempted to lure the delightful Cynthia but to no avail. He had contemplated going back to the UK in order to win her but he had eventually decided that he ought to spend some of his holiday tidying up his business affairs generally and, in particular, his finances.

Max had also decided to amuse himself with getting drunk on ouzo and chatting up the local taverna wenches who were not disinclined to pick up huge tips for their out-of-hours services.

Generally Max was respected by the locals because he frequently injected money into the area. His local architect and the builders of his residence, for instance, had certainly learned that it would serve their interests to greet him warmly on every visit. And they were handsomely rewarded for their diligence.

Max was fractionally older than the other members of Vendetta but this fact did not mean that he was more mature. He had, of course, wasted his youth somewhat before being plunged into the limelight but now he had as much interest in making money as he did in bedding women. And it was for this reason that money laundering was his primary forte.

Max imagined that his biological father had probably been an accountant or a banker because of his own interest in money. But as Max had actually never met his natural parents, he had no way of verifying his speculation. Max had been brought up by a series of foster-carers before being legally adopted by the Pollard family but he simply had no interest in tracking down his real parentage. He did not even know whether his parents were alive or dead.

Presumably any parent who recognised him would claim paternity or maternity as a means of extracting money from him but nothing had so far emerged in this respect. Indeed, Max only assumed that he must have had some parents somewhere at some stage – because most people did. It was the prevailing law of nature. But really he didn't much care. And maybe Max's upbringing was the reason why he was attracted to women of Cynthia's age – that is well past the age of consent.

Because of his money interest, Max had two accountants. One kosher and one not so upright.

His official accountant had a plush office in central London and handled only those clients who earned millions annually. They were, therefore, snotty and fussy but this suited Max right down to the ground because the Inland Revenue leapt when this firm spoke.

All Max's day-to-day bookkeeping was, of course, handled by the lesser minions on the staff at Prentice, Klevier and Degottle in London. And, when the end of the tax year arrived, Max felt reassured that his affairs would be conducted satisfactorily without too much hassle by the firm's partners who prepared his official accounts and his income tax returns.

While in Greece, therefore, Max assembled and despatched details of his expenses by courier to Prentice, Klevier and Degottle so that the bookkeepers could get busy with whatever they did on his behalf. Max was unusually efficient in keeping bills and receipts for this purpose. He was not exactly anally-retentive in this respect but he certainly was way ahead of the game when compared with the rest of his colleagues at Vendetta Ice.

Max, however, had another under-the-table accountant for a different type of deal. His name was Reggie and this guy knew a thing or two about money laundering. Reggie, therefore, was consulted frequently by Max when he wished to move brass around the globe in order to invest in property and in business enterprise which would disguise its origins and so evade detection.

Max and Reggie had met at an upper crust club-restaurant in London while Max was entertaining a high-class female whom he was endeavouring unsuccessfully to impress. Reggie, though, had gone to the restaurant on his own and he was seemingly looking for others with whom he could converse. The club's restaurant was of the kind whereby the menu did not have any prices printed on it because, if you needed to ask the price of the fayre, then you could not afford to dine there.

When the classy female elected to leave early and return to her own abode without Max to accompany her, he and Reggie thence consoled each other at the club with high priced drinks and upmarket cigars. Between then they downed several bottles of champagne at the kind of price which would normally require the consumer to take out a second mortgage.

During this first auspicious meeting, many financial plans were hatched while few questions were asked about the provenance of the funds to be laundered. Dirty money was seldom a topic which the big boys wanted to air publicly but for Max and Reggie this topic of conversation was all-consuming.

From this meeting, consequently, Max acquired a conspirator, a drinking buddy and a fellow crook who could efficiently take care of and maximise the profits from Max's drug-money.

Max, for instance, had, on the advice of Reggie, invested in property around the world and in offshore enterprise. Max was also assisted by Reggie to open accounts in various false names in several different countries around the world. Max did not know how Reggie managed these feats of amazement beneath the radar but he did know that Reggie was very useful in this respect and that the slush-fund was rapidly mounting.

Another useful occupation for Reggie was to transfer money to various creditors across the globe on Max's behalf. Max had, for instance, recently employed Reggie to send money across to Asia in order to pay off some of Gerry's contacts who had been working hard on the mule-train for the drug-scam. Max felt pleased that this trifling detail could be handled very successfully and, while he sat sleepily by the poolside in Greece, he congratulated himself on his own ingenuity.

The elusive Cynthia, meanwhile, back at the Hotel Splendora, was considering her next move in this game of chance with King Max.

ROUCHUKA'S RETREAT

Rouchuka's holiday was spent at her chateau in the south of France. She wanted to visit this property because it was being restored by some local workmen and she needed to check on progress.

So Rouchuka could kill two birds with one stone. She could get away from the razzmatazz of showbiz life while, simultaneously, supervising the work being carried out on her property and ensuring that its progress would be continuous.

Greta had escorted her mistress to France and she had stayed for a short period. Greta had then returned to the UK to the bosom of her own family in order to get a break. Rouchuka always paid for Geta's travel plans and she was happy to do so for such a sensitive and congenial companion.

Rouchuka also had some bodyguards in tow but she soon dispensed with their services. She felt that having a bodyguard team around would actually draw attention to her status. So she gave her friends a paid holiday in order to purchase some time in solitude.

The first week of Rouchuka's stay in France was taken up with supervising the workers, discussing plans for the further restoration work and sampling the delights of French home-cooking. One of the local women always came to the chateau when Rouchuka was in residence in order to cook, clean and launder for the mistress of the house.

Rouchuka inspected her small vineyard which the locals worked on and she discussed progress and profits with the site manager. The locals earned an appreciable percentage of the vineyard's profits as profit-sharing employees but the situation suited Rouchuka admirably for tax purposes, not to mention the favours it bought her. The local vine-workers, therefore, showed their employer the utmost respect and welcomed her on each visit with much in the way of merriment and French kisses on both cheeks. Rouchuka thus greeted her old friends and a newcomer to the team, called Roussel, who was gallant and courteous to a fault.

Rouchuka felt that, if she were ever able to retire from Vendetta Ice, she would want to make her home permanently in this part of the world. Perhaps with Greta by her side as a full-time live-in companion?

On Saturday nights, the vineyard team and the restoration workers always celebrated together with a lavish meal to which Rouchuka was customarily invited and she accepted gladly. She took along her own contribution of food and drink which was always gratefully appreciated during the festivities. The charade of initially refusing her generosity was quickly followed by grovelling acceptance. This scenario was regularly enacted and so was Rouchuka's premature exit from the scene on the pretext of needing an early night in order to allow the team to really enjoy themselves.

At the first Saturday evening party, Rouchuka noticed that Roussel had managed to engineer himself a seat next to her but that she was not that displeased. She retired early from the party as usual but the chivalrous Roussel volunteered to walk her home. Despite Rouchuka's protest, she caved in eventually because Roussel, like the rest of the crew, was not at all mesmerised by her fame. And some – perhaps including Roussel – were actually unaware of it. And this suited Rouchuka really well. Roussel escorted Rouchuka to her door, bowed graciously and then left abruptly with a courteous farewell. Rouchuka was surprised to realise that she was slightly disappointed when Roussel left.

The next morning, however, Roussel arrived on her doorstep with some wild flowers from his garden, some wine, cheese and hunks of bread. This was apparently a thank-you present from the team who were grateful both for her contribution to last night's bun-fight and for the profit-sharing income which they derived from her vineyard. Rouchuka found herself inviting Roussel back to share the produce with her over lunch in the garden.

Roussel spoke fairly good English and so Rouchuka was able to converse freely with him in her native tongue rather than in her schoolgirl French. In truth Roussel actually spoke excellent English with virtually no trace of an accent because he had lived for many years in the UK. But he prudently found it politic to accentuate his French accent when in the company of a British woman. They talked inconsequently over lunch about the vineyard and its output, the latest gossip in the village and the progress of the chateau's restoration.

Rouchuka also took the opportunity to show Roussel around her domain because he seemed to take a great interest in the restoration work and its authenticity in terms of French rural culture. He even volunteered to keep an eye on the workmen in her absence which Rouchuka found very reassuring and so she accepted his generous offer. She explained that she needed to travel with her work but she gave him her private mobile number so that he could report back to her as necessary. Rouchuka, of course, was evasive about the work which she undertook and she hoped that Roussel would not have any interest and/or a knowledge of the pop scene.

It seemed important to Rouchuka to keep her popular culture occupation a secret from Roussel because she believed that she would then appear more favourable in his eyes. This was surely a sign of her liking for the dashing Frenchman?

Because Rouchuka was also interested in classical music, she discovered an affinity with Roussel in that he was an advocate of the French impressionist genre from the early twentieth century. The couple, therefore, discussed Debussy at some length as well as his contemporaries, such as Ravel, Messiaen, Satie and Fauré. Rouchuka was happy to converse freely in this vein not only because she had found something in common with the fetching Roussel but also because it kept them well away from the subject of popular music which might inadvertently reveal her identity.

The holiday for Rouchuka finally came to a close but, while she was in France, she had spent a most exciting and restful break in the company of the attentive Roussel. She returned to the hubbub of life on the circuit with renewed vigour as well as with a promise to find a way of freeing herself from her current employment.

Rouchuka had, during the vacation, had time to think about the future and to decide in which direction she was aiming. But she was unable to put her schemes into viable practice until she had done some more research into the theatrical world in which she would like to reside. Rouchuka had begun secretly to harbour an ambition to sing in musical theatre and this notion had stimulated a train of thought which would not readily budge from Rouchuka's mind.

Roussel had been very attentive throughout Rouchuka's work-break but he knew how to play it cool by giving her the promise of future romantic attention but not moving things forward before she was really as ripe as one of the grapes in her vineyard.

KICKER'S ASTONISHMENT

Jenny and Kicker set off for a romantic holiday in Italy's capital city in order to recharge their batteries after the long northern tour of England. They were being worn down by the constant travel with Vendetta, on the one hand, and their need to semi-retire and to start a family, on the other. Jenny and Kicker had discussed this future but the pair had not yet formulated a plan of action for the way forward.

On their holiday they visited the Forum and the Colosseum in the heart of ancient Rome. The Roman Forum displayed buildings from which the roman empire had once been run and this notion gave them both the idea that their dilemma could be resolved with a bit of ingenuity. The Colosseum with its triple-tiered structure which had once been a medieval fortress similarly gave the couple inspiration about the way ahead.

When visiting the Palatine Hill, where the ancient hoi polloi had once lived and, legend has it, was the place on which Rome was founded by Romulus who killed his brother Remus, Jenny and Kicker could vividly imagine the vision which the founder of Rome harboured within his breast.

The majesty and splendour of the Vatican museums and the Sistine Chapel, wherein Michelangelo's legacy from the ancient world was viewed by the visitors with awe and wonderment, also rendered them both speechless.

"How can I get out of all my contract?" asked Kicker as if he were voicing his thoughts aloud when he and Jenny were sitting in a street cafe enjoying some coffee and tiramisu as an afternoon treat.

"Can you consult a lawyer?" replied Jenny in the hope of making a helpful suggestion?

"I think if I leave, the whole band will collapse overnight. It is unlikely that they will be able to replace me at short notice."

"Well, that's not really your problem, is it? All you need to find out if how you can get free," Jenny encouraged.

"Vendetta is already divided between us and them. So it will collapse if one of us leaves."

Kicker recalled the fact that he, Bluey and Rouchuka were really with Vendetta because they had been compellingly recruited by Rocker and Gerry who then signed them up to a long-term contract. Jenny and Kicker then reminisced about those early days but not in a wistful manner. At the time Kicker, Rouchuka and Bluey had been simply carried along on the tide of excitement but they had not really thought the commitment through. All had been tempted by the carrot of fame and fortune and, in the absence of a better offer, they had jumped at the chance without thinking out its implications. The scheming Gerry, of course, had stitched everything up tightly with legally binding contracts as if the three of them had been committed for life.

Kicker spoke at length in terms of "what if this?" and "what if that?" but the level-headed Jenny reminded her partner that the past was now all irrelevant and that they should think only about the future at present.

"I am also worried about being associated with the brat-pack," Jenny urged.

"I know they are a bit tedious but they are just a lot of kids really."

"I didn't mean just that," replied Jenny enigmatically.

"What do you mean, darling?"

Jenny then went on to explain that she believed that some of the brat-pack were involved in drug-smuggling. Kicker was dumfounded at this news because he had not picked up anything of the sort on the bush telegraph. Jenny reported that she had overheard some conversations between Max and Myra and between Gerry and Max. And she backed up her case with some plausible examples of the way in which they behaved. Max, furthermore, had let a few things slip when he was blotto one night.

Kicker now felt that he must definitely extricate himself from Vendetta as he in no way wished to be associated with criminal activity or, worse still, accused or implicated in such illicit trade. Jenny and Kicker were now even more determined to make a rapid exit from the band and, to this end, Kicker phoned his lawyer from Rome and made an appointment in order to discuss the termination of his contract as soon as the law would allow. A Zoom video conferencing session was accordingly booked for later in the week.

At the Zoom meeting, Kicker's London lawyer, Christopher Naddingley, had reassured Kicker that he could be extricated from his contract, albeit at a price, pretty smartish and that a sworn affidavit would, furthermore, assist him if trouble broke out in the Vendetta camp because of the nefarious dealing of the brat-pack and its business manager.

Christopher agreed to draw up the necessary documentation for Kicker to sign. The papers would be ready in a few days for despatch to Kicker's home in Bulgaria. Kicker could then sign the papers and return these documents to the lawyer who would keep them ready for action once Kicker had given the go-ahead.

The couple next moved on to Bulgaria for the rest of their vacation. Here they could enjoy the peace of rural living on their country estate and they could meet their many friends and neighbours. Here Jenny and Kicker partook of several congenial lunches and evening meals in an atmosphere which uplifted both their spirits.

A visit to a local notary in order to sign the legal papers, which had recently arrived from Christopher Naddingley, before a reliable witness then took place and Jenny and Kicker began to breathe again with relief following this event. Jenny and Kicker thus felt happier in their minds about the future away from the glaring spotlight in which Vendetta sat but they did, of course, have reservations about returning to the group and continuing their work.

The legal documentation was designed to release Kicker from his duties after Vendetta's tour of the southern counties. They had also instructed Christopher to hold off the presentation of the documentation to Vendetta until the last moment because they knew that Gerry and the others would hit the roof once they had learned of Kicker's intention to withdraw. Kicker did not relish the prospect of informing his colleagues of his decision but Jenny felt a secret pleasure at the thought of the discomfiture of certain members of the group. Both Jenny and Kicker then began to count the days before they could escape.

When the time was right, therefore, Jenny and Kicker returned to London in order to resume their work for Vendetta but with mixed feelings of delight, relief, pleasure and impishness. The flight home was uneventful and, on landing, Jenny and Kicker made their way to a convenient London hotel in readiness for resuming work.

On arrival in London, Kicker returned the signed documentation to Christopher Naddingley who had agreed to hold the papers until Kicker gave the word.

JULES' INFILTRATION

Jules Axminster lived in Agadir in Morocco with Hakim who fed him plentiful supplies of spiced chicken tagine and beef tagine served with couscous as well as oceans of gunpowder mint tea. Jules put up with being overfed because Hakim was easy-going and he allowed his live-in partner to come and go as he pleased. And wanderlust regularly grabbed Jules by the proverbials both in connection with his work and in order to assuage his continual boredom.

Hakim was attracted by Jules' long brown wavy hair and his brown eyes as well as his elegant gait and his carefree disposition. Jules was not, for instance, hidebound by rules and regulations nor was he concerned with the minutiae of life and this trait appealed to and complemented Hakim's home-loving and slightly motherly instincts.

Jules was an information technology whizz-kid with brains enough to sink the Titanic. He had acquired a PhD in Computer Science from Cambridge University by the time he was twenty years of age, having previously acquired degrees in Mathematics and Electronic Engineering. At thirteen years of age, moreover, Jules had secured a degree in Forensic Science from Dundee university. So you get the picture? He was a tad clever, right?

For Jules, stuffed with knowledge and a thirst to acquire more, his tolerance of fools was less than zero but he had married his laptop to which he had made an avowed commitment for life. Hakim was the only creature on earth with whom Jules was prepared to be consistently unfaithful to his laptop and this was probably only because the laptop could tolerate the ménage à trois. If Jules, at any stage, needed to upgrade his current laptop to another state-of-the-art beast, then his devotion would automatically be transferred and the commitment would be deemed to be ongoing.

When Jules needed to travel for work or pleasure, his language skills also came in handy. At an early age Jules had taught himself Latin, Greek, French, Italian, German, Russian, Arabic and Chinese and the rest of the world's languages could go hang.

Jules' incentive to bestir himself had now been fired up by a phone call which he had recently received from one of his major clients who wanted to send him on a special mission to east Asia. Jules relished the prospect of this trip because it would earn him a mint of money, it would engage his cerebral ingenuity and it would cater for his sexual proclivities. Three birds with one stone, eh?

Accordingly Jules kissed a tearful Hakim goodbye and jetset himself off for South Korea. At his destination, Jules soon identified a certain drug-courier with the aim of planting a bug on or around him somewhere. Jules was good at making hardware and software bugs which he could use in order to spy on this targets. He had even sold a few of his bugging devices online. And, of course, his client was a regular purchaser of these devices.

Jules found himself a suitably dodgy hotel in South Korea, explored the demimonde freely and then set about tracking down his quarry. He picked up the scent quite easily from the preliminary information which he had to hand and so he set about following his mark.

The mark was in east Asia in order to check up on a drug-traffic route and to generally have a good time. This augured well for Jules who was fully intending to have a good time himself too. Jules' prey was a cross-dresser who, on this trip, maintained that he could disguise himself by wearing conventional clothes. But Jules was not fooled by this disguise. He sniffed out the rat and stuck close to him. By this means, Jules could identify one of the vital links in the drug-chain and he could also observe the habits of his quarry.

After a day or three of snooping around, Jules observed that his target had a penchant for male strip-joints in South Korea's capital city, Seoul, as a means of making the evenings pass quickly. Jules, therefore, did likewise.

Jules' target entered the Asian Delight Club one evening in order to waste some of his time while checking up on the progress of the drugs through what Gerry had told him was an unorthodox route. Myra sat in an alcove where he could quietly watch the show and where he believed he could be stimulated unobserved. Or so he imagined. Poor sod!

Jules ordered a drink and acclimatised himself with his surroundings. The Asian Delight Club was obviously popular with both the locals as well as numerous tourists from many nations. Some of the tourists looked as if they had travelled the world going from one strip-joint to the next and doing not much else. From a good vantage point at the bar, Jules observed his prey and noticed that, while he appeared to be self-sufficient, there was almost certainly an air of loneliness about him.

After a word or two with the barman, Jules learned the fact that his intended victim was a British subject who had recently arrived and who had covertly been enquiring about the drug-scene. Jules then waited for his pigeon to start to look a bit bored before he made his approach.

"Do you mind if I join you? I understand that you're British like me," was Jules' opening line.

Myra looked up in surprise. He had not expected that his quiet space would be invaded. Myra was initially irritated by the stranger's intrusive assumption that he needed a friend. But when Myra met the newcomer's brown eyes, he decided that he would make an exception in this case.

The two men then sat quite close together but continued to watch the show while, all the time, trying to pretend that the other did not exist. But both men felt the same degree of stimulation not only for the artistes on the stage but also for each other.

Very soon Jules and Myra got chatting. They commented on the performing talent, the non-stop titillation and its obvious benefits for the audience. They ordered some more drinks. They even shared a bottle of champagne. They drank it indiscriminately. They moved closer together. They did a few drugs.

Myra learned that his new companion, Arnie, also lived in the UK and that he worked as a freelance writer for a number of publishers. Some of Arnie's work involved travel and research which was why he had found himself in South Korea. Arnie explained that he was currently doing some research on Korean history for one of his clients who was a scientific magazine publisher but that he was combining this task with a short holiday. As Myra knew nothing about science – and cared even less about it – he did not question what he was told by his newfound friend.

The duo moved even closer and eventually indulged in some under-the-table foreplay prior to retiring to Myra's luxury hotel bedroom for a night of bliss, kiss and nose candy. Heaven!

MEDICI'S INSPIRATION

They listened to the recording made by the bug, designed especially for the job by the Medici Squadron's resident whizz-kid, which Maisie had planted in Castle Lucia in order to snoop on the conservation between Rocker Blaize and Myra. The recording device had also been set to capture telephone calls and other conversations but none of this data was of any interest to the listeners.

Rocker seemed to be castigating Myra for his drug-dealing but Myra appeared bored by his interrogator's prudishness. Myra carefully explained that they had a foolproof plan but, when questioned, he refused to disclose either his accomplice or any other pertinent detail. No amount of badgering or threats from Rocker had made any difference to Myra's resolve.

At one stage Rocker lost it and grabbed Myra by the throat but the other had merely brushed Rocker's hands aside and sniggered. Myra justified his actions by stating that he, Myra, was in no way implicated in the latest bout of raids by the local customs officials who were currently mounting a clean-up operation in the Caribbean. Rocker argued that if Myra were caught red-handed at any time, then the whole of Vendetta would suffer devastation.

Myra was eventually told, in no uncertain terms, to get the hell out of St Lucia, even though Rocker had, at last, reluctantly agreed to store some gear in the bell tower for a limited period. Rocker had simply buckled under the pressure but, at the same time, he believed that he would not be incriminated if the paraphernalia were moved out pronto, as Myra had promised, in the next few hours.

Rocker was informed that a bodyguard-type messenger would call on the pretext of collecting a few items which Myra had inadvertently left behind. The password for handing this consignment over was revealed as "goodwill hunting" which the messenger would include in one of his opening sentences.

"But we don't know what the merchandise actually is, do we, sweet love?" began Barrington as he closed down the recorded file on his computer.

"Well, it must be heroine because Myra has already denied that it was coke," deduced Calendula.

They replayed the recording in order to verify this pertinent question.

"Only time will tell on this one. So this is another waiting game, eh?" added Barrington.

Calendula nodded her assent.

"But we have now played our trump card and he is in South Korea as we speak? Yes?" enquired Barrington's partner. "And he's hit the mark, I assume?"

"Not heard back yet from him but Jules would never fail us."

"And, of course, we have our very own US private detective. Haven't we, lion cub?" Calendula continued, almost musing to herself.

"Such an asset especially with her oscillating sexual preferences."

"So that's the team, then."

"Well, we may need to supplement it a bit, perhaps. But we'll see," Barrington mused.

"Shall we go to the Peacock's Feather tonight for dinner?"

Calendula wanted to change the subject and to distance herself from work.

"Absolutely."

It seemed to be a tradition at the commencement of any enterprise that the pair should celebrate their success in advance.

At the Peacock's Feather, the couple sat at a window table secured for them by Pedro the manager. Pedro always cared solicitously for Calendula Fortescue-Bligh and Barrington Flint because they were regular customers and, more importantly, they were handsome tippers. This meant that Pedro and his staff were able to supplement their income tax-free with the help of these diners.

Calendula and Barrington usually sat outside in the garden but the weather was inclement in early spring and thus a window table was secured for the pair as the next best thing to alfresco dining.

They ordered from the specials of the day which consisted of marinated sardines with chargrilled tomatoes and red peppers for starters followed by pan-roasted chicken breasts for Calendula and a beef wellington with a truffle and wholegrain mustard garnish for Barrington. The whole meal was washed down by a chardonnay which accompanied the starters and a red burgundy which complimented the main dish.

This fayre was substantial enough for both of them and so they skipped the desserts. Coffee for Barrington and hibiscus herbal tea for Calendula completed the meal.

Calendula and Barrington had previously been a couple of drifters before they had met in Paris many years ago but now, as a couple, they were both jet-propelled by their mission in life.

Calendula was a highly sought after fine artist, with oodles of talent, who sold her work worldwide with little or no effort on her part. She had started as a penniless artist in Paris, scraping a living initially before she hit the big time. Now she was the owner of Two City Designs – so called because she maintained an art studio both in London and in Paris. When she had been impecunious and living in France, however, Calendula had resorted to the seduction of various wealthy Parisian aristocrats and she found that this strategy constituted a feasible supplement to her meagre income. But it also made her restless and discontent. Now that the success of Two City Designs had taken root, of course, Calendula was more content with her progress and her financial rewards from her self-employment.

Barrington had been variously a corporate lawyer and a freelance business management consultant in the past who had travelled constantly with his work. While he managed to circumnavigate the globe and to acquire a few tricks along the way, he had also learned to be an aimless and disconsolate wanderer. It was, however, not until Calendula and Barrington had met up in Paris, and struck up a lasting intimate relationship, that both their lives had attained an even keel by doing an about-turn.

In Paris the pair came up with the idea of forming the Medici Squadron and, from that point onwards, they had never looked back. The Squadron had exposed many scams and much nefarious activity of the rich and famous and other personages who pretended to be so and as such cavorted accordingly.

Contentment for Cal and Bal was, therefore, now the order of the day. And they had thus settled in the UK with their main residence in Grove Naxton Cross in middle England and a supplementary riverside apartment in Vauxhall in London as well as a villa in the south of France.

PART 3
ICING ON THE GINGERBREAD

The Queen Of Hearts
The Queen of Hearts, she made some tarts,
All on a summer's day.
The Knave of Hearts, he stole those tarts
And took them clean away.
The King of Hearts called for the tarts
And beat the knave full sore.
The Knave of Hearts brought back the tarts
And vowed he'd steal no more.

HENRY'S RECRUITMENT

Wanda had, during the holiday respite, approached Henry with a view to asking him if he had a vacancy for an assistant stage manager. She knew, in principle, that John and Henry were looking for another member of the crew and she hoped that this knowledge was actually true. When Wanda received an affirmative reply to her enquiry, she invited Janice to make contact directly with Henry.

Henry had then asked Janice to come to the London office which he shared with Gerry Paxton and John Dawson as Vendetta's administrative headquarters. It made sense for Vendetta to have a London office suite which Gerry, Henry and John could share between them when not on the road. This was also an office expense which could be set again tax.

While Henry was not that keen on sharing an office with Gerry, he did see an advantage to this situation in that he could keep a keen eye on the business manager. And, in any case, they only came together in order to discuss business affairs but otherwise they did not get under each other's feet too much. John also had an office here but he seldom needed to visit it.

The offices of Vendetta Ice's administrative headquarters, known as Colossus Enterprises plc, were situated in the east end of London in order to be able to get a favourable rental while, simultaneously, not drawing attention to the nub of a burgeoning industry.

Janice Evans arrived in good time for her appointment with Henry. She was so early, in fact, that she had to walk around the block a couple of times. She was not really nervous about the forthcoming interview but she dearly wanted to get this particular job for reasons of her own. Janice thought this was a bit of a dodgy area and she did not relish the thought of working here while the cohort were not on tour but she decided that she would have to put up with the rough as well as the smooth in this case. Needs must when the devil drives.

When she approached the offices of Colossus Enterprises plc, Janice was struck by how uninviting the building looked from the outside but, once inside, she realised that this place was a sight for sore eyes. It was obviously a converted warehouse and the conversion had really spared no expense. The entrance hall was large and luxurious. The floor was obviously an engineered oak with rooms off it and a wrought iron staircase which led to an upper floor.

A receptionist greeted Janice warmly and enquired the nature of her business. Janice explained that she had come to see Henry Sissingford. She was then asked to complete a guest visitor's form. Once Janice had undertaken this token of officialdom, she was then given a visitor's badge which she pinned to her jacket while she waited patiently for Henry's arrival. Janice did, of course, appreciate that security would be of paramount importance in an enterprise such as this, despite her contempt for red tape.

Janice was impressed that Henry collected her in person from the reception area rather than simply directing her to mount the stairs to his office. Henry courteously thanked, Donna, the receptionist, and then led Janice up the staircase with a welcoming smile and a pleasant demeanour.

"You found us all right, then, Janice?" he began.

"Oh, yes, no trouble at all. Your directions were very helpful, thank you. I might not have found your offices without them," replied the candidate for employment.

"We try to keep a bit incognito here, for obvious reasons," explained Henry to his prospective employee, "and so, directions are usually necessary for those, such as yourself, who may not know the area well."

At the top of the stairs, Henry turned right and guided Janice into his private office. Here Janice noted that the room was neat and tidy and that the decor did not deteriorate the higher one went up the building.

Henry began the interview by explaining to Janice the nature of the business, the need for confidentiality and the rigorous demands of the job of an assistant stage manager. Janice listened with interest and then asked a few pertinent questions which she felt she was expected to ask in order to show interest.

"I gather from Wanda that I would be working mostly on tour, then?" queried Janice.

"Yes, of course. And during the breaks you would be based here but the work will not be as frantic as when Vendetta are on tour obviously. And, indeed, you may not actually be required to work here much at all during the breaks between tours because we have a small office staff here in residence. And, of course, you will be contracted and paid for each tour separately."

"I see," commented Janice.

"Your work here would mainly consist of planning and preparation with John Dawson, the crew's road manager and stage manager, but, apart from that, you would have earned a break after each tour."

Janice also learned that John Dawson would be her immediate superior in the job on offer.

"I see," Janice repeated because she felt that she ought to make a contribution to the conversation and she wanted to appear keen.

Henry continued his spiel with elaboration and clarification for his interviewee.

"Obviously, because you will be away from home during all the band's lengthy tours, we feel that you should not need to be here much at all between times."

I had better not say another "I see," thought Janice.

"I understand," she said instead which was merely a paraphrase of the same thing.

"I have studied your career resumé, Janice, and all looks in order. You seem to be no stranger at all to touring with a company obviously."

Janice laughed breathless but did not comment.

After giving out some more information about the nature of the job and the temperament of some of Vendetta's members, albeit in an edited version, Henry took Janice on a tour of the offices.

Gerry Paxton, the business manager for Vendetta, Henry explained, was out of the office just now. But Janice did get an opportunity to meet John Dawson and they seemed to hit it off quite well – much to Janice's delight.

A few days later, in consequence, Janice was asked to return to Colossus Enterprises for a second interview at which John explained a lot more about the demands of the job on offer and the personnel involved. Janice felt this augured well for her success. And eventually she was proved right.

Henry wrote to Janice officially the next day in order to offer her the job of assistant stage manager with Vendetta Ice at a miserable salary and the prospective candidate appreciatively accepted.

Janice then agreed to join the troop for the forthcoming video recording session at Hobart Studios in Kelleringham to be followed swiftly by the tour of the southern counties due to commence within a few weeks. Arrangements were then made for Janice to be picked up in south London with the other members of the crew who were making their way to Hobart Studios.

Janice was also invited to the reunion gathering which took place immediately before the recording session was due to start.

Janice was, of course, well briefed beforehand by John about her role in the near future for both the recording session and the tour. And she was grateful for this work induction course.

Janice found the prospect of her work with Vendetta very exciting and so she counted the days left before her job commenced. Janice, consequently, packed her handsome collection of whodunits to take with her for the months ahead.

VENDETTA'S REUNION

Rouchuka had been sorry to leave her beloved chateau in southern France but secretly she had been even sadder to leave the charming Roussel.

She was, of course, thoroughly refreshed after her break and so Rouchuka was thankful for this manna from heaven. She returned to the gang in London with a degree of sangfroid and with much renewed energy both for the forthcoming recording session and for the subsequent tour of the southern counties.

Rocker returned to his penthouse suite in London's docklands, which was his UK base, with some hope of seeing Diana again. He had tried to call her several times but her mobile phone seemed to be permanently switched off and, furthermore, he had no other way of contacting her. Pity, he mused. Oh, well. There will be other fish to fry.

Myra had beat a hasty retreat from South Korea just in time to rejoin the band. He had rather hoped that Arnie, his new inamorato, would accompany him but, unfortunately, Arnie had been detained on further business out in east Asia.

Myra's UK bolt-hole was a house near Brighton but he seldom visited it because it all felt too much like settling down. The house was fully staffed and so, when the master descended, Myra could soon get back into the routine. His house, however, would be a perfect place from which to start when the tour of the southern counties began quite soon. But, for now, he simply stayed at a hotel in London for the sake of convenience.

Gerry and Henry had organised a small gathering for when the troops reassembled. The get-together was a means of ensuring that all had returned from their various global excursions safely. Gerry also believed that a few drinks would ease them all back into an arduous work-routine. Such events were usually a hugging, kissing and back-slapping affair when everyone recounted their adventures over the past three weeks and they then discussed their tactics for the next eight.

Most of what the band had done with their time was predictable but the real spice of the holiday experience was mostly left unsaid.

Rouchuka merely skimmed over the details of her restoration project and its viniculture. Roussel was not mentioned at all to the assembled company.

She wanted to keep this secret to herself and she even kept Greta in the dark about Roussel.

Rocker told of the way in which he had spent his time in St Lucia with the women in his life but he neglected to mention Myra's untimely invasion of his little love-nest.

Myra simply stated that he had just gone travelling across America and Asia and that he had met a few interesting people and seen some exciting places. Myra also did not give any specific details about where he had descended or who he had encountered.

Max spoke of his trip to Greece which followed the usual pattern of his getting drunk every night on ouzo, shagging the local talent and doing a few drugs with the inhabitants. Nothing new there! Max too had provided a similarly edited version of the actual events. Cynthia didn't even get a mention.

The boring Bluey mentioned his tedious holiday in Wales with Wanda and his demanding parents but no one was really that interested to hear Bluey's news. Bluey was more or less customarily ignored by all present anyway with the exception of his friends Kicker and Jenny who knew where Bluey and Wanda had been anyway. Rouchuka, although not considered to be a close friend of Bluey, was also deemed to be part of Bluey's circle and she, as always, listened with interest.

Kicker and Jenny told of the wonderful time which they had spent in Rome and they outlined some of the tourist attractions which they had visited prior to descending on their estate in Bulgaria where they indulged in country-style living. Again most members of the team had heard this all before and, therefore, they were not that attentive. Kicker, of course, also omitted to mentioned the subtext which had resulted from his holiday with Jenny.

The three boiled sprats in the band, of course, were really only interested in themselves and their own lives and so very little attention was paid to anyone else's story.

Gerry soon turned the attention of the members of Vendetta Ice back to business by reiterating that there would be a video recording session over the next two weeks so that Vendetta could release their new video album, to be entitled *Captive Audience*. Gerry also reminded the team that the rehearsals for the recording session would begin tomorrow morning at 9.00 am sharp in the Hobart Studios in Kelleringham. Groan!

John announced that transport would be arranged for all parties and that a couple of minibuses would leave from two points in south London. He asked each member of the team to provide him with details for the pick-ups. That is, where they would join the travelling circus and at what time.

John also informed the team that the bodyguard contingent would join them all at the two pick-up points but he asked whether anyone needed a protector prior to this embarkation. No one requested an overnight bodyguard even though Gerry was not happy with this level of exposure for the clan.

Gerry ran through the typed schedule which detailed the rehearsals for each video item and the proposed running order which Eve Rushford and Tad Green distributed to both the band-members and the technical crew. Rocker's eyes followed Eve on her voyage around the room but Eve's eyes made sure that they purposefully avoided his. Tad, however, had been instructed by Gerry to deliver Rocker's copy of the schedule. Gerry was determined that his female staff would not fall under Rocker's spell and so he had organised this scheme in consequence.

Henry took the opportunity to give the final briefing to his technical crew and to inform Vendetta of any arrangements which were vital for them to know about the forthcoming recording session.

Henry and John invited questions on certain technical minutiae but the room remained silent. The assembled company was, in fact, divided into those who took due note of administrative details and those who ignored them as a matter of policy. While the brat-pack hated these tiresome meetings, most of the others in the room appreciated the necessity of ironing out minor details in order to ensure the smooth running of their working schedule.

John also introduced the new member of his backstage crew, Janice Evans, who had just joined them. She was welcomed by the brat-pack who sized her up as a potential bedfellow while the mature members of Vendetta were more genuine in their greeting.

Janice felt that she was now officially part of the team and that she had been given ample opportunity to identify and to study the characters involved in the set-up. She had, of course, previously met the other members of the backstage staff before the band-members had arrived on the scene.

The meeting then broke up and Gerry as always urged all to get some sleep and to stay clear of all stimulants in readiness for a hardworking couple of weeks ahead. This advice was, of course, summarily ignored by those who did not feel inclined to comply with Gerry's wishes.

ROUCHUKA'S ENLIGHTENMENT

The video recording session for the *Captive Audience* album began in earnest the next day. And miraculously all the members of Vendetta actually arrived on time at the London pick-up points and they collectively reached their final destination at Hobart Studios without undue delay and entirely sober for once. Well, almost. Wonder of wonders!

A larger studio complex was required for the video recording because the band, for the first time, were to have an orchestral accompaniment as a backing.

Rouchuka, in particular, was very excited at the prospect of working with an orchestra.

Rouchuka was also delighted by the studio premises which she had not seen before because Vendetta normally worked from a smaller studio in the north west of England. But she was impressed. Vendetta's own studio premises were currently being built with state-of-the-art equipment in Hertfordshire but the completion of this project was some way off yet.

The singers in the band had to get used to a different set of acoustics and so the initial rehearsal period took longer than Gerry, Henry and John had previously anticipated.

Rouchuka, however, found the experience to be an eye-opener for her. With a full orchestra, she discovered a new dimension to her career and her existence. Rouchuka found that she could project her sonorous alto voice above this full and rich sound booming out behind her. Thus Rouchuka began to discover things about herself and her talents which set her mind gyrating as well as her body. Both John and Henry were keenly aware of the fact that Rouchuka thrived in this setting and they were only sorry that she was not, at present, in her natural habitat with the band.

The orchestral experience, indeed, was a game-changer for the whole band. And some never really fully recovered. The orchestral musicians and its conductor were all freelancers who had been commissioned especially for the occasion. The numbers and the jingles written by Rocker and Max had been arranged for the orchestra in order to provide accompaniment for certain numbers as well as backing tracks generally for the band.

Rocker and Max listened with interest to the ways in which their music, originally composed in St Lucia, had been transformed by this means and they were generally impressed with the results. Their music could now stand on its own as worthwhile music rather than being just a load of strumming and drumming.

King Max came into his own because his keyboard skills and his clarinet playing were much appreciated by the orchestra. He was also provided with a grand piano on which to perform. Max found initially, however, that the piano needed more effort and strength to play than a plug-in keyboard but, after a bit of polite nagging from the conductor and some minor adjustments from the technical team, he accomplished the task relatively easily. He had learned the piano as a child but he had not been near a proper piano for many years. A microphone was thus placed inside the fully opened lid of the grand piano in order to assist Max. But his innate musicianship was a great advantage which stood him in good stead throughout the session.

Kicker Sax also flourished in this new environment because his instrument, the saxophone obviously, could blend well with the rest of the orchestra.

Bluey too faired quite well on percussion and earned much respect from the orchestral players but the rest of the team were somewhat overshadowed and overwhelmed.

Rocker did not, for instance, command the stage as he would normally expect to do. Myra also had to have an extra microphone pinned to his chest in order to amplify his somewhat feeble voice. Personality was not everything here obviously, although Rocker and Myra managed to blag it as usual. But the real musicians were not at all duped. While Rocker and Myra's noses were put out of joint somewhat by the experience of working with proper musicians who could actually read music, they also held their peace so as not to increase their slight embarrassment.

Vendetta spent most of the first three days in rehearsal and no attempt was made to start any actual recording because of the adjustments which needed to be made by both performers and technical crew.

The addition of an orchestra had been Gerry's brainchild but, by the end of the second day, he was beginning to have his doubts. Poor sod! Accordingly Gerry threatened the team with fire and brimstone in order to encourage them all to up their game. And he was backed up by the orchestra's conductor luckily. Drink and drugs at the end of the day were, consequently, taboo and most of the team obeyed this edict.

The advantage about doing a video recording was that it could be done piecemeal and, therefore, the cohort would be able to complete their recording within the allocated two weeks. Henry had worried at the start of the session that the group would have to extend the time allotted for hiring the Hobart Studios but fortunately the day was eventually saved.

Recording proper began in earnest on the third day. Rouchuka, Max and Kicker were asked to do mini solo numbers because of their ability to work with the orchestra.

Bluey, Vendetta's drummer, was also invited to do a trio with the orchestra's two percussion players which he, Bluey, found incredibly exhilarating and inspiring because of its improvisatory opportunities which sparked and fuelled his creativity. The rest of the musicians and the Vendetta team were also impressed with Bluey's contribution. Blimey!

John and Henry cunningly arranged for Rocker and Myra to be spotlighted for their stage presence rather than their performing skills in order to appease their vanity. Rocker chose to ignore the sleight while the laid back Myra was not really fazed much in any case because he did not always seek the limelight when on the stage.

Rouchuka really came into her own and she was much appreciated by the orchestra and its conductor both for her singing and dancing skills and for her general stage presence which the proper musicians admired. During the lunchtime breaks, Rouchuka even elected to sit with and to converse with some of the players and, it was at this point, that she began to discover that there could be life of a very different nature long after Vendetta might have become but a distant memory.

Some of the string players and the woodwind players actually found time to seek out Rouchuka and to educate her about musical theatre performance opportunities which she stored in her ample brain for future reference. The orchestral players to whom Rouchuka spoke were, moreover, delighted to learn that the female lead singer of a pop group also had an interest in proper music. Rouchuka, at this time, also decided that she ought to learn to read music because it would add a new dimension to her work and it would assist her when she entered any new performing platform.

The orchestral experience and the discussions with the players had, furthermore, reminded Rouchuka of her love of the classical genre and her meetings with the gorgeous Roussel in France. This recollection of her holiday in France, however, made Rouchuka somewhat wistful and nostalgic. She recollected her discussion with Roussel in France about Debussy and his pals in the evenings which she had spent in his delectable company.

Janice's initiation

Janice was pitched in at the deep end in no uncertain terms from the first day at Hobart Studios and, by the end of the first full day, she was totally exhausted both mentally and physically.

John had assigned her to the role of floor manager for the duration of the two-week recording session at Hobart Studios. Janice was thus given the typed schedule to follow and she had to organise the rehearsals and the performances for the various recording slots. She also had to keep an eye on the time which was threatening to run behind schedule.

Janice was, moreover, asked by the boys to get coffee and cigarettes on demand and to fetch mobiles phones from coat pockets, to leave messages for girlfriends and/or boyfriends and even to collect some dry-cleaning at lunchtime. She realised, of course, that these errands would probably be an integral part of her job for such a high-profile crowd. But she didn't really like it.

Rouchuka, Kicker and Bluey caused Janice very few insurmountable headaches but the brat-pack were generally a nuisance. Janice soon knew which half of the team she preferred.

When John realised that Janice was being put upon, he gently asked the band-members to keep their demands to a minimum. He knew, of course, that they were, in fact, simply trying it on. John also instructed one of the stage hands and a few of the bodyguards to help out with the errands required for the performers.

The Vendetta performers were required to work in costume and so Janice had to organise the wardrobe mistresses and make-up artists as well in order to ensure that all performers arrived on the set on time, properly dressed and ready to go. Lighting and scenery, even though this was part and parcel of the set dressing, was, fortunately, not Janice's concern.

Rocker, by force of habit, of course, chatted Janice up but she was seemingly invincible and, in any case, she was far too busy with sound cues, lighting cues and costume changes to even notice him. Rocker, however, saw Janice as only a mild distraction from Eve and, of course, from Diana who was still in the back of his mind.

Lunchtime eventually arrived and then Janice noticed that John cleverly managed to chaperone her away from the brat-pack's attention in order to ensure that she was refuelled in readiness for the afternoon's onslaught. Janice was grateful for John's consideration of her needs.

Janice sat with Wanda and her friends over lunch. Janice, by this means, got to know Greta as Rouchuka's assistant and Jenny who also helped out backstage. The girls decanted to the on-site cafe-restaurant for lunch where the specials of the day were shepherd's pie with a macédoine of seasonable vegetables or a lasagne with mixed salad. Janice thoroughly approved of her new working environment once lunch had been sampled. And the lunchtime company was so congenial that Janice felt that she was really going to like working with this group of girls.

Janice, however, gained the impression from the midday chat that most people connected with the band were put upon most of the time. Those who had been with the band for some time all warned Janice to get wise. Once she started agreeing to cater for the lads' petulant demands, she would be digging her own grave. Janice took these words on board as wise advice. She realised that John could only protect her some of the time and so she was grateful for the additional guidance from those who had learned from experience.

The weekend brought Janice more into the company of her co-workers in the backstage crew as well as with Wanda and Jenny. The girls had rooms near each other in the same hotel which were was, by design, some distance from the rooms occupied by Rouchuka and the boys. It was during this first week that Janice struck up a close friendship with Greta, Wanda and Jenny which was destined to assist her greatly in the future. These compatriots had much in common. They all depended for their existence on the members of Vendetta Ice but they were not at all about to be taken advantage of by any of the brat-pack.

Janice, therefore, learned how to carefully tiptoe through the tulips and to keep everyone sweet but not to suffer humiliation in the process. She also learned how to avoid the advances of Rocker and she acknowledged and respected Rouchuka's need for solitude when not in the spotlight.

Janice, moreover, became an expert in how to read everyone in and around the world of Vendetta Ice and this talent was not only useful to her but it also made her refreshingly popular within the inner sanctum. Janice, of course, rapidly got Gerry's measure. And she soon realised that he was the king-pin in many ways and that he might attempt to push her around. She resolved, however, to be a match for Gerry if he thought for one minute that she was a pushover.

The Janice who could stand up for herself hence duly emerged during her probationary period with Vendetta Ice. Essentially then Janice was the ultimate survivor. She could survive in the world of work, she could survive in the social world and she could survive by understanding other members of the herd known as the human race.

By the end of two weeks, *Captive Audience* was finally in the can and so the Vendetta performers and its attendant retinue could now disperse. The album, of course, still had to undergo the long and tedious process of editing in order to prepare it for the anticipated market which would certainly be a captive audience.

Janice rested in preparation for the forthcoming tour by taking life very easy. But she also congratulated herself on how well she had performed and on what she had achieved in the first two weeks of employment with the notorious Vendetta Ice band. Janice silently thanked providence for providing her with this heaven-sent opportunity and this occupational experience.

JULES' CONSOLATION

Jules didn't really feel like returning to Hakim in Agadir just yet. He would have loved to renew his acquaintance with beef tagine and chicken tagine, for which he had now acquired a taste, but the thought of gunpowder mint tea was frankly nauseous.

After Myra had left him in South Korea, Jules had ambled about a bit and had continued to follow the drug-trail, as much for this own amusement as for his business mission. Jules had to use his ingenuity in order to discover the next stage of the journey and this activity had stimulated his capacious brain cells for a while. The wayfarer's meanderings, however, soon started to pall for Jules and he decided that there must be an easier way of following the trail of fairy-dust. So he considered what to do next.

Jules sat at his laptop computer amusing himself while contemplating his next move. He did some work in his own website for Inter-Galactic Expeditions Incorporated which was his online company with its own server. The creation of this site had meant that Jules could exercise his information technology musculature in odd moments when either he was bored or he needed to think.

Right now, of course, Jules was both bored and needed to think. And so he invented a new computer game for Inter-Galactic Expeditions. This game required that the player should follow a snakes-and-ladders-type route across the cosmos in order to win the prize of a gold jewel-encrusted crown and sceptre. In the process of this journey, the player would need to fight with alien tigers, hack through the dense jungle, swim across shark-infested oceans and risk imprisonment by the forces of darkness. Jules considered how similar his own life was to this new game, entitled *Moon Mountain*. Well, well!

Once this particular distraction had exhausted Jules' boredom threshold, he was now at a loose end but his problem still remained unsolved. Jules, therefore, treated himself to a night on the tiles and here, fortuitously, he got his lucky break. Jules ambled around the bars, the clubs and the backstreets of Karajani City where drugs could easily be obtained after a few discreet enquiries. And Jules happened to run across a couple in one of the disreputable bars who luckily pointed him in the right direction.

"Where do you see the action around here?" asked Jules who could speak the native tongue to perfection and knew all the possible dialects.

"What kind of action are you looking for friend?" asked Pisquito.

Jules' correspondent had answered Jules' question with another of his own. How annoying, thought Jules.

"Well, I am looking for something which would give me a bit of a lift tonight. If you know what I mean," came the rapid response.

Pisquito and Ichiro, Jules' latest acquaintances, were thus able to tell the questioner what he needed to know and, even more beneficial, Jules learned a few names. Jules already knew the established routes and, more importantly, the unestablished routes for the drug-trade but what he had not yet discovered were any names of the sellers and the couriers. And this information was vital for his mission.

Jules learned, for instance, the name of one Nipisos who was the contact whom he needed in the vicinity. Nipisos, Jules also realised, was part of the drug-scam which he had been following assiduously. But Jules contained his delight under his poker-faced expression. With gratitude, however, Jules bought Pisquito and Ichiro another drink in payment for such useful information.

Then Jules thought he ought to reward his informants in a more appropriate manner and so the three men left the bar, painted the town red and later retired to Jules' hotel room. Nipisos could be contacted on another occasion when Jules was unaccompanied by his two latest friends.

By this time, of course, Jules was shagged out in every sense of the word. The combination of Myra, Pisquito and Ichiro was really too much for him to withstand. He found it necessary, therefore, to sleep the whole of the next day in order to recharge his batteries.

The next evening found Jules in covert conversation with Nipisos in a back alley and the dealer accommodated Jules' needs and provided him with much relevant information.

Jules then sauntered through some of the other Asian and Russian routes, therefore, seeking further contacts so that he could start his dossier of names, job descriptions and pertinent locations. This information all added to the database in Jules' mind, as well as the one on his laptop computer, and thus rendered Jules in a position whereby his knowledge could be of great value to his employer and of substantial monetary benefit to himself.

Back in his backstreet hotel, Jules made a call to his client. Jules was thus able to keep Calendula and Barrington abreast of his discoveries in Asia and to state his intention to return to the UK for further investigation. Barrington expressed much gratitude and he then promised to reimburse Jules handsomely for his out-of-pocket expenses as well as to increase Jules' coffers with a payment for the information which he had resourcefully gathered to date.

Jules now decided that it would make more sense for him to return to London because the next part of the expedition could be conveniently sewn up there.

Jules soon located Myra in a posh hotel in London and he was subsequently to acquire certain supplementary pieces of information which he could put to extremely good use.

Myra's rejuvenation

After the video recording session was complete and the performers had been dismissed until they were needed again for the tour of the southern counties, there was a moment of respite for the band and its attendant team.

Myra contemplated retiring to his residence near Brighton for a few days of rest before the next offensive began. But he kept putting it off in favour of the delights of the capital city. He had booked his hotel for a long weekend and then intended to make his way homeward before the start of the midweek tour.

Because he had drunk himself stupid on the previous night, Myra had slept late that morning and he had missed breakfast. He, consequently, ordered some coffee to be brought up to his room as a means of subduing his hangover. Myra lazily sipped his black coffee in bed and wondered how he might spend this rest of the day – well what was left of it at any rate. He decided, however, that he would just let the day go by and so he turned over with the intention of getting some more shut-eye. Then his mobile phone rang.

"Oh, fuck," Myra said under his breath as he tried to ignore this untimely interruption to his slumbers. But the ringing was persistent and, at last, curiosity got the better of Myra and he picked it up.

"Hello, baby," said a soft and mellow voice.

Myra sat up instantly. He was awake at last.

"Hello, honey," he replied.

"I'm home and in London," said the caller, "and I was wondering if we could continue where we left off last time, maybe?"

"Bang on the nail! When can we meet?"

Myra had intended to sound cool and evasive but his libido got the better of him. Myra recalled the nights he and Arnie had spent together in South Korea. The drink, the drugs and the sex. If sex had been rationed for every individual on the planet, Myra reckoned, he and Arnie would both have used up an entire lifetime's supply in one week out in Asia during his vacation there.

Myra had been heartbroken when the couple had to part with what he thought were nothing but merely vacuous promises to do it all again soon in the UK. But Myra felt that he had now got lucky because here was Arnie's voice at the other end of the line.

So arrangements were made between the two men for another night on the tiles which would not disappoint. Hence Myra dismissed his personal bodyguards as he prepared for a night to remember. The duo did a couple of male strip-joints and celebrated their reunion with champers and weed. They then returned to Myra's hotel slightly stoned in order to continue what had been started in South Korea.

"How do you get hold of this stuff so easily?" enquired Arnie who seemed amazed at the ready availability of the Big C both here in London as well as at Myra's holiday location.

"I have my suppliers," replied the suppler of drugs himself but without revealing his sources.

"Do you have some decent contacts in London? I live in the north and rarely venture this far south."

Myra read the implication in Arnie's words as being that he, Myra, was the attraction which had brought Arnie to London. And Myra was actually flattered by this idea. Poor sod!

"Well, I can get you whatever you need, sweetie. You just say the word. I have many contacts in London."

"Just in London," asked Arnie.

"What the hell do you think I was doing in South Korea, babe? Studying palaeolithic history?" replied Myra ignominiously.

Arnie smiled at the joke. But he didn't really think the gag was that funny.

"Why South Korea, then?" he asked.

"Well, don't tell the cops, but South Korea is one part of an unknown drug-traffic route."

Arnie smiled again. This pillow-talk was beginning to become interesting and Arnie was alert to its outcome.

"And a bleeding good one," continued the boastful Myra.

"Where does the route go to and from," Arnie asked trying hard to feign a singular lack of interest, "and why is it so bleeding good?"

Myra, in extant bragging mode, continued to explain to Arnie the ingenuity of the scheme because of its lengthy overland route which took in all the backstreets and byways rather than the highways which the customs people were normally patrolling in earnest. Myra was obviously trying to impress his new conquest. Myra indicated the general direction of the route but he also claimed that he had a map of the world which showed the cunning passage of the cargo.

Arnie lay back on the pillow and closed his eyes. Would Myra actually show him the map? Or would he just continue to tantalize his me? I must box a bit clever here or I will lose my advantage.

"I don't believe you," said Arnie with his devil's advocate hat on.

This stance cut the mustard. Myra sprang out of bed, went to a drawer of the desk in his room and brandished the map on which Arnie could feast his eyes. But Arnie now changed tack and feigned a lack of interest by distracting Myra with some more sex-play to which his partner responded willingly.

Arnie smiled inwardly when Myra visited the bathroom for a prolonged soak after their latest round of sexual antics. Now he would have to take his chance. And he did. Jules, consequently, got out his mobile phone and clicked the camera icon. And with practised skill and nerves of steel, Jules gained his prize. He also fished around under the bed in order to retrieve the bug which he had placed there previously and which had recorded their recent conversation. Jules was famous for his bugging devices which had served many a useful purpose in the course of his work for the Medici Squadron.

When Myra returned to bed, there was a cat-that-got-the-cream grin on Arnie's face which Myra interpreted as an overture for some more lewd fun and sex-games.

The next day saw the pair parting again for a while with promises to renew the arrangement as soon as work commitments permitted. Myra was sincere in his promise and his desire to renew his acquaintance with Arnie in the near future after Vendetta's tour. Arnie was, conversely, not so genuine in his claims. Jules, therefore, left Myra in peace while Myra was in pieces at their separation.

Jules was so pleased with the way in which things had gone for him in the latter part of his fact-finding mission that he decided to return to Agadir. Accordingly Jules boarded a plane from London Gatwick to Agadir because he had managed to get a cheap flight on the internet.

Hakim was delighted that Jules had returned to the fold and he instantly set about making some beef tagine. When Hakim made some gunpowder tea, however, he discovered that his lover was not that thirsty. Strange? Hakim was, therefore, glad to see Jules back but was somewhat disappointed that he would not join him in celebrating with mint tea.

It also appeared that a welcome-home sexual encounter was not on the agenda either for Hakim because Jules claimed that he was very jetlagged. Hakim, of course, had no option but to buy this lame excuse in the absence of any further information to the contrary.

VINCE'S PERAMBULATION

The skeletal muscles of the human body are made up of muscular fibres. Every human being on planet Earth has a blend of Type I (or slow-twitch) fibres and Type II (or fast-twitch) fibres.

Slow-twitch fibres, as the name suggests, are slow to react but they have more inherent endurance potential because they resist fatigue and are built for sustained movement and postural maintenance. Slow-twitch fibres have a naturally aerobic metabolism with a plentiful blood supply for energy generation. Because of this good blood supply, slow-twitch fibres are sometimes referred to as red fibres.

Fast-twitch muscular fibres, conversely, quickly respond to human activity and are designed for strength and power during rapid bursts of energy although they do, however, tire easily. These muscular fibres are more anaerobic in terms of metabolism and, therefore, they demand less blood supply because they require less oxygen. Fast-twitch fibres are often called white fibres because of their meagre blood supply.

Vincent Craven was miraculously born with an optimum ratio of slow-twitch and fast-twitch muscular fibres which made him the envy of his admirers and rendered him in an ideal position for maintaining a physically active lifestyle. Vince had, consequently, run the odd marathon, had scaled a mountain or two and had won a few rowing contests and tennis matches in his time.

He was also not averse to a bit of hang-gliding and bungy-jumping when he felt in a particularly dare-devil mood. So Vince was not lacking in courage either. Courage, strength and stamina. An unbeatable combination. James Bond would have envied Vince in many respects.

As Vince was also no stranger to the gym, he was able to optimise his physical attributes and to put his body to good use. Vince had, indeed, worked as a fitness instructor at the local gym for a number of years before turning to freelance work which provided him with more variety of physical activity in his occupation.

As well as working as a self-employed fitness instructor, Vince was now a much sought-after freelance diving instructor in both scuba diving and deep-sea diving in St Lucia where he lived. He also amused himself with being commissioned to dive professionally for television films and documentaries and with sprinting around the well-known racing circuits on the west coast of St Lucia. Bliss!

Vince was, however, not just a load of efficient muscular strength and stamina, he also had a brain which functioned in a remarkable capacity and he had a succulent curiosity which needed constant and regular feeding. Again, James Bond, eat yer heart out, matey!

So when Vince was asked to attach a number of packages to the bottom of a pleasure craft harboured in St Lucia late at night on several occasions, his curiosity was stimulated. Even though he took the abundant supplies of money for the job, he was also studiously careful to ask no further questions.

Vince then decided that about now might be a good time for him to take a break from his regular work. He also felt that the female whom he regarded as his casual girlfriend was beginning to get a bit clingy and so a rest from her for a while might not go amiss. His life needed a bit of excitement, he felt, and an exploratory mission might just fulfil his need. Vince, therefore, began an internal dialogue with himself and he finally agreed with his first thought. So let's give it a whirl, he determined. And take a break.

And so it came to pass that Vince decided to follow the *Ocean Spray* yacht on its voyage to the mainland in order to discover where the vessel was going and who would be collecting the cargo at its destination.

He called in a favour from a friend who lent Vince his powerboat. Vince then set off one evening in order to keep pace with the yacht at full throttle. The consignments, Vince noticed, were destined for Venezuela where they were unloaded and passed on to an overland courier.

Vince wondered about his discoveries and he contemplated the prospect of doing some more research into the excursion on which these packages might be embarking together with the reasons for the expedition. After Vince's initial sea-going voyage when following the yacht, consequently, he decided to make some additional enquiries.

Vince thus returned to St Lucia, gave his friend back his launch and then bided his time. He next mounted a surveillance operation in order to discover when the packages were attached to the bottom of the transporting yacht either by himself or by others like him.

When the moment was ripe, therefore, Vince elected to travel across to Venezuela in the seagoing vessel in question because he knew the owner vaguely. So he asked Rowan Boyd-Fuller if he could accompany him on one of his nocturnal voyages. Rowan agreed because extra money was always welcomed and this injection of funds would allow him to court Rosemary more easily without facing financial embarrassment or perhaps even ultimate ruin.

Vince discovered that the *Ocean Spray* initially meandered around the Windward islands near St Lucia and then made its way to Porlamar on the coastline of Isla de Margarita. From here it was a short distance to Puerto la Cruz on the mainland of Venezuela. It took a whole day and night's journey but Vincent stuck to his mission diligently.

Vince disembarked on the mainland and thanked Rowan for his transportation across the Caribbean Sea at the start of his supposed holiday.

Now the mysterious consignment was taken by truck across to Caracas and it then began a lengthy cross-country journey, changing hands many times and taking well over a week to reach its destination. Vince was able to hire a series of vehicles in order to follow the procession until he got bored with his undertaking.

Vince eventually determined that his curiosity had been satisfied sufficiently for his needs and so he made a note in his efficient brain of what had occurred.

Vince then returned to St Lucia by another route which entailed a judicious admixture of hitchhiking, long-distance swimming and stowing away on another vessel bound for St Lucia.

Vince believed that his so-called holiday had done him a power of good once he was safely back in his wooden shack on the non-tourist side of the island.

His former girlfriend, moreover, had given him up as a lost cause and Vince was quite satisfied with her conjecture.

Vince did, however, elect to make a transatlantic call to the UK in order to sort out one or two things concerned with his finances.

ROSEMARY'S CONQUEST

Gemma Gallagher lived in New York and worked as a private detective in her own agency.

But her work was not as exciting as most people erroneously imagined. She spend most of her time, for instance, in tracing errant spouses and locating stray cats. But, nevertheless, she enjoyed self-employment and she had an office staff who undertook the administrative work while she was away on business. Gemma was also in the process of endeavouring to recruit an assistant who could carry on with the mundane detecting work while she was away but this prospective newcomer had not yet reached her shores.

Gemma, in fact, took every opportunity to travel in connection with her work because she regarded the world as her personal playground when out of the office, whether on business or for pleasure.

Recently she had kissed goodbye to Bertrand with whom she had for some time now been having a fling. She found Bertrand most accommodating because he had been trained never to ask any questions about her confidential work and he also allowed her to travel whenever she pleased. Very convenient for Gemma.

Gemma needed to visit St Lucia in the Caribbean because she was detailed to undertake a special assignment. She rejoiced in the carefree atmosphere of the Caribbean and the friendliness of its people. Gemma, therefore, booked herself into a mid-range hotel in St Lucia because she planned to have some fun while working officially for her client.

The next day Gemma's mission was to take a trip around the islands in order to spy out a few locations where unsavoury business might occur. Accordingly Gemma boarded a motor-powered yacht which enabled her to obtain a view of most of the Caribbean islands from offshore. Gemma had come across the *Ocean Spray* vessel as a likely means of transport and she had managed to book a place for a full day's round trip.

The weather had been glorious and the vistas were breathtaking and so Gemma had thoroughly enjoyed her day on the yacht. The trip had encompassed the surrounding islands to the north and the south of St Lucia – from Martinique in the north down to Barbados in the south. Gemma had thus seen a great deal of Caribbean life from a new and distant perspective in a very short space of time.

She had spent much of the day chatting idly to a group of elderly, yet spritely, ladies who were obviously well heeled and enthusiastic for such adventures. They all managed to keep up a running commentary on the sights which had supplemented the narrative of the boat's owner as the official tour guide. Gemma had also dined with these ladies when the launch stopped for lunch at midday.

Gemma had, furthermore, spent some time talking with the tour guide himself and he had seemed to be very pleased to converse with her. This may have been because Gemma's disguise and her cover-story was that she was on a mission to discover places where conference delegates could spend their leisure time in the Caribbean.

At the end of the day's excursion, the tour guide had invited Gemma out for a drink with him and she had gladly accepted. Rowan steered Gemma towards one of the bars in St Lucia which displayed local colour rather than sophistication. But Gemma regarded this as all part of the experience and she complained not one iota.

"What will you have to drink, Rosemary?" enquired Gemma's host. "A cocktail is usually what people order in this part of the world. Will you indulge?"

Gemma confessed that she knew very little about Caribbean cocktails and so she allowed herself to be advised by Rowan. Gemma's host then gave her a fleeting tour of the cocktail menu from which she chose a Planter's Punch. The Planter's Punch concoction consisted of local rum together with a blend of citrus fruits and, of course, lashings of ice. The cocktail was then served in style with a curly multi-coloured straw and a little paper umbrella because that was what the tourists expected. Gemma smiled both outwardly and inwardly at this pandering to the tourist trade.

Rosemary appeared delighted by this cocktail experience and Rowan Boyd-Fuller seemed to be uplifted by her obvious appreciation. When Rowan enquired whether Rosemary would like another cocktail, Gemma responded that it was her turn to buy the drinks. Rowan tried not to look too relieved by this suggestion. Gemma had, in fact, realised that her host was almost certainly penniless and so she had made this considerate gesture.

Because Gemma had told Rowan that she would only be in the Caribbean for a couple of days, he was emboldened to ask her for a dinner date on the following evening.

"I would like to see you again, Rosemary," Rowan pleaded.

Gemma wondered whether Rowan could actually afford to take her out to dinner and so she suggested that a light meal in an inexpensive restaurant would fit the bill. Gemma explained that she ate very little in the evenings but that she would appreciate sampling some authentic food. The colour returned to Rowan's face at this welcomed proposal.

On the following evening, therefore, the couple visited Mama's Caribbean Kitchen, a beachside cafe, which was full of local colour and scrumptious food but, otherwise, it had very little with which to recommend it as a swanky setting.

After a joyous evening with plenty of outrageous flirting, Rosemary invited her companion to dinner with her on the morrow in order to reciprocate his hospitality. Rowan seemed somewhat reluctant to accept her invitation because he was of the old school whereby the fellow was supposed to foot the bill. But Rosemary stood her ground and explained that she had more than enough money to be able to return his favour. Finally Rowan could not resist the temptation which Rosemary was offering. And, in any case, Rosemary had told him that she could swing it on expenses. That comment convinced the only slightly reluctant Rowan to break the habit of a lifetime and to accept Rosemary's well-intentioned charity.

Gemma felt that things were going in the right direction with Rowan. And Rowan, in turn, couldn't believe his luck as the evening progressed and the two of them began to get closer and closer.

ISABEL'S ENTRAPMENT

Gerry was extremely pleased with the way in which the last press conference had been conducted and received. The press reception had hailed the end of a successful video recording session for *Captive Audience* and it presaged the start of the southern counties tour for Vendetta Ice.

The video of *Captive Audience* was in the can and the editing process had started in earnest almost immediately. And as the inclusion of the orchestra had been Gerry's brainchild, he was justly pleased with the way in which he had pulled it off.

The team briefing which followed on from the press function was then short-lived and succinct and the team seemed ready and eager to start the upcoming tour. And so Gerry felt that all was safely done and dusted in readiness for the next lap of Vendetta's journey. After the epic event of the press conference and the subsequent team briefing, therefore, Gerry considered that he had earned himself a drink in the bar of the hotel in which the press reception had taken place.

The rest of the troop had at last dispersed and Gerry now had a quiet moment to himself. He ordered himself his favourite champagne cocktail and a cup of black coffee for his self-congratulatory celebration of a job well done and a rosy future ahead to behold.

There were several journalists still hanging around the hotel bar but Gerry chose to ignore them and to select a quiet table in an alcove away from the general throng. After all, Gerry was not really the main attraction at the press conference and so, Gerry thought, he could remain unmolested. But he was wrong. Poor sod!

"Mr Paxton, hello there, my name is Isabel Franklin. I was wondering if you received my email sent yesterday?"

"No, I don't believe I did," Gerry lied.

Gerry, in fact, remembered having received an email begging him for a press opportunity but he had chosen to shelve it for the time being.

"Sorry to disturb you here but could we have a quick chin-wag now? It won't take very long. I just wanted to . . ."

Gerry began to protest.

"I'm sorry, I am not sure who you are and, in any case, I am off duty just now. Could I please have some space? Thank you."

Gerry considered that this authoritarian statement would do the trick. But again he was wrong.

Isabel Franklin then smiled and this occurrence changed the ambience quite considerably.

Gerry was not really a man for the ladies. He was too busy working. His marriage had gone down the pan, indeed, because he was always working and he had certainly not been that attentive to his wife. The separation and final divorce had cost him a packet but he was not at all upset at not having a woman to go home to these days. And where was home, anyway? On the road usually. The smiling Isabel, however, stirred up ideas in Gerry's mind which he had not experienced for some time.

"I sent you an email yesterday because I am a freelance journalist and I wanted to write an article featuring you for several of my regular clients in the glossy magazine trade," persisted Isabel.

Gerry still stalled.

"Sorry, what did you say your name was?" he asked as a form of prevarication and a put-down.

"Isabel Franklin," came the reply as she handed him her calling card. And another smile crossed her face.

"Well, it's not convenient right now. Sorry."

Gerry was actually disconcerted by this female and he was dismayed that he had found the need to apologise to her so many times in the space of just a few seconds. Well, Gerry, that's the way of the world, you know!

"I just wanted to make a date to interview you and possibly with my photographer present."

Gerry, for the first time, then noticed an unobtrusive man with a flashy camera hovering in the background.

Gerry positively waived. He looked at this Isabel women and studied her appearance. She was very beautiful. Gerry observed her perfect cheek bones, her grey eyes, her brown hair, her slender shoulders and those inviting breasts. And he liked what he saw.

Gerry tried, however, to concentrate on the matter in hand and persisted with, "Please, not just now, Miss . . . er." He looked down at her business card for a prompt.

"Franklin," she supplied, "but do call me Isabel."

"Please, then, Isabel, I do insist on a bit of quiet time alone for a while. Thank you."

Isabel was not to be put off by the blustering Gerry. And so she smiled once again.

"Well, may I buy you another drink before I leave you in peace, then?"

"I'm OK, really," Gerry explained.

Isabel then moved away and Gerry sighed with relief. But he was again deceived.

"A champagne cocktail isn't it, Gerry?" she said as she headed towards the bar before Gerry could protest any further.

Perhaps I should just agree to a short interview and be done with it, Gerry thought. I can always cancel at the last moment and be shot of her finally. But, on the other hand, it might be a very good promotional opportunity for the band. And, of course, it will bring me well into the spotlight which may pay dividends in the future. Perhaps a bit of limelight for me for a change might open a few doors? I am not necessarily going to be tied to Vendetta forever and maybe this could put me in an advantageous position should I ever find myself out of work? Gerry was good at convincing himself where Isabel might have singularly fallen short.

Isabel sat down and handed Gerry his favourite tipple. Again she smiled. And she looked into his eyes.

"So could we make a date, Mr Paxton, then?" she said in her soft, seductive voice.

Gerry found himself short of breath and so he inflated his lungs. And he definitely did not invite her to call him Gerry. In spite of himself, Gerry, however, found himself taking his mobile phone out of his pocket and looking in his electronic diary. He was obviously all of a fluster while Isabel remained calm and in control.

"Well, I am rather busy for several weeks. Vendetta is just about to go on tour, as you know. I assume that you were at the press conference just now?"

Gerry, of course, had noticed her and her photographer but he did not want to divulge this nugget of information to this relative stranger.

"Oh, yes, I was. And, at one point, you looked directly at me," came Isabel's rejoinder.

Gerry fumed. Bugger! Hell and damnation!

Gerry felt that he would need to tread very carefully in future with this one. She would not be as easily controlled and manipulated as most of the females in his immediate orbit. Caution Gerry!

An hour of Gerry's time, however, was allotted to an interview with Isabel and so Gerry's nell was rung. Poor sod!

Isabel and her hovering photographer then obligingly left the hotel bar both wearing a self-satisfied grin on their faces. The two linked arms as they walked out towards the hotel car park and their waiting car.

Gerry, meanwhile, was allowed to resume his quiet moment but in his inner mind he was not all that serene.

Vendetta's Jamboree

Vendetta's tour of the southern counties began in earnest midweek.

Vendetta's forthcoming eight-week tour was scheduled to begin in Hastings in Sussex and then the company planned to visit Brighton, Chichester, Portsmouth, Southampton, Bournemouth and Exeter. The jamboree was then scheduled to culminate with a bang at the Wave Crest Theatre near Newquay in Cornwall.

There had been, of course, another choreographed pantomime press conference at the end of the *Captive Audience* recording session and just prior to the start of the new tour. After this charade, Gerry had arranged for the final briefing of the unit in order to review the transport arrangements for the tour and the proposed schedule of performances and rehearsals. But most of the details of the tour were already known to the band-members and all transport arrangements had previously been confirmed at the end of the recording session. Hence this briefing was short and so was the temper of the brat-pack who had heard it all before.

The programme for the southern tour was really a carbon-copy replica of the northern circuit excursion. The programme, hence, consisted of ten numbers which featured various members of the band but with the emphasis on showcasing Rouchuka and Rocker with Max, Myra and Kicker as supplementary soloists.

The programme consisted of *Lonely Planet Without You*, *Metro Magic*, *Fevered Nights*, *Only My Heart*, *Wild Girl*, *Rhyme and Poetry*, *Once Again*, *Travelling Solo*, *Storming and Stomping* and *Day and Night Blues*. All these items had been number one hits for the group, they had remained in pole position for several weeks and had broken many all-time records.

Only My Heart and *Wild Girl* brought Rouchuka into the spotlight while Rocker was the soloist in *Travelling Solo* and *Storming and Stomping*.

Rouchuka and Rocker then both featured in *Metro Magic* and *Rhyme and Poetry* whereas *Lonely Planet Without You*, *Fevered Nights*, *Once Again* and *Day and Night Blues* were a group effort. Max on clarinet and Kicker on saxophone, however, had a special spotlight duo within *Fevered Nights* and Myra was supreme in *Lonely Planet Without You* with a guitar solo.

The tour consisted of a couple of days at the venue for rehearsals and performances and then a day of travel to the next appointed place for another show.

The show in Hastings got Vendetta Ice off to a flying start. Everyone was on top form and the fans delivered the goods in the expected manner. No surprises there!

Between Hastings and Exeter everything was singularly uneventful in terms of what was expected of the artistes. The fans still screamed and wet their knickers but the performances went well.

Rocker habitually trawled in the talent after each show, Myra continued to make improper suggestions to Hal who deflected them cunningly and Max persisted in hankering after Cynthia but with no result. Still nothing new there!

Rocker rang Diana a few times but she did not return his calls and so he reluctantly decided to keep looking elsewhere – which he did in any case.

Eventually Gerry took Hal away from Myra because Hal was looking as if he were on the point of losing it and resigning from the post. Myra, of course, had a forceful altercation with Gerry about Hal's defection. He tried desperately to assert his authority and to maintain his dignity. Myra's business manager, however, was impervious to his empty threats and his pathetic postulating.

Gerry managed calmly and skilfully to keep Myra in order by not giving in to his demands. There were no flies on Gerry – or, if there were, they didn't stay long. Myra characteristically didn't like being prevented from getting his own way but he soon realised that he had to toe the party line sometimes. He was, when all was said and done, just plain Nigel Dulse from the back end of nowhere.

Max, in turn, wondered why Cynthia was so evasive in not returning his calls even though she had raised Max's hopes decidedly while he resided in Greece. When Max finally got through on the phone, Cynthia told him, once again, that she could not get away from her work and that, in any case, she was not looking for a new relationship, however transient, just now. Max, therefore, had to swallow this snub and to look elsewhere for his sexual exploits. The tour would obviously provide this opportunity which Max planned to exploit to the hilt with relish.

Rouchuka also kept herself to herself as usual and only Greta was permitted into her personal space for a short while after each show. Rouchuka, however, used her me-time to consider the rest of her career. She was now determined to make some radical changes but her first steps would need to be to find a way of extracting herself from her contract and then to engage a new promoter. Rouchuka obviously had to keep her thoughts to herself but her thoughts did not dry up while she did so. Perhaps I should consult my solicitor first so that I can extricate myself from Vendetta's contract without too much egg on my face? Yes, this route was the way ahead, Rouchuka decided.

Bluey seemed troubled for some reason throughout the entire tour. Gerry astutely observed Bluey's state of mind but no one so far could discover the source of his worries. And most of the brat-pack did not care anyway. Gerry, therefore, kept a watchful eye on Bluey because Gerry had noticed his reticence in joining in with the others at the end of each day. But, as Bluey's performance work had not deteriorated in any way, Gerry did not waste too much head space on this form of contemplation.

Hal was subsequently assigned to guard Bluey because Gerry felt that they would be a much better match. Gerry also believed that Hal would have a calming influence on the seemingly troubled percussionist.

Kicker seemed his usual happy-go-lucky self and so he was not a cause for any concern on Gerry's part. How wrong could one man be?

The girls, Wanda, Jenny and Janice, seemed to jog along just nicely and Gerry was glad that the new member of the backstage team was settling in easily and that she was well liked by all. Greta, moreover, never seemed to cause Gerry, or anyone else for that matter, any headaches and so he largely ignored her.

Gerry believed, of course, that it was important for all these girls to get on well together and to be happy in their work. And so he did not pay them too much attention unless there appeared to be trouble at that particular mill.

The apex of the tour, eagerly anticipated by all, was at Newquay. Here the stay was longer and Vendetta were joined by the orchestra with whom they had worked on the recording of *Captive Audience*. This stratagem was designed to give the fans a sneak preview of the forthcoming album and to heighten the hype for the concert itself.

Predictably the final performances at the Wave Crest Theatre were over-subscribed and Gerry and Henry were more than delighted. Both surfers and non-surfers showed up in their droves.

At Newquay the tribe settled into the splendour of the Sea Front Grand Hotel – suitably christened because it was on the seafront. Nothing original there!

Gerry and the brat-pack were provided with rooms which overlooked the sea and which were at the far end of the hotel's west wing. Gerry could, by this means, then keep the troublesome boys in order and he could also steer them away from the less riotous members of Vendetta Ice.

Because Gerry's accommodation was away from the general hubbub but near to the wild boys rooms, it was conveniently located for some late-night meetings which Gerry believed it would be expedient to conduct.

REGGIE'S SPECULATION

The website for Home Spun plc extolled the virtues of designer-label natural wool garments from the highlands of Scotland and the Scottish Isles.

The home page contained a mission statement from Sandy Sinclair as the enterprising and charismatic founder of the company. The prose of the founder's message to the world was peppered with catchphrases, such as "all natural and organic", "undyed and unbleached", "return to the cottage industry" and "roots of our British heritage". References were also made to the natural lifestyle of the islanders from Shetland, Orkney and the Hebrides which should be the envy of the world.

Another page on the website displayed photographs of models dancing through summer meadows or walking along windswept beaches wearing "ultra-warm but infinitely lightweight knitwear for bracing winter days". The models consisted of both men and women and all appeared fulfilled, contented and blissful whether either posing alone or gazing lovingly into a partner's eyes.

Other pages showed well-lit photographs of old ladies knitting and spinning with a degree of unbelievable contentment and satisfaction in the comfort of their own homes. And sheep lazily and happily grazing in luscious green fields and on hillsides. An array of highland bagpipers, *Cervus Elaphus Scoticus* (Scottish red deer, to you), rugged mountain glens and wild and windy coastlines also graced the remaining pages of Home Spun's website. The message on these website pages focused on life north of the border and endeavoured to make the rest of the world envious that they did not share this rural idyll despite the uninviting and bone-perishing weather.

A whole page was, of course, reserved for those wishing to shop online and to spend exorbitant amounts of money in so doing.

Home Spun, the website stated, had been founded a few years ago and its success had soared to dizzy heights because of its ethical principles, its ability to provide work for many dedicated cottagers and its wholeheartedly sincere mission. The website, moreover, was riddled with glowing testimonials from satisfied customers both from the UK and from across the globe.

Home Spun's website, in fact, was a positive extravaganza of self-indulgence for all those who visited it and who perhaps lost some money in the process.

All this bla di bla was, of course, a load of old bollocks because it was just one of Reggie's scams.

Reggie had spent a thoroughly productive weekend designing Home Spun's website and he was justly proud of his inventive copywriting skills. He then rewarded himself with a glass of sherry and a few chocolate bars as a result. He also felt extremely proud of his inventive talents, although he could never actually boasted to anyone of his creations.

Reggie had registered the Home Spun company some years ago and, on the surface, it was extant but, in fact, it had never done any trading at all.

Although the website did not have a high search engine profile, it did attract some customers. Potential purchasers, however, were simply told – with profuse apologies from the management – that their requested products were "out of stock" because the cottage-industry could not keep pace with the exceptionally high demand. Or that "the line had now been discontinued" for the foreseeable future because the sheep were not producing the goods fast enough. Reggie, of course, managed to keep a note of all the debit or credit card details of the prospective purchasers in case such information should prove useful in the future for any reason.

Over the weekend, Reggie had also managed to compile an impressive brochure which he was easily able to get printed on demand. He then finalised the draft of a prospectus with a view to requesting a grant for funds from the Benefice Charity Trust. The grant proposal, on the trust's official application form, of course, answered all the right questions and was destined to simply wow its readers.

The proposal documentation emphasized the ethics of the Home Spun business, the harvesting of natural resources, the generation of income for the cottagers in outlying areas of the UK and its ecological angle. Alistair (Sandy) Sinclair had also included his own mission statement and his personal vision for the enterprise's future. Sandy Sinclair, indeed, looked as if he were a reincarnation of Reggie himself with his steel-grey hair, dark eyes and ruddy complexion but Reggie, in fact, did not recognise the similarities.

The grant proposal, of course, had borrowed heavily from the website because its wording had attracted many customers and so Reggie assumed that the same magic would work on the Benefice Charity Trust. The proposal was also accompanied by a set of accounts which demonstrated sensible business practice but fell short on the working capital front and the need to supply the homeworkers with capital equipment for their services.

The final step was to present all this documentation to the Benefice Charity Trust which Reggie was able to accomplish with ease now. He had perfected the art of slipping these items into the pile of other applications which the Board of Governors would consider at their next meeting.

In due season, therefore, the Board of Governors approved the official application from Home Spun wholeheartedly and with one accord much to Reggie's delight and relief.

Madeleine again wondered, however, how this application from Home Spun had found its way into the bundle for consideration by the trust. This occurrence got her thinking but she was still undecided what to do about it. After all, if Reggie was the culprit, she could hardly inform him of her suspicions.

Madeleine, therefore, once again, just let her thoughts roam but she was still in a quandary and she was filled with indecision. I'll think about that tomorrow, she concluded, and then she ploughed on with the rest of her day. There was always work for Madeleine to attend to and so, for the time being, she forced herself to become absorbed by her normal administrative duties.

MEDICI'S DISSEMINATION

The landline on Winston Blakefield's desk rang early one morning and he answered the summons with a freshness which he did not naturally feel. Winston had felt rather jaded lately because no exciting scandals had come into his field of vision.

The phone call from a very reliable informant, however, changed Winston's perspective on life totally. His gloomy world turned 360 degrees in an instant when he recognised the voice at the other end of the line.

"How are you Winston, you old bugger? Working hard and feeling the pressure or just down in the dumps at the lack of scandal around just now?"

Winston's caller had hit the nail on the head as always. Winston felt that he was decidedly short of scandal in the celebrity world right now and he was worried that his readers might desert him because of this deficit. The superstars and the royals seemed unusually and unfortunately well behaved for this time of the year for a change.

"Well, things are a bit slow, you know," was Winston's honest retort.

Barrington regarded this remark as an over-exaggerated understatement.

"I could change all that for you, Winston, old boy, and probably put you on the map for all time. Interested?"

"Silly question! What have you got for me you old scoundrel?"

"Winston, please. I am not that bad."

"No, usually much worse."

The badinage continued for a while until Winston could not contain his curiosity any longer.

"Spill the beans, you bastard!" he exclaimed.

"Well, it's about Vendetta Ice. A nice juicy scandal."

"An exclusive?" enquired the cautious editor.

"Absolutely," came the prompt reply.

Winston squirmed in his chair with excitement but he realised that Barrington was going to savour the moment and that he could not be hurried. Winston, consequently, tried another tack.

"Do you fancy a quick drink and a bite at lunchtime?"

"OK. When and where?"

Barrington happened to be at his London riverside penthouse apartment in Vauxhall right now. And he was not at all hostile to the notion of a bit of chit-chat and a few drinks because Calendula was out shopping and that would mean that she would be away for some time. Barrington was a lost puppy while his love was away, even though he had attempted to assuage his boredom with some piano practice. But, as this ploy had not, unfortunately, worked, he was game for any other ways of killing time.

A time and venue for lunch were duly agreed on by the two men. And both looked forward to the occasion.

When the meeting commenced at the Wheatsheaf near Winston's office in Powton Street in London, Barrington explained what he had on offer but he warned his chum that it would take some time for him to winkle out the news-fodder.

"We know that the stuff comes from St Lucia, crosses the Caribbean overnight and then takes an overland route through South America and eventually lands up in South Korea. But we haven't traced it further than that as yet," Barrington reported.

"And where does it end up?" asked Winston.

"In London, of course. But we need to verify the Asian route and the European route before the picture is complete."

Winston had listened to all this information very attentively. He was more excited than a newborn spring lamb on a sunny day and he knew that his correspondent would not be unaware of his inner feelings.

"And how long will your investigations take, do you think?"

"Hard to tell. The tactics are to take a long time over the journey and to shed some of it along the way. But, basically, they are playing the long con in the hope of evading the attention of the customs laddies. Our investigation, therefore, will, of necessity, take some time. And collecting watertight evidence for you is no speedy process."

"I understand," Winston replied and nodded his agreement, "but are we talking weeks or months?"

"Probably weeks – but who can tell? It would be worth waiting for, of course."

Again Winston could not disagree with this statement of fact.

Their meals arrived and Barrington ordered some classy wine with which to accompany their posh ploughman's lunches. The malt whisky which they had ordered earlier had more or less been consumed and they were ready for some additional liquid refreshment.

Winston already had an inkling about the fact that Vendetta Ice were prone to fishy deals but this lunchtime meeting was beginning to clarify his thoughts on the matter. One of Winston's staff at *Public Enquiry* had hinted at some skulduggery in connection with Vendetta's doings in St Lucia, where the front man, Rocker Blaize, had a villa, but no concrete facts had so far come across his desk.

And so Winston's elation grew because he knew that Barrington, of all people, would be the one to extract the truth and to supply him with the concrete evidence which he needed before he could publish his findings. If Barrington could fish out the facts meticulously and then hand them over to Winston on a plate, it would be well worth the investment.

Winston had been the chief editor of the public profile section of the *Public Enquiry* magazine for some time now but. as yet, he had not particularly distinguished himself in his career. Admittedly he had investigated and unearthed some pretty hot scandals before now but nothing major or earth-shattering. This news could change all that, Winston thought.

Once financial terms had been agreed between the two, both returned to their respective places of work.

Winston went back to his Powton Street office with an uplifted spirit. Powton Street was the central core of the periodical and magazine publishing industry in London and the competition here was fierce. Winston knew that if he wished to retain his position in such a lively centre, then he would need to be ahead of the game. And this opening to which he had been exposed at lunchtime could be the key to his guaranteed success and the furtherance of his career.

Barrington returned to his penthouse apartment in Vauxhall which commanded a superb vista on to the River Thames. He too exhibited a similarly optimistic outlook.

Barrington looked at his white upright piano but decided against another attempt at the Schubertian lullaby on which he had been working for several months. Instead, Barrington made his way to the Lagunita Spa Leisure Complex which was open only to his immediate neighbours. Here Barrington enjoyed spending time in the gym, in the pool and, of course, in the jacuzzi, sauna and steam room following his strenuous yet worthwhile exercise.

When in the steam room, Barrington contemplated the way in which he and Calendula could discover how Vendetta's traffic found its way across Asia and Europe and how they could prove it. Barrington, however, acknowledged that his love-partner, as the creative brains of the outfit, would have a better idea of how to solve this equation than he might.

Barrington then returned to the flat in Vauxhall in order to be ready for the return of his beloved Calendula from her shopping expedition. He then prepared a fragrant Thai curry for them both to consume when Calendula arrived home. And while waiting he did, in fact, manage to do some piano practice.

JOHN'S REVELATION

Henry and John were both delighted with their new recruit. They were pleased that Wanda had found Janice so unexpectedly and in the nick of time. They also congratulated themselves on their own discernment in making such a sensible choice. Janice had certainly saved their bacon by materialising for the *Captive Audience* video recording and for Vendetta's southern tour.

They both found Janice Evans to be competent, efficient and always willing to go the extra mile as a dedicated professional. Another vital asset was Janice's ability to handle herself when the brat-pack tried it on. She had managed to evade Rocker's overtures with a smile and without offending him in the process of rebuttal. She had not allowed herself to become a skivvy for Myra or Max's every tiny whim but again she had not made an enemy of her colleagues in doing so.

John had endeavoured to protect Janice in the early days of her employment when she was assigned to the role of floor manager during the recording of *Captive Audience*. But now his services were no longer required. Janice had got the measure of the exhibitionist-types and she knew very well how to teach each one that she was in charge without ruffling any plumage. Janice had, in fact, now begun to command the total respect of her colleagues.

Janice had also made many friends in the team. Wanda, Jenny and Greta were frequently seen with her at lunchtime and she and John would often share a drink at the end of the day.

Janice and John had a good working relationship and, moreover, they had become friends. Their friendship was of the platonic variety and it would never be otherwise because both had differing sexual preferences. And because of this fact, there friendship could grow strong.

One day when Janice and John were having an after-hours drink, the conversation turned unexpectedly yet quite naturally to discussing the members of the team in a conspiratorial manner. Each member of Vendetta was paraded in front of their minds for a kit-inspection and a judgement.

Rouchuka, Bluey and Kicker were spoken of with affection and consideration.

They both knew Rouchuka was probably in the wrong business even though she maintained a brave front. But because she always performed as a consummate professional, she commanded their sympathy and their admiration.

Bluey, who was considered by most to be a boring wimp, was pitied but not unkindly. Kicker was deemed to be underrated yet he was acknowledged as much loved by all – including Janice and John.

But the little horrors in the band were a different kettle of fish.

Rocker came in for his fair share of criticism in that he only really had eyes for himself, although outwardly his eyes never left the females in his orbit.

"I have managed to keep him well at bay," announced Janice proudly.

"Yes, I congratulate you on that. You have engineered him very well," responded John with admiration.

"He's really an overgrown infant at heart."

"I think he is still trying to prove to his parents that he's OK. But, unfortunately, they are not taking much notice."

"I thought it would be something like that," admitted Janice.

John went on to fill Janice in on the background to Rocker's parentage and their general lack of ability either to praise him or to even acknowledge his success. John mentioned how ungrateful Rocker's parents had been even after he had bought them a large house as a testimony to his wealth. Both Janice and John sighed with dismay at this state of affairs which accounted for most of Rocker's outlandish behaviour.

The next candidate for gossip was Myra. Janice confessed that she suspected that there was certainly something strange about him and about his relationship with Max and Gerry.

"I notice that they all three seem to have these secret late-night meetings," asserted John.

"And they appear to have some urgent business to discuss when they do so. It's as if they are all attending a board meeting."

"Yes, I've noticed that too," agreed John.

John thought for a moment before he spoke his next thoughts aloud.

"What do you suppose they are talking about? It cannot be anything to do with the band because the others are not ever invited. I think it's something illegal, though. And I'm sure drugs are involved."

Janice and John were silent for a moment but both were curious to know more about these clandestine meetings.

"Could we spy on them, do you think?" asked a mischievous Janice.

"Hm, I notice that the meetings often take place in Gerry's room at night. Perhaps we could eavesdrop at the door?" remarked John.

"We could also ask around to see if anyone else knows," mused Janice.

"Actually we could also ask one of the bodyguards. Like Hal, for example. I bet he'd know. He is treated like wallpaper but I think he keeps his ears open and flapping," returned John.

"I could do a bit of snooping, myself, if you like," decided Janice.

"Yes, but be careful," warned John.

"I won't do anything dangerous but I could ask Hal casually."

They both laughed at the prospect of their scheme, each having a different agenda. John wanted to hear the latest scandal about Vendetta while Janice had her own reasons for wanting to get her suspicions confirmed. And, indeed, John had just inadvertently endorsed her previous conjectures.

So Janice was now on a mission and she had a good idea of the way in which she would set about it.

John, on the other hand, just relished a bit of speculation but he was not particularly concerned to discover the finer details for himself. He would leave that to Janice. She will decode the mystery far better than I could. And so Janice can save me the trouble. How prophetic were John's words? Hm, very!

BLUEY'S APPREHENSION

Hal Caxton was back on bodyguard duty for Vendetta's tour of the southern counties. But this time he had been assigned to protect Bluey. Gerry had engineered this switch because Myra was getting restless and Hal seemed to be the target of his truculence.

Hal was quite relieved that he no longer had to fend off Myra's overtly promiscuous advances. Bluey, moreover, was undemanding and, while not exactly as lacklustre as he was made out to be, he was generally quiet and unassuming. For Hal, therefore, guarding Bluey was easy money. Bluey did not, for instance, have a plethora of riotous sexual adventures every night and so Hal was able to take life easy and even to get a bit of elicit shut-eye while on duty.

In the Sea Front Grand Hotel, where the flock were staying in Newquay at the conclusion of the tour, Hal was given a room which adjoined Bluey's.

This meant that Hal could stay near Bluey but he could still manage to sleep lightly while actually getting paid to stay awake.

One night a tentative knock came on Hal's interconnecting door and, because he was practised in the art of lightly sleeping, Hal woke instantly and responded immediately.

"Everything all right?" Hal enquired as he sprang off his bed and rubbed his eyes vigorously before opening the door. Hal was, of course, fully clothed and so there was no embarrassment in that quarter.

"I thought I heard someone at my door," replied Bluey, "would you be able to check for me?"

"Certainly," replied the hunk of flesh.

Hal was galvanised into action and so went to check on behalf of his charge. Once Hal had assured himself and Bluey that all was quiet on the western front, the two men began to relax once more.

Bluey suggested that they should have some beverages in order to calm down the situation. Bluey drank some camomile tea in order to get back to sleep while Hal opted for coffee in order to keep himself awake.

And then they started to chatter. Bluey was obviously worried about something and Hal encouraged him to get the burden off his chest in the night watches. Hal had noticed Bluey's preoccupation and thus the subsequent revelation did not come as a complete surprise to his bodyguard.

"I'm worried about the band," said Bluey as he commenced his narrative.

Hal enquired whether Bluey was worrying about the bodyguard presence but he was assured that the work of the bodyguard team was not being criticised. Bluey, moreover, confessed to feeling very safe on this tour with Hal at the helm. Hal breathed a sigh of relief that his charge did not suspect him of any dereliction of duty because he occasionally snatched a bit of sleep during the night when he was supposed to be on duty. But then Bluey was unlikely to be in danger anyway, thought Hal, because he is not one of the key figures in the band.

Bluey then continued his narrative while Hal kept schtum. Hal noticed, however, that Bluey's state of mind had given him a slightly ashen complexion which contrasted with his reddish brown hair.

"I am worried about certain members of the band. Oh, not about their safety but about their outside activities."

Hal murmured but still said nothing. Bluey was now in confessional mode.

"You see, I think, there are some funny things going on."

There always are, thought Hal.

"Oh, I don't mean just all the high jinks and sex and drugs and all that. No, I think that some members of the band are up to something suspect."

Here it comes, Hal reflected. Keep your mouth shut laddie! Remain disinterested!

The one-way conversation was thus prompted to continue unabated.

"Well, to be more precise, I think Gerry, Myra and Max are up to no good."

Hal decided that now was the time for him to interject.

"Well, Myra and Max are a bit wild, I admit, but Gerry seems OK."

Hal believed that his lame rejoinder would encourage more from Bluey. And his calculation was accurate as it happens. Strange that!

"Can I speak in confidence, Hal?"

"Of course, it is part of my duty as your bodyguard, you know," he replied because confidentiality was usually an unwritten law in the safeguarding world and most guards were above corruption.

Hal felt that things were going quite well now and he was eager for Bluey to reveal more. Bluey kindly obliged and he delivered the goods on a platter for Hal.

"Well, to be honest, I think that Gerry, Myra and Max are operating a drugs-racket."

Bluey felt so relieved at having voiced his suspicions and Hal was very aware of Bluey's degree of divine deliverance.

"Blimey," responded Hal, "That's quite serious. Are you sure?"

"I am."

"They all seem a bit over-the-top, even for pop stars, but I would not have thought Gerry would indulge in anything illegal. Are you really sure?"

Hal had managed somehow to feign incredulity.

"I have overheard things," continued the sober Bluey, "but I have nothing to prove it."

"Well, that's very serious!"

Hal could think of nothing better to say and he wondered how to play his cards from here on in. But Bluey gave Hal a helping hand at this juncture.

"I am not about to shop them to the police or anything but it will mean the break-up of the band if it was ever found out. And I don't see what I can do about it. No one will ever listen to me."

That much was true, thought Hal.

"Well, if this is true, you are in a sticky situation yourself, of course." Hal was no comforter. "What are you going to do about it?"

"I really don't know but it's very, very worrying."

"Can you have a word with Gerry?" asked Hal trying to sound innocent yet helpful.

"I could but I don't see that it would do much good if he's part of the inner ring. And he's probably the ringleader anyway."

"Hm, difficult, I see."

"I am going to have to give it some serious thought," continued the distressed Bluey because an impasse had resulted for him.

"I'm not sure what to suggest," said Hal, as if considering Bluey's position. "Does anyone else know, do you think?"

"Not sure."

Bluey was beginning to look really troubled now.

"Well," suggested Hal, "perhaps you ought to think more about it and then decide what you want to do."

Believing the conversation to have dried up, Hal changed the subject.

"But, for now, I think you ought to get some sleep. You have a heavy day ahead tomorrow, you know, Bluey."

Bluey, of course, agreed and the two men parted for the rest of the night.

Bluey, however, failed to get much more in the way of sleep that night. The camomile tea had not worked obviously.

Hal returned to his adjoining room with a wry smile on his face. This has been a good night's work, he mused. And he then settled down to some more elicit slumber. The caffeine did not keep him awake at all.

MADELEINE'S TEMPTATION

After a long and hard day at the office one day, Madeleine had elected to treat herself to dinner in a nearby restaurant.

She sat at a small table in the Orchard Garden restaurant which was near her office but not too far away from her home in Braxmere Mews. The Orchard Garden served typically British fayre and it was not too expensive and so it suited Madeleine admirably. She ordered a sweet potato soup as a starter and this delight was followed by lamb cutlets with mashed potato and fresh seasonal vegetables.

While consuming her sweet potato soup, Madeleine was now really beginning to relax. As she progressed with her appetising and comforting soup, she found that thoughts of work and its accompanying worries could now be banished from her mind.

"Are you Miss Jenkins, by any chance, madam?" a cultured voice from out of nowhere asked.

Madeleine looked up because she was startled by the appearance of this stranger who had approached her table unexpectedly and, for a moment, she was lost for words. Once Madeleine had overcome her initial surprise and her tongued-tied reaction began to subside, she replied in the affirmative quite automatically.

The stranger then presented Madeleine with a large bouquet of red roses which he put into her arms with a flourish. Madeleine, by now, had dropped her soup spoon because she was so bemused by what had occurred.

"I don't understand," she proclaimed.

"These were ordered for you from Floral Creations and I was told to deliver them to you here," explained the courier.

"I still don't understand. I didn't order any flowers and who would know that I am here?" she protested.

"I believe there is a card inside," responded the other, "but my job was merely to deliver them."

Madeleine looked at the card which told her nothing except that the flowers came from a well-wisher and, as far as she knew, she did not have any well-wishers in her life.

"There must be some mistake," she exclaimed more vehemently.

By now Madeleine was beginning to recover from her initial shock and correspondingly she became assertive.

"I cannot accept these because there is some mistake on your part," she stated forcefully.

The courier then checked his mobile phone log and he politely confirmed that his information was, indeed, correct.

"Miss Jenkins, yes. The Orchard Garden restaurant, yes," he asserted.

Madeleine, however, was far from being reassured by this so-called confirmation from the courier's phone log. She had told no one that she would be dining out this evening. Madeleine also wondered about this man because he was very expensively dressed and he seemed too polite and well-spoken to be a courier, although she did not consider herself to be a snob. How misguided can you get?

Undaunted, Madeleine stood up and then forcibly handed the bouquet back to the courier who had no option but to accept the rejected delivery.

"Thank you but I cannot accept them. And my soup is getting cold," Madeleine gave her final word.

The courier then left with the promise to look into the matter further and to report back to her. Madeleine ignored this statement and continued her delicious meal.

Nothing much happened during her main course except that she enjoyed it enormously and she forgot about the intruder with his bunch of stupid roses. The other diners in the Orchard Garden restaurant by now had lost interest in watching the contretemps between Madeleine and the courier and so they all had resumed their meals. Madeleine had not, in fact, even noticed that she had attracted any attention from those nearby.

Madeleine was not normally the kind of woman to whom men sent red roses and so she shrugged the whole episode off as she continued with her evening treat. Madeleine was fairly attractive but not really much interested in pursuing the opposite sex and having fun. She took her work seriously, she kept her mortgage payments up, she went to a keep-fit class once a week and she only treated herself to dinner occasionally. In short, that was Madeleine's life and she had no wish to rock the boat with complicated and unnecessary relationships. No one, consequently, would ever wish to change places with Madeleine because her existence held very little in the way of excitement and jollity. Madeleine was obviously unmarried and, because youth was but a vague recollection nowadays, she seemed unlikely to alter her marital status for the foreseeable future. And so the roses were undoubtedly an error on the part of Floral Occasions or Creations or whatever they were called, she determined.

Madeleine declined a dessert course because, by now, she had eaten enough. She did not, moreover, want even to risk an increase in her waistline, despite the fact that no one would normally look at her figure. She paid her bill, she thanked the waiting staff graciously and she made her way homeward.

Once outside the Orchard Garden restaurant, however, Madeleine was astonished to see the courier again still holding the now-famous red roses.

"Not you again," was Madeleine's instant response.

"I have a confession to make, sorry," he retorted.

Madeleine walked on trying to ignore him.

"I do not work for Floral Creations and no one has sent you any flowers," the man remarked.

This much I know, thought Madeleine, as she walked on trying to evade this nuisance of a man.

"I just wanted to meet you and get to know you and I could think of no other way of approaching you."

Madeleine now wondered whether to call the cops even though the stranger did not seem to be threatening her at all.

"Please accept these flowers. They are from me and no one else."

Madeleine quickened her pace but so did this annoying stranger.

"Do say you'll have dinner with me one night? I think you are very beautiful and I would like to get to know you better. I am sincere and mean no harm."

Madeleine still kept walking but her pace was beginning to slow down.

The charade continued for some while yet with Madeleine walking away and the man running to catch up with her and making yet another attempt to woo her.

"Please say you will have dinner with me one night. We can go to a better restaurant than the Orchard Garden if you like. I do so want to get to know you better. And please accept these roses from me."

Madeleine at last stopped walking and came to an abrupt halt.

MEDICI'S COGITATION

Calendula and Barrington were sitting on the patio of their home in Grove Naxton Cross after a lunch lovingly prepared by Barrington from homegrown garden produce.

Calendula had spent most of the morning at work in her studio on her latest creation, entitled *Temperate Climbs*, earmarked for a rich punter. This was a painting in her inimitable style for which she was well known. Her painting consisted of an exquisite blend of oil pastels and gouache and its hallmark was bold opacity in contrast with transparent sub fusc impressionism. It conjured up an atmosphere of mountains, seas and sky in no place which was recognisable on this planet. But the intended buyer was not at all concerned. Indeed, Calendula's purchaser wanted to be taken out of himself.

Calendula was excited because her buyer would be paying a hefty sum for her artistic creation and his money would keep her in champagne and jewellery for some months ahead.

Barrington had also been hard at work in the garden, cleaning out the small pond which had recently been constructed in order to surprise and delight the great love of his life.

Barrington had organised for the pond to be built at a time when Calendula was abroad on business so that the surprise was even more appreciated when the traveller returned home. And Barrington was justly proud of his efforts and his forethought. The pond was now well stocked with both flora and fauna but this garden feature still had to be tended and the wild-life respected accordingly. Both Calendula and Barrington had espied *Corixa Punctata* (water boatmen, to you) and *Gerris Lacustris* (pond-skaters, to you) in evidence in the pond but they still hankered after inheriting a frog.

Calendula and Barrington had also contemplated purchasing some fish for their pond but they had not yet decided what they wanted to acquire or whether this would be a practical proposition when they were on their frequent travels.

Calendula had suggested that their housekeeper, Gladys Taylor, could feed the fish when they were away but Barrington had vociferously demurred at this suggestion. It was then quite plain to Calendula that if they acquired any fish, Barrington would have wanted to have the exclusive right to feed his babies.

"Well, we do need some more facts and some concrete evidence," announced Barrington trying to overcome their obstacles yet again. "Particularly for the path through Europe. We have most of the rest sewn up."

Calendula agreed with Barrington.

"But we need to decide how we are going to achieve our goals and join up the dots," stated Calendula who would obviously brook no argument.

Barrington considered for a moment.

"Well, let's take stock of the situation," he suggested. "Do we know whether Janice has got the job yet for the next tour?"

"Absolutely! She has done her stuff with Wanda, beautifully," asserted Calendula.

Calendula turned to face him directly and then she began to enumerate their options.

"Well, we now have installed Janice successfully near to the nub of the problem. But her info will take some time to acquire. Hal has the run of the place and so that should help. And Jules has done some sterling work so far."

"And, of course, I'm pretty sure we can crack Gerry," Barrington interjected with a knowing grin which Calendula deliberately ignored.

"And Gemma and Tom are doing well too," continued Calendula.

The two of them considered what was left to do and they then decided that, even though the remainder was simmering nicely, they still needed to explore the European section of the drug-route.

"We could, of course, just hire a camper van and do it ourselves," suggested Barrington.

"Over my dead body!" replied Calendula.

Barrington realised that the idea of slumming it would definitely not appeal to Calendula and so he felt suitably rebuked.

"But we must get someone else out there," remarked Calendula with finality.

And so now the discussion had come full circle. They had made progress admittedly but there was still much work to be done and some vital information to be obtained.

"I will have to give this stuff some serious thought," Calendula concluded.

Barrington realised that she was troubled by the impasse and he wanted to soothe Calendula's brow and to stop her from fretting.

"Let's go and visit Chantal?" he suggested. "This weekend, say."

Calendula seemed to wake out of her deep reverie at this brilliant suggestion.

"Yes, I could think better in Paris, of course.'

Barrington was delighted that his recommendation for a trip to Paris, where Calendula had an art studio, had been taken up so readily because this excursion could be the solution to their predicament.

Calendula's eldest daughter, Chantal, lived and worked in Paris and this occasion would provide an excuse for a visit. Chantal worked there as a freelance fashion designer who was forging ahead in her chosen career. She worked principally for an international fashion house but she had recently acquired another prestigious client in the city. Calendula was justly proud of the progress which Chantal had made so far and she was delighted that her eldest daughter was following in her own footsteps in the artistic profession. And because Calendula had an affinity for Chantal's work, the suggestion that they spend a weekend in Paris was heaven-sent.

Calendula's younger daughter, Juliet, was also doing quite well in the teaching profession as an academic. But Calendula understood nothing much about this occupation.

And so some expensive flights and a stylish hotel were duly booked for the weekend adventure and Chantal was warned about their impending visit.

Chantal was relieved that her mother and her chosen life-partner would not be staying with her because she did not want the extra work of housing and entertaining any guests. Chantal was thus thankful to learn that Calendula and Barrington were proposing to stay in a hotel nearby so that she could visit them both easily while they were in the city.

Chantal was very fond of Mum and Barrington and so their impending visit gladden her significantly. In anticipation of their arrival, therefore, Chantal replenished her wardrobe and waited expectantly.

PART 4
BLACK ICE

JANICE'S EXPLORATION

Janice was very thoughtful after she had discovered that John had suspicions about Vendetta's drug-running enterprise. She had resolved to find out more about these activities if she could and so, to this end, she approached Hal whom she understood had his ear to the ground.

"Do you fancy a quick pub lunch?" invited Hal.

Janice replied in the affirmation and she took this invitation as a token of Hal's intended co-operation.

The tour had by now reached and settled in Newquay for two weeks at the culmination of the jaunt. Once Vendetta's tour of the southern counties was actually on the road, it meant that both Janice and Hal had some free time during the day prior to working their fingers to the bone in the evenings. Lunch could, therefore, easily be arranged because they both were on the spot and were free in the daytime. Janice, moreover, had no longer agreed to run errands for the boys and so she had even more leisure time.

Both Janice and Hal had learned the repetitive routine for the tour management off by heart and so preparatory work during the day was virtually unnecessary. This routine had thus given the supporting crew a bit of breathing space. So when they had found a gap in the fence in terms of time that day, Janice and Hal then decanted to the local hostelry, safe in the knowledge that nothing would collapse if they took their eye off the ball.

Janice had a couple of sandwiches at the pub while Hal fed the inner man on Kate and Sidney pie and chips. They both, however, stuck to soft drinks in order to ensure that they would be wide awake for the evening's offensive.

When the business of the lunchtime meeting commenced, Janice and Hal swopped stories and exchanged notes. Hal admitted that he had overhead a meeting between Myra and Gerry in Myra's room on the last night of the previous tour in the north. Janice also confessed to her conversation with John during which time he had voiced his suspicions.

So now the cards were really on the table. Both were pretty sure that a drug-scam was in full swing within the members of Vendetta Ice and both were worried by the knowledge and its implications.

"Even though only Myra, Max and Gerry are involved, their drug-dealing could affect all the Vendetta mob and its hangers-on, like us," affirmed Hal.

"But are we sure that the culprits are just those three? Who else might be in the team? What about Rocker, for instance?"

"I'm pretty sure it's just those three but it might still be worth checking for certain, though."

"I'm worried for my job," stated Janice decisively while slightly changing the subject. "If the caper were discovered then everyone on board will go down with the ship. And I would be on the dole again. Even unemployable via implication."

"Yeah. They're a selfish bunch and it's not as if they need the readies."

"They do everything for kicks, so this is just another example of the same, I reckon," Janice asserted.

Hal was as frustrated about the situation as his colleague.

"I can easily get a job elsewhere, through the agency," he maintained, "but I do get some kudos from working for a high profile band."

"Even though their profile may not work in your favour if the criminals are exposed and caught," Janice replied.

"Doesn't bear thinking about," Hal agreed.

Janice sighed in sympathy with Hal.

"I can, of course, give you the names of a number of agencies in London who could help you out if needs be. And they could certainly help you when your current contract comes to an end when the southern tour concludes," continued Hal.

"Thank you," retorted Janice, "that might come in very handy."

"Obviously, I hope that they will renew your contract for the US tour, at least, provided that you are not sick to the back teeth of them by then."

"No chance," affirmed the affable Janice.

Both Janice and Hal now halted their narrative in order to mull over their predicament. But it was as if the pair were still communicating because there was a companionable silence between them both.

"But what are we to do? How can we prevent the rot from getting any worse?" Janice had now voiced her quandary aloud.

"We can start by verifying the facts and then taking some action," replied Hal.

"What kind of action?" enquired a curious Janice who seemed to feel that her colleague-companion might have the answer.

"Well, I can keep listening at doors and you could continue to make conversation with those close to the boys. Because other team-members must know something. We cannot be the only ones with the gossip."

Janice felt that this was good advice from Hal who seemed a level-headed sort of chap.

So plans were made between the two of them to keep a watching brief on the situation and periodically to report back. If sufficient evidence were collected by them both, it was agreed, they would then be in a position of power as a result. They could, for instance, expose the scam and be rewarded. Or they could simply jump ship before it sank irretrievably. Or they could sell the information which they had acquired.

The options would be available to Janice and Hal once their suspicions had been either confirmed or denied after some information-gathering activity. There thus seemed to be a way forward from which the two could benefit and then emerge from the sticky situation unscathed.

"I will report back when I have more data following our discussion today."

"Good thinking, Hal. I would like to come out of this smelling of roses rather than with my career down the drain," concluded Janice.

The pair then returned to work with a lighter frame of mind now that the air had been cleared and a useful plan had been formulated.

Hal, moreover, also felt that his conversation with Janice had sparked thoughts of a different kind. Janice could be useful to his endeavours with his other employer in many ways.

Thus Hal put a call through to Barrington Flint in order to recommend that they recruit yet another member of the Medici Squadron team. The results of this conversation, however, were interesting.

GEMMA'S TRIUMPH

Gemma sat in her room at the Caribbean Lodge awaiting a call which would announce the arrival of Rowan as her dinner date.

She had made herself ready for this evening with a new hair-do at the hotel's on-site salon and she had carefully selected an eye-catching red dress which would show off her nearly black hair to startling effect. One might almost have taken Gemma for an islander as a result of her looks. Her beauty had, indeed, caught many eyes in the past and she had known many feet following her footsteps.

She idly flicked through the pages of a tourist magazine in order to familiarise herself with the delights available for the hardy and determined visitor to the islands. Gemma also wanted some conversation-fodder for the evening ahead and tourism seemed as good a topic as any as far as she was concerned. And talk of tourism would also add verisimilitude to her cover-story as Rosemary Devlin.

At last the telephone rang in order to announce the arrival of Gemma's date.

"Mr Rowan Boyd-Fuller to see you, madam," announced the hotel receptionist.

"I'll be right down," replied the hotel's guest.

Gemma then continued to read her magazine for a few more minutes before descending to the ground floor reception area in order to greet her guest. Gemma felt that keeping Rowan waiting would endorse the cliche about making men work hard for their rewards.

Rowan sat somewhat nervously in reception. Gemma's hotel, the Caribbean Lodge, was, in fact, far from being pretentious and so Rowan was not too embarrassed that a girl should be paying for his meal. He did, however, feel a little under-dressed in the establishment but no one seemed to sneer at his casual attire. Rowan's jeans and shirt were actually the best in his wardrobe but he hoped that Rosemary would not realise this embarrassing fact.

"Rosemary, delighted to see you," said the hopeful and expectant Rowan when his date arrived in reception.

Gemma kissed him on both cheeks which incorporated a promise of more enchantment to come later on. Rowan melted at the thought of the evening ahead.

Gemma acknowledged the receptionist with a nod and thanked her for announcing her visitor's arrival.

"Would you like to dine at the Caribbean Lodge or shall we do the town? Still my treat, of course. I can swing it on expenses," she emphasized.

Rowan was lost for words and so Gemma took the initiative and proposed that they went out in search of a restaurant instead of being confined to her hotel. Gemma had apparently discovered a beachside bistro which served traditional island fayre and which she knew would be atmospheric. Rowan was relieved because he knew that they would now be going down-market.

Gemma opted for a lobster paella while Rowan chose curried goat accompanied by rice and peas for their main dishes. Gemma also had a starter which resembled an Iberian gazpacho while Rowan selected an appetising shrimp and mussel platter.

Gemma tried to remember not to eat too much because she had previously told Rowan that she only partook of light evening meals.

The evening seemed to be going well for both parties. The outrageous flirting of the evening before continued and, indeed, became more serious.

"I shall miss you very much when you return home, Rosemary," said Rowan who looked as if his heart was already broken.

"I shall come back frequently, if only to see you again, my sweet Rowan," stated Gemma with what seemed like heartfelt sentiment.

"That would be delightful. And then we can meet up again, I hope."

Outwardly Rowan looked a lot more than hopeful but inwardly he actually felt desperate.

"Certainly. I shall be back very soon on business anyway," Gemma reassured her adoring suppliant.

"I'm so glad."

"Meanwhile, let's make the most of my time here now."

Gemma could be very tantalizing when she chose to be and Rowan appeared to be putty in her hands.

"How will you be spending your time while I'm away?" enquired Gemma.

"Oh, same old thing. Just working on the yacht, you know."

Gemma didn't know and so she asked, "What kind of work do you do on the yacht? Just day-trippers?"

There was a slight hesitation before Rowan said that day-excursions were his main source of income. He didn't want to give too much away obviously.

"Nothing else? No cargo transportation, say?" said Gemma trailing her coat nonchalantly.

Again Rowan hesitated before saying, "Not much really."

Gemma decided to hedge her bets.

"Do you do trips or transportation to the mainland, for instance? I ask because I may have need of some transportation services myself," she probed casually.

Gemma's last enquiry did the magic and thus opened the floodgates.

"Well, I do take some stuff regularly across to Venezuela. Overnight sometimes."

"Could you let me know the next time you are planning a trip across to Venezuela, Rowan dear? I may want to visit the mainland briefly myself while I'm here. Or send some things over there, perhaps."

Gemma knew now that she was on to a winner and so she instantly pressed home her advantage.

"Of course," Rowan dear replied obligingly.

Rowan could see an opportunity now to take two consignments across the Caribbean sea and to earn twice the money. He was snared in the man-trap. Poor sod!

The evening continued with dancing, with the couple clad in Caribbean garlands, to the accompaniment of a steel band. The spirit of reggae, salsa and calypso added glamour to the evening. The duo then danced most of the night away and were virtually locked in each other's arms by the end of the evening.

The next morning, Gemma asked for more details of Rowan's trips to Venezuela and she was furnished with some interesting data. She learned of the nights, for instance, when the trips were made and the possibility of an illegal cargo.

Gemma also realised that Rowan was concerned about what he was transporting because the ask-no-questions policy seemed to be essential for his business contact. Someone called Sid apparently, Gemma gathered, was the one who had initially approached Rowan who had then agreed to carry the consignments across the sea at night because he was on skid-row at the time.

They had an early breakfast together before Rowan had to hurry away to work. Rowan felt on top of the world now that he had met the rich Rosemary and she had invited him into her life.

Gemma, on the other hand, felt proud of her achievements on this short visit to St Lucia and she returned to New York with the information which she had set out to acquire and which she immediately fed back to her wealthy client. Gemma, in return, received many thanks and a goodly of sum of money in order to cover both her out-of-pocket expenses for the trip and her high-pitched fee.

Everything in her private detective agency seemed fine when Gemma checked in at the office on her return to the US capital.

A number of applications for the vacant post of another private eye were, furthermore, sitting on her desk and they were eagerly awaiting perusal. Gemma scooped up these applications and a few other important messages. She then told her trusted secretary that she would be in on the following morning but that, at present, she needed to recover from her jetlag hangover. Gemma trusted that her efficient secretary would keep the pot boiling steadily until she was officially back in harness in the office when she would be raring to go.

Gemma then rang Bertram to announce her return and her desire to see him again that evening. Bertram came around like a shot once he knew that his latest concubine was back in business in New York.

MADELEINE'S DILEMMA

Madeleine seemed to be beset by many worries these days. She was worried at work because she was pretty sure that her boss, Reginald Trevelyan, was up to no good in his position of Chief Executive of the Benefice Charity Trust.

This state of affairs offended Madeleine because she was fundamentally honest and she wholeheartedly believed in the charity's mission. But she could not think of any way in which she could resolve the situation and there was no one to whom she could confide her knowledge or her suspicions.

Madeleine had contemplated approaching one of the other members of the Board of Governors of the Benefice Charity Trust but she was unsure which one to approach and, if she were setting the cat among the pigeons in the process, whether her revelation might rebound on her. Obviously Madeleine did not want to seek alternative employment but to remain in her present post seemed fraught with difficulty. So Madeleine was at a crossroads here.

Madeleine, moreover, had met this Nicholas Benson nuisance who was very persistent in wanting her to have dinner with him one night soon. And that was a worry too.

While she was, in essence, attracted by the idea of dining with Nicholas, she also felt nervous about dating a virtual stranger and, perhaps, taking things a little further. Madeleine was certainly not an object which men had sought after in the past and, therefore, it was something of a new experience for her. And so Madeleine was not sure that she could handle the encounter wisely. This situation was a dilemma for Madeleine consequently.

While all these thoughts were mulling around in Madeleine mind, the phone on her desk rang. Talk of the devil! It was the devil himself – that Nicholas Benson again.

"Can I still not persuade you to have dinner with me one night? I won't bite, promise," he jested.

Madeleine laughed in spite of her desire to remain impassive and serious.

Nicholas tempted her with some very expensive restaurants and also invited her to watch a show with him at the local theatre.

Madeleine was definitely tempted by this latest proposition. She dearly wanted to go the Newbridge Theatre in the centre of town in order to see a production of the comedy *When We Are Married* because she was a great fan of its author, John Boynton Priestly. But Madeleine wondered whether the title of the play might not give Nicholas the wrong message.

Eventually Madeleine's resistance crumbled and she consented to go to the Newbridge Theatre with Nicholas on the coming Friday evening. Can't do any harm, thought Madeleine, because there will be plenty of other people around. And so she thought nothing more of it. She even volunteered to pay her whack but Nicholas was adamant that it would be his treat. Madeleine had hoped, of course, to be able to pay for her own ticket as her way of not being beholden to him. But that strategy had obviously misfired. Blast!

On Friday evening, in consequence, Madeleine left work slightly early in order to doll herself up for the occasion. She was a trifle disturbed by her actions because Madeleine considered that she was taking the occasion just that much too seriously.

Madeleine had wisely arranged to meet Nicholas outside the theatre at 6.30 pm rather than allowing him to collect her from her house. She thought that if he knew where she lived, he would become even more of a nuisance.

Just before the appointed hour, therefore, Madeleine duly arrived at the Newbridge Theatre where she found Nicholas patiently waiting for her. It soon transpired that damn Nicholas had already bought their tickets and that the show did not, in fact, begin for another hour yet. Blast again!

The couple were thus obliged to have a drink in the theatre's bar at this early hour. Madeleine cursed her silliness in not realising that the show would be unlikely to begin at 6.30 pm in the evening and so she blamed herself for the fact that she had fallen into Nicholas' trap.

She ordered a fruit juice because she did not want to lose control this evening even though Nicholas pressed her for something stronger and, indeed, he bought himself a glass of red wine as a token of his willingness to enjoy the evening.

Nicholas gazed attentively at the subject of his interest but their conversation appeared to be hard work because Madeleine was relatively uncommunicative. While they were waiting for the play to begin, Madeleine seemed to be tongue-tied and so much of their time in the bar was taken up merely with drinking their drinks and eating some nuts and raisins which Nicholas had also purchased unbidden. Because Madeleine had refused an alcoholic drink, the wheels had not been oiled. Nicholas had hoped that some alcohol would serve to loosen both her tongue and her disposition.

Eventually a voice on the loudspeaker invited the audience to take their seats as the performance was about to commence. Madeleine felt the relief of this move away from the bar and into the theatre because she then did not feel it necessary to make any polite conversation with her gallant and adoring host.

When We Are Married was written in 1934 and the play enjoyed much success in London when it opened. And the work has been a firm favourite in the repertoire with theatre audiences ever since. The play has also been a stalwart of the amateur drama repertoire which was how Madeleine had been introduced to the work initially. Having seen the play done on the amateur stage, it then became one of Madeleine's all-time favourites and so to experience Priestley's work on the professional stage was an added treat for her.

The play opens with three well-to-do and supercilious couples celebrating their joint silver wedding anniversaries in Victorian splendour in Yorkshire. Things take a turn for the worse when the three couples are informed by a humble church organist that they are not, in reality, married because of a clerical error. Those within the orbit of the three couples then make capital out of and poke fun at the misfortunes of the embarrassed sextet which generates much laughter from the audience. Essentially the comedy exposes the shallowness of people who consider themselves to be a cut above the rest of the underlings in the wider population.

Madeleine was delighted with the performance of the play and Nicholas was pleased that he had persuaded his guest to come to the theatre on their first date. Perhaps the first of many? Can't really tell at this stage.

It was quite dark by the time Madeleine and Nicholas left the Newbridge Theatre and the obvious question now was what would happen next. Nicholas would have wished to have a late-night meal but he did not want to chance his luck. He then offered to drive Madeleine home but she told him that she had brought her own car. Another of Madeleine's defensive-barrier strategies. And this one paid off.

Bloody hell! Nicholas felt that he had not thought this one through sufficiently well and the whole caboodle could blow up in his face. Undaunted, however, Nicholas then asked Madeleine if they could have dinner one night soon but again she was evasive. She would be a hard nut to crack, thought Nicholas. But he was not about to give up.

"I shall track you down and keep asking you out until you say yes," he persisted.

After thanking him for his generosity in taking her to the theatre, Madeleine relented somewhat and suggested that Nicholas could ring her some time so that she would have a chance either to make up her mind or to stall him indefinitely. Madeleine had, in essence, enjoyed the evening and so secretly she was not averse to further dates but she did not want to commit herself or to give him too much encouragement.

Madeleine had barely recovered from her evening with Nicholas before he was on the telephone again and this time using her home number. How the hell did he get hold of my landline number?

She scowled at even the thought of Nicholas' audacity, although she did admire his persistence and his resourcefulness. Perhaps he is a private eye? Or a police officer? Perish the thought.

"I did enjoy our theatre trip last evening," he began, "and I think you enjoyed it too.

"I did enjoyed the play, yes," retorted Madeleine pointedly.

Madeleine was rather non-committal about yesterday evening's date. She had thanked him last night after all was said and done. What more did he expect? Well, she knew the answer to that one, at least.

"So when can we do it again then? I'm really keen to see you again."

If Madeleine had been a gambler, she would have put money on his asking this question and then she would have simply raked in her winnings. But what could she say in reply?

"I'm not sure," was her pretty lame response.

CALENDULA'S CREATIVITY

It was a tad breezy up on the top floor of the magnificent *Tour Eiffel* (Eiffel Tower, to you) in Paris on the Left Bank on the Champ de Mars.

The *Tour Eiffel*, built by the engineer Gustave Eiffel between 1887 and 1889, is nicknamed *La Dame de Fer* (Iron Lady, to you) by the locals. The tower has now become France's cultural icon and the monument attracts millions of visitors annually as perhaps the world's most sought after tourist attraction. Because it is 324 metres high, visitors to the top can see much of Paris below and thus they can get a new perspective on life as a result.

The Eiffel Tower consists of three levels. The first floor is 57 metres from ground level, the second floor is 115 metres high and the top floor boasts 276 metres in height. Visitors can climb to the first and second floors if they are energetic enough but they must take the lift to the very top floor. The lift can, of course, be taken all the way if visitors are lazy or lacking in stamina.

Calendula and Barrington wanted to climb the many hundreds of steps up the Eiffel Tower so that they could get some exercise but, as the flesh was weak, they took the glass-walled lift to the first and the second floors and, finally, to the top level for the breathtaking view. So the pair did the full circuit in order to see life from a different viewpoint.

On the second floor, Calendula and Barrington stopped off at the Jules Verne Restaurant for lunch. Here they sampled the gastronomic delights of a Michelin-starred restaurant as well as the awe-inspiring view of the Champ de Mars, the indigenous cultural art museum of the Qual Branly and the gardens of the Trocadéro.

When they reached the top floor, of course, Calendula wanted to visit the Champagne Bar just so that she could say that she had fully partaken of the experience. The numerous gift shops were of little interest to the couple and so they gave them merely a cursory glance.

Having previously lived in Paris, both Calendula and Barrington had visited this iconic monument several times before but it was now for them a trip down memory lane which they relished to the full.

On the top level of the Eiffel Tower, Calendula and Barrington gazed up at the upper antennae which reached towards the sky and they looked down from the God's-eye view on all Paris. Here Calendula and Barrington also observed the reconstructed office of Gustave Eiffel with its wax models of the main protagonists and they visited the summit model of the tower itself. They likewise studied the various maps which indicated their location with reference to the rest of the world.

When on the breathtaking open-air platform of the top level, suitably ringed-fenced in order to prevent people jumping off after too much vin rouge, Calendula gave a loud cry which startled Barrington and everyone else in the near vicinity.

"I've got it!" she exclaimed sibilantly.

"Eureka," mumbled her partner under his breath.

Barrington gave an indulgent smile to those around who were staring with a puzzled expression and perhaps some concern at the antics of these crazy English people. He knew what Calendula's exclamation proclaimed and his smile also reflected his satisfaction.

"I knew we'd find the answer here in Paris. This is my second home and it inspires me," announced Calendula.

Once back on the ground, the couple then spent some time walking around the gardens of the Champ de Mars and the Trocadéro while Calendula explained her plan in detail. Barrington was extremely impressed but then he always admired his lover's creative brain in addition to her body, of course. From the Champ de Mars, they could view the Iron Lady at a distance from ground level and hence they could see yet another angle on life. The pair also had the opportunity of seeing the Military Academy (École Militaire, to you) on the south eastern side of the park close up.

The two next sought out some of Calendula's old and much loved friends in the Place du Tertre in Montmartre. Calendula and Barrington had, in fact, visited here recently when conducting another enquiry which exposed some political intrigue. Calendula had then been instrumental in unearthing a fox on that occasion too.

Calendula was easily able to track down her beloved friends who greeted them both in the traditional French manner with kisses on both cheeks. Two of her friends, Philippe and Claudette, who were not unfamiliar with the drug-scene, were able to explain the ways in which dealers and couriers could be tracked down in a big city like Paris. This vital information was thus stored in the minds of Calendula and Barrington for future reference.

The couple's next port of call was Calendula's studio in Paris where they found that everything was ticking over nicely and that no crises loomed which might demand Calendula's immediate attention or might need to detain her at present in the French capital.

Then Chantal, Calendula's eldest daughter, was honoured with an impromptu yet somewhat fleeting visit.

Calendula was delighted to see what her daughter had created in terms of fashion designs for her two principal Parisian clients. The two women discussed their work in detail while Barrington merely listened, looked interested and topped up their drinks.

The three of them then went out to dine in an authentic French restaurant which Calendula knew her daughter would seldom frequent but which she would much appreciate. At the little known Parisian restaurant, which Calendula had visited with some of her ex-lovers who were in the know, the three were treated to the delights of traditional French fayre.

The three diners at La Bella Place between them managed to consume haute cuisine in the guise of bouillabaisse, croche monsieur and French onion soup complete with croûtons croustillants fromage (crispy cheese croutons, to you) for starters. These delights were then followed by chicken confit, salmon on papillote and boeuf bourguignon. The whole extravaganza was washed down with some Pouilly-Fumé, Colombard and Cabernet Sauvignon.

Their eats and drinks were all the usual stuff of traditional French cuisine without the pretentiousness of adventurous chefs who strived to titillate the palette of the unwary. But all three diners preferred traditional fayre and regular iconic favourites as they did not really consider themselves to be tourists. Both Calendula and Barrington had lived for a spell in Paris and, indeed, Chantal still did.

Calendula and Chantal delighted in their gastronomic experience and their reunion meant that they could talk non-stop during the meal. Barrington really did not have much to contribute to the conversation except a few nods and smiles. But, of course, he paid the bill willingly and he was gratified by the reunion of his dearly beloved and her dearly beloved daughter.

Exhausted the couple bid farewell to Chantal and made their way home with optimism and satisfaction. Once home in Grove Naxton Cross, after the unpacking had been completed and the washing had been consigned to the linen basket ready for Gladys Taylor's ministrations, Barrington came into his own.

Accordingly Barrington rang two of his friends and spoke at length about the next phase of their latest project. One friend was located in St Lucia and the other in Morocco. Calendula listened into their conversation and she was pleased that her inspiring plan could be put into action so efficiently and expertly.

At the end of the day both Calendula and Barrington crashed out in their double-aspect bedroom and, more importantly, their ensuite shower room where Calendula utilised some more Rose Garden Mist for the occasion. Where did they get the energy from? Why not climb the Eiffel Tower instead?

HAL'S CONTRIVANCE

Hal had been disturbed by Bluey's admission that he was worried about the drug-trading with which Gerry, Myra and Max seemed to be involved. Hal, in fact, knew that what Bluey had claimed was, in fact, true because he had overheard Gerry and Myra plotting himself. But he certainly did not divulge his insider knowledge to the troubled Bluey.

Hal had then been even more astonished when he discovered from Janice that she and John had also had their suspicions and that they were intent on investigating the matter.

What a lot of nosey people there are about the place? Hal then thought more about the situation. And, if this drug-scam became common knowledge, then my job would be threatened and my position as an informant for the Medici Squadron would also be down the pan.

When Hal had his lunchtime meeting with Janice, furthermore, an idea had struck him. If Janice could be counted on as a reliable snoop then perhaps he could recruit her into the fold? When he spoke to Barrington, however, he learned, to his amazement and glee, that Janice was already on board as an operative which was why she had taken the job of assistant stage manager in the first place. Barrington had, of course, apologised for not keeping Hal informed of events but Hal was not that put out as it happened.

Hal had now been given carte blanche by Barrington to carry out some further investigation and Hal relished the prospect of using some of his ingenuity in order to earn another packet of dosh in the process. Hal had naturally continued his eavesdropping routine but now he felt that he needed more tangible evidence and that he should be more proactive in unearthing and snaring the fox.

After some serious contemplation, therefore, Hal formulated his plan of action. He noticed, for example, that the clandestine meetings of the triumvirate took placed usually about twice a week and the boys tended to favour Tuesday and Thursday nights for these events. Accordingly Hal decided to find a means of recording these meetings with his sophisticated bugging equipment. As he knew that the gatherings took place in Gerry's room in the Sea Front Grand Hotel in Newquay, Hal decided that this would be where he could place his ticking timebomb.

And so, one night, when Vendetta were on stage and in full swing, Hal crept up to Gerry's room and entered with a pass key which he had borrowed from one of the reception staff. He had explained to the receptionist that he needed to enter Gerry's room because someone had reported a stranger possibly lurking thereabouts and Hal, as one of the bodyguard team, needed to investigate this rumour promptly.

Janice had aided and abetted Hal by backing up his story for the receptionist and by showing the appropriate concern for the safety of the band in the process. Janice had managed to organise the other members of the backstage team in such a way that she was able to get away for a few minutes in order to assist Hal.

Now all Hal had to do was to find a convenient location in Gerry's hotel room for his recording device and then, once the die had been cast, just let the natural course of events take over. He also retained the services of the accommodating Janice who kept guard outside Gerry's room while Hal did the deed.

Hal soon found an appropriate location for his black box bugging device beneath a chest of drawers near Gerry's bed. This device was really state-of-the-art in that not only would it record Gerry's clandestine meetings but also Hal and Janice could listen to the proceedings of the meeting remotely if they wished.

The next stage of the operation, unfortunately, was slightly trickier in that Hal needed access to Gerry's computer on which, Hal believed, some vital information would have been stored. Hal, therefore, took advantage of his illegal trespass into Gerry's room in order to locate Gerry's laptop.

Then fate stepped in and prevented Hal from being able to continue his stealthy work.

Janice tapped rapidly on Gerry's door which was the warning signal to Hal that danger was approaching. A member of the hotel waiting staff had been asked to deliver a room-service meal to one of the other residents and this had caused Janice to alert Hal.

Hal immediately came to the bedroom door with what he assumed was a relieved expression on his face and he stated that everything was in order and that it had just been a false alarm. Janice and Hal had prepared for this eventuality and, as such, they had their cover-story ready. Janice explained to the waiter, in case he was the curious type, that there had been a report of a stranger lurking outside Gerry's room and so she and the official bodyguard had gone to investigate.

Hal and Janice had, by this means, covered their backs and had managed to get away with it successfully. So as not to rock the boat, however, they decided to abandon their reprehensible activity and to leave it until another night.

Then fate intervened again but, this time, the cosmic powers were in Hal's favour.

Later the next evening, when the Vendetta team were having their evening meal, Gerry found that he had left his cigarette lighter in his room. Gerry was just about to return to his room, when Hal stepped forward and suggested that he could act as the errand boy on Gerry's behalf.

It came to pass, therefore, that Hal was able to enter Gerry's hotel room legitimately for once in order to locate Gerry's laptop computer, to plant a permanent bug on the hard drive and to download the entire contents of the hard drive on to a USB stick. And Gerry, lucky man, got his lighter in return.

Just before leaving the hotel after the final night there, Hal stole a pass key from one of the cleaners in order to retrieve the bug which he had previously placed beneath the chest of drawers in Gerry's room. The USB stick was then promptly couriered across to Barrington Flint together with the recording taken by the bugging device.

Hal reported his actions back to Barrington who praised him for his ingenuity.

Hal had now more or less completed his espionage work and so he awaited further instructions from the Medici Squadron before making another move.

Barrington, in due season, was delighted to receive his parcel of goodies which consisted of recorded meetings and the contents of Gerry's laptop. This information constituted a significant part of the evidence which the Medici Squadron were busily accumulating on the project. Calendula and Barrington, hence, began to think that the end was not that far off.

BARRINGTON'S WARNING

Andrew Ormerod was the chief political editor of *The Times* and, although he usually specialised in the activities of parliamentary personnel, he also had responsibility for general news about those who had violated political correctness.

Andrew and his wife, Maureen, were good friends of Calendula and Barrington and they all often spent an evening over dinner together.

Calendula and Barrington frequently found themselves entertaining Maureen and Andrew usually at a London restaurant because Maureen found the ordeal of cooking somewhat taxing and embarrassing. Barrington, however, seldom cooked for Maureen and Andrew because it always covered Maureen with shame at her own lack of culinary talent. So there was a downside to the relationship in a way but its existence was not significant in the overall scheme.

Calendula and Barrington, of course, found Maureen's cooking virtually inedible. Sometimes, however, Calendula and Barrington simply had to bite the bullet, to dine reluctantly at Maureen's table and to make the right complimentary noises in the appropriate places so as not to embarrass Maureen too much.

Andrew was permanently on an abstemious diet and a punishing health regime and Barrington always felt that this would have been his way of avoiding facing Maureen's disastrous efforts in the kitchen. Calendula also secretly believed that the Ormerod family usually dinned on ready meals or in restaurants in order to sidestep Maureen's gastronomic fiascos on a regular basis.

But the two couples still remained close friends who met up on a regular basis for dinner engagements of some description – pleasing or otherwise.

Barrington, on this occasion, however, sat patiently waiting in the Braided Duck in Tooley Street in London for his friend Andrew. They had arranged to meet this lunchtime for an informal chat in one of the upstairs rooms in the Braided Duck in order to discuss business. Andrew often slipped the innkeeper a backhander so that he, Andrew, could buy himself and his business associates some private space for confidential discussion.

Andrew arrived, as ever, puffing and panting after his sprint from the office as part of his fitness programme. Barrington, as usual, gave Andrew a hearty thump on the back in order to exacerbate his condition with a grin.

"Well, what have you got for me this time, you old rogue," began Andrew.

"I'm not an old rogue," protested Barrington. "You're as young as you feel."

"Yeah."

"And how's the old fitness-freak stuff doing these days? I notice you're not dead yet."

"It was all going well, Barry you old bugger, until you slapped me on the back."

"I was congratulating you on your safe arrival here."

"Well, what is it this time?" persisted Andrew.

But Barrington, Andrew knew, did not like to be rushed. Barrington grinned and savoured the moment mischievously as was his wont.

"A little snippet," said Barrington giving nothing away.

"How little?"

"Enough to interest you somewhat, I would imagine."

"Get on with it, for God's sake!" Andrew was now running out of patience.

"Let me get you a drink," prevaricated Barrington again cheekily.

"I've ordered one already. A bottle is being brought up from the cellars as we speak," replied the other.

Barrington decided to put Andrew out of his misery.

"It doesn't directly affect anyone in parliament but it does affect the government in a way," he resumed enigmatically.

Andrew waited and listened.

"It's a charity scam," continued Barrington.

"Which one? That is, which charity?"

"The Benefice Charity Trust. They get a few grants from the government."

"I see."

"Their head honcho is a bit dodgy, we believe. But we are looking into it, of course."

As Barrington was obviously getting into his stride, Andrew took a no-comment stance so as not to interrupt Barrington's flow, although he murmured his appreciation here and there.

Barrington then uncharacteristically remained silent for some time. Andrew eventually decided that it was time to prod the dormant tiger.

"And when will you know for certain, then?" asked Andrew.

"Pretty soon and, of course, you will be the first to know," came the reply.

Some more silence ensued which prompted Andrew once more to fill the gap.

"Right."

Andrew's response was not original but he could think of nothing better to say. Then came a shot across Andrew's bows.

"Of course, we also believe that Benefice's Chief Executive is into a lot more underhand stuff and this is what we will expose and have for sale eventually."

Andrew now listened more intently because Barrington, as always, had dexterously managed to whet his appetite well and truly.

But Barrington changed the subject by way of teasing his pal even more.

"How's Maureen? Still going to cookery classes, I imagine?" quipped Barrington.

"Ha! Ha!"

This was a sore point with Andrew and he often felt as embarrassed about Maureen's cooking as she did.

The drinks arrived and Andrew elected to be Mum and pour them out. He had ordered a malt whisky which he knew was Barrington's favourite and he hoped that this treat would loosen his friend's tongue a bit more. But Andrew had legislated without accounting for Barrington's penchant for bantering. The result was that no further information was forthcoming from Barrington for the rest of the lunch break.

Before the waiter left the room, however, Barrington ordered a lunch of steak and chips while Andrew, not to be outdone, had also asked for a cottage cheese salad.

"Cottage cheese salad! God, you really are desperate!"

Andrew grimaced while his friend chuckled and, once again, gave him a hearty slap on the back.

"Why do I tolerate you?" Andrew asked himself aloud rhetorically.

Barrington smiled.

"Cos I got want you want, matey!"

And that was lunch accounted for and the carrot had been dangled. Andrew ate some of the carrot with his miserable cottage cheese salad and he just had to like it that way.

Andrew returned to his office, consequently, encased in the knowledge that Barrington would soon have a tasty morsel for him with which he could satisfy the insatiable appetite of his readers.

The essence of Barrington's discoveries, in the meantime, would not be made known to Andrew until it was time for the information to go to press. But Andrew was OK with that premise because he was sure that the news-fodder would be worth waiting. Especially if the information had been supplied by the notorious Barrington Flint.

VINCE'S DISGUISE

Vince Craven made his way across the continents of South America and Asia in order to end up somewhere remote in the Ukraine. He took a plane from St Lucia to Odessa International Airport where he then put up in a nearby hotel and waited for events to unfold.

Vince had arranged to meet with Jules Axminster who was due to make contact with him once he himself had arrived in the Ukraine. So Vince had some time to kill before his associate telephoned him.

Being a dedicated fitness-freak, Vince thus spent much of his waiting time jogging several kilometres in the early morning and long-distance swimming in the Black Sea during the day. He also spent some time familiarising himself with the layout of the city and learning how to find his way about expertly. After this exploration, Vince could probably have got a job as a tour-guide. Vince, however, did not have to wait very long for his compatriot to ring and to announce his arrival. Jules' sullen voice was heard loud and clear on Vince's mobile phone.

Vince and Jules made a very complementary team. They were the perfect double act. Jules could masquerade as a down-and-out which was not, in fact, far from the truth while Vince disguised himself as a brash American tourist. Vince was thus ready to talk jovially to anyone who came within his orbit and his disguise was complete with panama hat, sunglasses, binoculars and camera.

They stayed in separate hotels in order to make it appear that they did not know each other. But, of course, they could keep in regular contact by phone. They then discussed their future plans and they agreed on their next move. And thus their scheme evolved.

The drill was largely that Jules would go about on the town and he would explore all the back alleys and dodgy places. He would also visit a few bars and clubs and ask a few pertinent questions of likely suspects. Jules would accordingly make contact with a dealer while Vince followed on request in order to take photographs of the culprit. Often the blokes whom Jules encountered directly were obviously those who as children had taken delight in blowing up frogs with a bicycle pump or playing football with the dog's testicles.

The twosome would then follow the appointed dealer in order to ascertain where the goods were stashed and where the stuff might then be transported to on the next stage of its journey.

In the course of this investigation, Jules and Vince discovered that the drugs were transported in a series of farm trucks, tractors and four-wheel drive vehicles mostly belonging to the local farmers or simply hired for the purpose. The transport route was decidedly circuitous and often Vince had to hone his sprinting skills in order to keep up or else to hitch a ride on the vehicle itself. Jules also followed at a safe distance and often took a different route from his associate after consultation by phone.

Once the goods were stored in situ awaiting either local distribution or for the next stage of the journey, Vince and Jules would approach the storage venue late at night or in the early morning in order to acquire ample video and photographic evidence. For this mission, of course, Vince ditched his brash America attire and donned a burglar's black garb together with a face-concealing balaclava.

The duo, by this means, managed to compile an impressive dossier of the names of the principal contacts, places where the gear was distributed, locations of the storage facilities and evidence of the means of transportation.

Both agreed that they had certainly had an adventure in the Ukraine and that they had definitely earned the handsome reward which they both anticipation from the Medici Squadron in due season.

Following the same trail, the two snoopers then moved on to Poland and Germany and to various other locations in western Europe where a similar pattern of operation was in evidence. By now the two had become adept at following their quarry and maintaining their disguises effortlessly and effectively and, in so doing, unravelling the mystery and amassing some damning evidence.

Finally Vince and Jules neared the end of their trail when the goods were transported across the English Channel to the UK. The stuff was taken in a small fishing boat from France late at night over to Dover in Kent. At this point Vince swam the Channel while Jules, the less energetic of the two, opted for the comfort of a bucket-shop flight to East London Airport. This separation of travel plans also served a useful purpose in that it would deflect suspicion away from any prying eyes who might think that Vince and Jules knew each other and thus were in cahoots somehow.

Once in the UK, the cargo made its way again by a series of farm trucks and tractors to the outskirts of London and, from here, the stuff was transported by a convoy of vans owned by a security company and a removals firm both of whom had no idea what they were transporting. Poor sods!

GRETA'S DISCOVERY

One evening after the show, Janice was tidying up the communal dressing rooms as part of her work as assistant stage manager for Vendetta.

In the costume store, Janice hung up some of the costumes, most of which had been left on chairs or simply dropped on the floor. Bo-Peep's costume, for instance, had fallen into this latter category. Janice also piled some costumes on top of the ironing board in readiness for the wardrobe mistresses who would religiously press these crumpled garments prior to the next performance.

Janice then made her way into the make-up room where each of the performers were adorned every evening by the make-up artists so that they would not look pale under the high-voltage stage lighting. While busying herself in the make-up room with her tidying-up routine, Janice heard some hushed voices in a room across the way and the echo of what sounded like someone in distress. She, therefore, stopped her work and listened more intently.

Janice could make out the sound of Greta's voice but she did not recognise the voice of her companion. Janice, therefore, went to investigate.

The dressing room from which the voices were coming was that of Rouchuka's and so Janice hesitated before entering in case the star of the show was too distressed and she would be embarrassed to see her. Janice hence tapped lightly on the door and gently opened it only a fraction. Here Janice found Wanda in floods of tears with the gentle Greta at her feet attempting to comfort the weeping girl.

"Come in, please," said Greta who rose in order to usher Janice into the room and then to close the door immediately afterwards so as not to invite any other curious visitors into the room.

"I'll lock the door," stated Janice who promptly threw the bolt across in order to prevent any further interruptions.

Janice too sat at Wanda's feet and held her hand in an effort to comfort Wanda in her agony. But Wanda continued to snivel uncontrollably.

"What's wrong?" asked Greta who so far had not managed to obtain any information from Wanda.

Greta and Janice speculated silently together as if they were mendicants at the feet of the anguished one. A series of questions were then variously, albeit gently, posed in order to elicit information about Wanda's obvious misery.

"Has something happened to you?"

"Have you had a row with someone?"

"Has one of the brat-pack been pestering you?"

"Has Gerry made life difficult?"

"Has Rocker been a pain?"

And the questioning continued in this vein but with no obvious result. Wanda shook her head as each of these enquiries came to her ears. Wanda had tried to speak but her weeping and gasping had largely prevented any strenuous action like speech.

"Is there some trouble with Bluey?" asked Greta.

Wanda nodded her head as her tears became louder and they flowed more abundantly.

Greta and Janice looked surreptitiously at each other as if conducting an unspoken conversation about what to do next. Greta then stroked Wanda's shoulder gently.

"It often helps to talk about it. Can you tell us what's troubling you?"

Wanda spluttered and sniffed.

Greta and Janice waited patiently and lovingly for Wanda to begin telling her tale. Greta even pulled up a chair and sat beside Wanda with her arms around her distraught friend.

At last Wanda had recovered enough to shed her burden.

"It's about Bluey. He's worried about Gerry and the brat-pack because he thinks they are into drugs."

Well that much was obvious with regard to the brat-pack but neither Greta nor Janice were aware that Gerry had ever indulged. But they certainly did not give voice to their thoughts aloud.

"Even Gerry?" prompted Janice.

"I don't think so," added Greta.

Wanda continued her narrative.

"No, I mean they are dealing in drugs," she wailed.

"Bloody hell!" said Greta and Janice virtually in unison.

The story then proceeded to tumble from Wanda lips in a torrent but, as it poured out, the relief for Wanda was palpable and paramount. Moses had parted the waves of the Red Sea and the Israelites were able to pass across to safety while the Egyptians were all drowned. God was obviously prejudiced and cruel.

Wanda spoke of what Bluey had overheard recently of the activities and the clandestine meetings of Gerry, Max and Myra. She related Bluey's conversation with Hal. And she mentioned her own discussions with her brother who was in a complete quandary about what to do next.

Janice, of course, had known about Hal's conversation with Bluey but she kept this secret to herself.

"Is Bluey quite sure of his facts?" Janice enquired.

"Absolutely," came the stark reply with conclusiveness in its intonation. No one attempted to argue.

Greta was astounded, of course, because this was the first that she had heard of any unsavoury activity. And the news shook her to the core.

The debate now was concerned with what could be done about the situation. And, for this reason, both Greta and Janice understood implicitly about Wanda's distress. Greta and Janice, after all, could simply get another job if the balloon went up but Wanda was in a very different predicament. Her fortunes were tied up with her brother. And her brother's fortunes were tied up with his fellow band-members. Sticky, eh?

The next obvious question, therefore, was "What will Bluey do, do you think?" and it was posed by Janice while Greta acknowledged the relevance of the question with a firm nod of her head.

"He's not sure what to do."

What a dilemma this was thought Greta and Janice silently to themselves.

The meeting continued with comforting words from Wanda's friends, some platitudes about not worrying about the future and a general agreement to discuss the matter further. But nothing was, as yet, resolved. It was a watch-this-space situation which left much food for thought.

Janice resolved that she would discuss the matter with Hal as soon as an opportunity presented itself. Greta had other ideas but she needed time and space in order to mull over her thoughts.

On a practical note, Greta went to get Wanda some tea and cake while Janice continued to hold Wanda's hand and deliver what cold comfort she could.

The future was, therefore, anybody's guess but a lot of contemplation would need to take place before long and some decisions would need to be put on the agenda for the near future.

ROUCHUKA'S DETERMINATION

The offices of Valentine, Dramber and Dramber were situated in York where Rouchuka had once lived for a while. She had been unable to visit these offices in person because of her current work commitment but this firm of solicitors were amenable to her having a Skype discussion because Harriet Chantry, known to the world as Rouchuka, was their most prestigious client.

Rouchuka's appointment with Kenneth Valentine was fittingly set for one morning towards the end of Vendetta's tour of the south. Rouchuka sat in her hotel room safe in the knowledge that no one could overhear her from this vantage point. Greta also kept watch in the corridor in order to ensure that Rouchuka would not be disturbed.

The meeting discussed the fact that Rouchuka wanted to extricate herself from her contract with Vendetta Ice before the start of the forthcoming US tour later in the year. Kenneth was doubtful about the outcome of this course of action and so he expressed his doubts in grave terms and with a wrinkled brow.

"I do realise, of course, that I will have to pay the punishing penalty-clause fee because I would be ducking out of the US tour scheduled for November."

Kenneth then confirmed that Rouchuka had, indeed, signed her contract to this effect.

"Well, as long as you realise that there would be a high financial penalty, it should not be too difficult."

"Could you let me know what the cost would be roughly?" asked Rouchuka who felt that the meeting was going well.

"I can tell you precisely if you can wait a moment, Harriet."

Rouchuka agreed to comply with this request as a short wait now would save time in the long run. Kenneth did not normally answer his client's enquiries so promptly but with the famous Rouchuka he made an exception to his normal practice rule.

And so Rouchuka waited while Kenneth searched through her contract with Vendetta Ice and Colossus Enterprises plc in order to calculate the sum which she would have to pay for departing from the band. In anticipation of such an eventuality, Kenneth had actually retrieved the contract from storage prior to the meeting.

Kenneth mumbled to himself while making his calculations on an expensive scientific calculator. He also checked and doubled checked the figures and at last he verified the fact that Rouchuka would have to pay several million pounds to Colossus Enterprises plc. When announcing the sum in question, Kenneth was careful to caution his client about the inadvisability of any rash decision on her part. But Rouchuka was adamant in her resolve.

When she heard the sum in question, Rouchuka shrugged, although she was prepared for this eventuality. She knew that she would have to pay for her exit-visa but she felt it would be worth it. She had decided some while ago to sell some property, or even one of her restaurants, and so this sale would cover the cost easily even if she did not have enough petty cash for the purpose. Even after paying the crippling penalty clause sum, she would still be able to live in a manner to which she had not been accustomed at the start of her career.

Once Rouchuka had learned from Greta that Gerry, Max and Myra were up to no good, this information had finally determined her once and for all to leave the band for good as quickly as possible at whatever the cost.

The two parties also discussed the implications of Rouchuka's departure from Vendetta but Rouchuka assured Kenneth that her reputation would not suffer as a result of her defection. She informed Kenneth that pop bands split up on many occasions and that it was par for the course generally.

The question of a sworn affidavit which Rouchuka would sign as her means of distancing herself from the drug-dealing enterprise was also discussed and Kenneth agreed to draft this document. When Kenneth heard this information about the illicit drug-trading, he was reassured that Rouchuka's exit was indeed a wise move. But, as it was only a rumour, he could not really advise her to go to the police.

Kenneth then agreed to prepare the papers which would extricate Rouchuka from her contract and he told her that he would arrange for all the documentation to be despatched to her hotel in Newquay for signature.

Rouchuka thanked Kenneth for his time and the Skype meeting came to a close after some inconsequential and friendly discussion.

Rouchuka stated her intention to have a holiday before seeking any further work but she also maintained that the pop music industry was really not going to be a part of her world in the future. Kenneth then wished her luck in whatever she decided to do in the future. And he also secretly relished the prospect of eventually sending her a substantial invoice for his services.

After the meeting Rouchuka called Greta back into her room. Greta reassured Rouchuka that no one had been anywhere near her hotel room and so her legal business would not have been overheard.

Rouchuka had previously briefed Greta about her intentions and she had also invited Greta to continue working for her both as her companion in France and as her assistant when she resumed work. Greta, of course, was sworn to secrecy about Rouchuka's departure because she, Greta, was one of the few people whom Rouchuka could trust.

When Rouchuka had been working with the orchestra during the *Captive Audience* video recording session, she had acquired from one or two of the orchestral players the names of several agents who could assist her in transferring into musical theatre.

Rouchuka, to this end, had sounded out a couple of prospective agents and she had then selected one with whom she felt she could work and for whom she had more respect than she had ever had for the conniving Gerry. Her experience of working in the professional world with Vendetta had rendered Rouchuka very astute when it came to dealing with theatrical agents.

Because Rouchuka was so well known for her work and her talent, the agents whom she had contacted were all ready and more than willing to jump at the chance of acting for her. Rouchuka was hence earnestly assured that there would be no difficulty in obtaining an engagement in the musical theatre arena.

Rouchuka then looked forward to an extended holiday before even contemplating relaunching her career and repackaging herself as a star. This holiday would, of course, result in another meeting with the delectable Roussel and this temptation seemed to be the prize which Rouchuka sought most of all.

The rest of Vendetta's performance nights in Newquay then took on a fresh sparkle for Rouchuka because she knew that there were brighter prospects ahead and that she could count the days before the tour concluded.

Greta was delighted that her mistress would shortly be withdrawing from the crazy world of pop music and even more delighted that Rouchuka's future career would take a more exciting turn and it would include her. Greta had come to regard Rouchuka as a sort-of mother-figure from whom she did not wish to be parted for any length of time and for whom she was content to work in virtually any capacity.

Greta, consequently, also drafted her notice to quit from the employ of Colossus Enterprises plc and she planned to hand her letter in to Henry at the end of the tour.

GERRY'S AGGRANDISEMENT

Gerry was waiting in his London flat for an auspicious occasion which he felt would make his fortune.

He was also excited at the prospect of meeting Isabel Franklin again. He remembered her invitingly sparkling grey eyes and her luscious brown hair as well as other tantalising features which stimulated his desire. Gerry, of course, bravely fought his inclinations in the interests of his own sanity but it was essentially a losing battle. Cupid was a canny and determined fellow.

Eventually the buzzer to his flat sounded and Gerry got up rapidly in order to answer it with a high degree of expectation.

When the door was opened, Isabel gave him her winning smile again. Gerry was delighted. But, on the other hand, he was chagrined to realise that she was not alone. Her bloody photographer had accompanied her. Fuck!

"Oh," cried Gerry, "I didn't realise that you would be bringing anyone."

Again Isabel smiled because she knew what was going on in Gerry's mind. It was obvious.

"Well, we are like the police, you know. We never travel alone. Always in pairs. Company policy these days," she lied.

Gerry had no option but to invite her into the flat along with her bloody photographer.

"You'll be all right with Brian taking a few photographs, won't you?"

Isabel's surface-level question was more of a truism which she affirmed rather than a genuine enquiry. She had cunningly circumvented any objections which Vendetta's business manager might raise as she walked determinedly into the flat. Brian did likewise. Gerry found that, at this stage, he could not object.

Brian, blast his eyes with hell fire, now proceeded to take a couple of quick shots.

"Very nice place you have here, Gerry," interposed his visitor.

She had obviously discarded her resolve of addressing him formally but he let the familiarity pass. There might be other more important battles on the horizon which he would need to fight.

Gerry invited Isabel to take a seat on the sofa while he grabbed a comfortable armchair some distance away from her. She then proceeded to set up her recording equipment without asking him. But again Gerry did not feel like objecting in the circumstances.

The interview began by Isabel asking Gerry about his past career and what had led him to the role of business manager of a pop group.

Gerry then briefly related his career to date. Gerry spoke of his introduction to the field of theatricals by being a runner for a travelling company and then moving on to become an assistant in an agency which specialised in discovering latent unrecognised talent. Isabel seemed impressed, Gerry thought, and this gave him the incentive to embellish his narrative somewhat. Poor sod!

Isabel then asked about his early life and his schooldays but this was a time in Gerry's life when he did not have much to relate which would be of any interest. He had not given a particularly good account of himself when at school. Isabel thus smiled enigmatically because she could detect Gerry's reluctance to admit much about his upbringing and his unremarkable schooldays. And so she tactfully passed on to another subject.

Brian, all this time, was taking the odd snapshot here and there and moving freely about the flat much to Gerry's dismay. Then bloody Brian had the audacity to ask if he could use the bathroom and Gerry was forced to consent.

Next the ostensibly casual conversation with Isabel turned to the fact that Gerry had branched out into his own business and so had eventually ending up as Vendetta's Ice's business manager. Isabel still seemed to be impressed, Gerry felt. Isabel, Gerry noted with pleasure, seemed actually to be in awe of his achievements and his effortless climb to precipitous heights in his chosen profession. And, of course, he felt that her praise was highly justified.

Isabel also asked Gerry about his inner feelings on the matter of his achievements which was a question which he found difficult to answer. Emotions and feelings were not matters which one shared with others, Gerry felt. Did she not know this? But, she's a journalist! So what do you expect, ducky?

After a short while, Brian emerged from the bathroom looking pleased with himself.

Isabel, however, carried on regardless of this interruption. What did Gerry feel about Vendetta's future? How could he be instrumental in driving the bus forward? What did he think of Vendetta's meteoric rise to stardom? Was Gerry pleased with Vendetta's fame and fortune? What did Gerry's colleagues feel about his success? Were Gerry's family proud of his enormous achievements? And so it went on.

The hour which had been allotted to Isabel in Gerry's diary was soon used up, although Gerry had not even noticed the time.

Eventually Isabel invited Gerry out to lunch once her interview was drawing to a close. Gerry, of course, wanted to dine with her alone without the annoying bloody Brian in the company.

"I have to be getting along now," remarked the obliging Brian and Gerry jumped at the chance of now getting Isabel alone despite her gimlet-type stares and her nosey questions.

But Gerry still believed that the publicity which he would gain from this experience might well secure his long-term future. Gerry was good at reasoning with himself but his rationality was not always as judicious as his business decisions.

And so bloody Brian left thankfully and Isabel and Gerry walked to a nearby restaurant for lunch.

Lunch, on Isabel's expense account at her insistence, consisted of more champagne cocktails and a lavish meal of caviar, smoked salmon, potted lobster and gravlax together with asparagus and artichokes. Such posh nosh, however, had not been served in Gerry's childhood home but his palate had by now become fully acclimatised to upmarket living.

Isabel, who had herself sampled the high gastronomic lifestyle in her early days, was, however, not at all deceived by Gerry's nonchalance but she considerately feigned ignorance of Gerry's dilemma for her own reasons.

Over lunch, the pair discussed more stuff about Gerry but Isabel seemed artfully to resist any attempt on his part to enquire more into her background. She asked, for example, about each member of Vendetta Ice and she was particularly interested in the individual personalities involved.

Gerry was, at this stage, quite guarded in his responses to Isabel's supplementary enquiries but his companion somehow had an insidious way of phrasing her questions so that Gerry revealed much more than he had originally intended. Bugger! Gerry consoled himself, however, with the knowledge that Isabel was not now recording their conversation and so he began to relax. How naive can anyone get?

When the lunch came to its natural conclusion, Gerry asked to see Isabel again on an informal basis and she consented willingly. But, at present, pressure of work would prevent her from putting any dates in her diary, she stated.

Gerry then said that he would ring Isabel in due course once the northern tour was over. Gerry, therefore, looked forward to seeing this delightful lady again and then being able to entertain her on his own account. Gerry also expectantly looked ahead to the sky-rocketing promotion of his career when Isabel's articles actually appeared in print.

Isabel said that she could not, at this stage, reveal which magazine publishers would be taking up her article but she assured Gerry that their interview would be widely publicised in all the best periodicals and that Gerry could only benefit from this meeting.

Gerry was, therefore, well pleased with the fact that he had survived the ordeal, that his career would burgeon as a result and that he had also met a beautiful woman with whom he could spend more of his leisure time.

ROUSSEL'S ENCHANTMENT

One day when Rouchuka had one of her quiet moments in the day during Vendetta's southern tour and when all around her were sleeping off the effects of the previous night's indulgence, her mobile phone rang.

Funny, she thought, I'm not expecting a call. Who can this be?

Rouchuka was not prone to getting calls while on tour mainly because those who were likely to ring her would be unlikely to want to disturb the busy star.

"Good morning," said the unmistakeable tone of Roussel's voice.

Rouchuka's heart skipped a beat.

"How nice to hear from you."

Her heart had initially skipped a beat because it was Roussel whom she heard but she then began to worry that something might be wrong at the chateau or in the vineyard. But her fears were soon allayed when he reported admirable progress on the restoration work and continued success of the viniculture. Rouchuka was much relieved because problems at this stage of the tour would only be an unwelcomed and worrying intrusion.

Roussel's next consignment of news was, however, unexpected and rather disturbing.

"May I come to see you in your show?" he enquired.

"My show?"

Now Rouchuka was really worried. How does he know that I am in a show? Does he know what type of music I perform? Would he find pop music nauseating? Would I be embarrassed? Would I lose him forever? Oh, Christ! Rouchuka stammered, flustered and blustered. What can I say? How can I make an excuse? Who had let the cat out of the bag? I wanted to keep this from him!

The lack of response from Rouchuka prompted the dashing Roussel to confess that he knew of her work and that he was not at all worried that she was a pop star because he had a broad taste in music. Roussel, moreover, stated that he had a few days off work and that he wanted to talk to her more about the vineyard. So Rouchuka somewhat reluctantly agreed to obtain a VIP ticket for her guest.

Roussel thus flew across to the UK in order to join Rouchuka in Newquay for the extravaganza. And a nervous Rouchuka upped her game during that night's performance when she knew that she had a special guest in the audience.

Roussel was effusively complimentary about Rouchuka's performance when he visited her dressing room after the show and when they had a late-night meal together in a private room at her hotel.

"You were marvellous. I was so impressed with your energy, your delivery and your effect on the audience. They all loved you, as I did."

Roussel continued in this effusive vein for several minutes while Rouchuka simply stammered and blushed. Roussel explained that he loved pop music and jazz just as much as Debussy and his friends but Rouchuka was not sure whether to believe him. Was he sincere or was this just his French blarney?

The meal was leisurely and Rouchuka's heart fluttered throughout in Roussel's presence. But soon she began to worry as make-your-mind-up time drew closer. Where will he be staying? Does he have accommodation already booked here or elsewhere? Will he expect to stay here with me? Oh, God!

Roussel had obviously taken lessons in telepathy because he read her thoughts. Roussel gently touched her hand and kept hold of it. Rouchuka's knell was wrung now without a doubt.

A night of tender and heavenly bliss ensued. The Frenchman was an attentive lover and Rouchuka was prepared to believe all the rumours which she had ever heard about the chivalry of this breed. He caressed her thick hair and gazed into her blue eyes with admiration and sincere affection.

"I can see that you like your work," began Roussel while consuming their room-service breakfast still in bed the next morning.

"I do but actually I'm thinking about a change of genre."

It then all came pouring out. Rouchuka confessed to her desire to enter the world of musical theatre, to leave Vendetta and to spend more time in France. She spoke at length about her career and the way in which it had evolved without much effort on her part but with little in the way of sober career decisions. She spoke of the difficult personalities within Vendetta and the tediousness of the brat-pack.

As she knew that Roussel would not betray her confidence, Rouchuka also voiced her suspicions about the extra-mural activities of some of the band. Eventually she told Roussel about Gerry, Myra and Max but the fact that she had nothing in the way of proof was a stumbling block. Her suspicions were, as yet, only based on rumour but it left her little alternative but to get out of the game damn quick. She knew that she would go down with the ship if the drug-dealing activity were ever discovered and so jumping ship was probably her only option before it was too late.

Rouchuka also explained about the legal steps which she had taken in order to extricate herself from her contract with Vendetta and to set up a damage-limitation solution in the form of a sworn affidavit.

Roussel listened attentively to Rouchuka's narrative while, simultaneously, stroking her hair, kissing her intermittently and gazing into her eyes. These attentions emboldened Rouchuka and encouraged her to take full confessional advantage of her enthralled confidant.

Roussel then praised and endorsed Rouchuka's wisdom and lent his support in such a way that she felt reassured and convinced that she was taking the correct course of action for the future. Rouchuka had now finally made up her mind and nothing would deter her.

Eventually the couple got up, after yet another round of obviously expressing their love, spent a leisurely time in the jacuzzi-style bath but they then had to go their separate ways.

Rouchuka promised to visit the chateau as soon as the tour had ended and both parties looked forward to this reunion.

Rouchuka then had to prepare for the evening's performance while Roussel made his way to the airport in readiness for the return journey.

Rouchuka now had more confidence and optimism about her future while Roussel looked as if he were the cat who had lived his entire life on cream.

NICHOLAS' ACCOMPLISHMENT

Madeleine continued to play hard to get with Nicholas about a dinner date every time he rang her at work or at home.

One day she did, however, agree to a lunchtime walk in the park where they could eat their midday sandwiches together in the hope of satisfying him sufficiently with this gesture. Madeleine was not sure where Nicholas worked or even what he actually did for a living but she was not about to ask any questions because she might give him the wrong impression. But she knew for definite that he was not a bloody courier.

The couple then met a few times on a casual basis, still with Madeleine always being evasive and not agreeing to a dinner date. Nicholas, by this time, was beginning to feel exhausted with the effort of trying to court the impenetrable fortress known as Madeleine Pearson and so he had to muster a bit more enthusiasm.

"I'll go on pestering you until you say yes to that dinner date, you know."

Madeleine decided that she needed to play it straight rather than all this pussy-footing around.

"Really, I am not interested. I have told you this already. Many times," she stated quite categorically.

The night at the Newbridge Theatre and a few lunchtime meetings had somewhat belied her words and had weakened her argument.

Nicholas, however, much to her amazement, changed tack.

"Well, I'll tell you what. You have my number. So why don't you give me a call if you change your mind but, if I don't hear from you further, then I will know that you are definitely not interested."

"Oh, all right then, yes."

Madeleine tried not to sound too disconcerted but Nicholas did just manage to detect a weeny fraction of disappointment in her reply. The conversation then concluded.

Madeleine now realised that without an admirer in her life, however annoying he was, she actually felt stranded. I meant to merely play hard to get but I didn't actually mean "no thanks". Oh, dear. She was now regretfully hoisted by her own petard.

She tried to concentrate on her administrative tasks during the day but this did not seem to distract Madeleine sufficiently from her unexpected disappointment. And her disenchantment seemed to be increasing by the second. What a dilemma!

But Madeleine soldiered on. She had work to do. She wanted to keep abreast of the filing and to update the personnel database. She needed to draft a list of those applicants who had applied for grants from the Benefice

Charity Trust this month. She was required to undertake some of the record-keeping for the stationery supplies. And, generally, Madeleine wanted to be efficient and organised. But her mind kept wandering in uncalled for directions. Never mind, she told herself, keep working hard because it will take your mind off him. Madeleine was still restless, of course, because she was preoccupied with thoughts of Nicholas Benson.

In the evening Madeleine watched a film on the box but this activity simply reminded her of their visit to the theatre recently. The next evening Madeleine chose to wash her hair and to set it with curling tongs but this routine only made her feel that she ought to go out on a date in order to show off her new hairstyle. The evening after Madeleine went to her keep-fit class in order to keep trim but, once it had concluded, she began to wonder who would be around to notice her slender and toned-up figure.

Madeleine, in short, felt dejected and at a loose end. Life had passed her by and, then when fate did brush her gently, she managed to fend off the foe. What a fool I've been. And it would only have been a bit of fun, surely?

Madeleine went gradually downhill and she was heading for rock bottom and the doldrums of all time. Just before she started taking the anti-depressants, however, which her doctor had prescribed for her recently, the phone rang. It was him again! But, this time, Madeleine responded very differently and the anti-depressants were flushed down the loo.

They finally had that dinner the next evening and this event was the start of more interesting things generally. Nicholas took Madeleine to his much publicized stylish restaurant which was certainly a couple of notches up from the Orchard Garden restaurant where they had met in such auspicious circumstances.

She dined on eggs florentine and a roast mutton cassoulet with green beans and sauté potatoes garnished with sprigs of rosemary while Nicholas partook of a black olive tapenade on rye bread followed by beef stroganoff with spinach tagliatelle. They also consumed a couple of bottles of riesling between them. So a good time was had by all.

A similar process was repeated on a number of other occasions over the next week and a trip to the cinema also came into their orbit. They went on romantic walks in the countryside at the weekend and also took a picnic prepared loving by Madeleine for their lunchtime treat.

This was getting to be a bit of habit. But another issue was beginning to loom on the horizon of Madeleine's mind and she was really unsure about this decision. Eventually Nicholas took the initiative by casually putting his arm around her while she was attempting to pack up the picnic things and he then nestled his head into her neck. God, help me, thought Madeleine, although God wasn't that interested in listening. After a night of bliss Madeleine was never the same again.

A spring holiday was also planned and Madeleine was dare-devil enough to take a week off work and to career off to Lanzarote for a rest-cure. They enjoyed the beaches and the sunbathing, the nightlife, the conviviality and the fairly sleepless nights in the suite of their hotel.

It was at this point in her life that Madeleine began to open the casket of her thoughts about Reggie. Nicholas proved to be a very attentive listener as well as a shoulder on which to cry. Madeleine had hitherto had no one to whom she could turn and so Nicholas opportunistically filled that gap. How convenient?

Madeleine felt so relieved and really rested once she had returned to the office after her enjoyable holiday, having off-loaded a heap of her troubles on to her lover.

Nicholas, of course, advised her to leave her job but Madeleine was still uncertain that this would be the right course of action for her. I'll think about that tomorrow, she reasoned.

ROUCHUKA'S PROCLAMATION

The southern tour eventually came to a grinding halt after a long and exhausting run. Vendetta's brat-pack, especially, were then eager to start the end-of-the-run proceedings while the rest were just looking forward to having something to eat before their night's rest.

Gerry and Henry, of course, had made the usual arrangements for the shenanigans of the concluding party. The strobe lights, the balloons and the streamers had all been lined up. And, as usual, the sex-objects had been marshalled for the occasion. All the now-expected froth of stardom, in fact. No surprises there!

The behaviour of the brat-pack could also have been predicted by the keen observer.

Rocker surveyed the local talent which the bodyguards had assembled in serried ranks for him in order to service his body and its masculine needs. And he earmarked those whom he wished to reserve for later entertainment. Myra looked around as always in order to deliberate on what might take his fancy in the way of masculine company. Max, who had now completely forgotten about Cynthia from up north, was similarly on the lookout for sex-fodder.

Drugs, moreover, were one of the key invitees to the party now that the brat-pack did not need to be warned by Gerry about abstaining in the interests of performing requirements.

Bluey and Wanda, together with Kicker and Jenny, sauntered into the ballroom reserved in the Sea Front Grand Hotel in Newquay for the banquet. Their intention was merely to replenish their supplies of food before retiring for the night but they were not really taking a full and active part in the evening's fun and games.

The usual feast was, of course, prepared for the invited guests but, this time, the chef had given the extravaganza a seafood theme because of the hotel's proximity to the sea front.

The main banqueting table was hence strewn with gourmet dishes of lobster, salmon, moules marinière, langoustine, scallops, dressed crab and oysters. Stilton, camembert and brie also accompanied these dishes in the hope of catering for those with fish allergies. Fresh salads and spring vegetables for those who had a healthy disposition also graced the tables.

An opulent choice of desserts from ice cream gateaux to fresh fruit dowsed in alcohol with meringues appeared for those who were not that weight conscious.

Obviously the full quota of bubbly and fine wine naturally put in an appearance at the party as well.

The waitresses were clad in red dresses and short skirts on this occasion and they created quite a stir in the assembled company. Max was particularly interested in these creatures and they seemed to remind him of the last party but he was not sure why.

Rouchuka was one the last to arrive with Greta. The two discreetly took a place at one end of the long dining table near to where Bluey and Kicker and their associates were sitting.

Greta, as usual, volunteered to fetch Rouchuka's meal for which she, Rouchuka, was extremely grateful. Rouchuka, however, did not look that tired following her high-energy performance which had only ceased a short while before. Rouchuka had, of course, had her usual snooze in her dressing room after the show but now she seemed almost alive here as if she were still on the stage.

Gerry kept a watchful eye on the troops in the hope of averting any disaster and by way of ensuring that the brat-pack did not over-indulge this evening and thence ruin tomorrow afternoon's press conference as his special pride-and-joy event. Gerry felt, for once, however, that the team were relatively well behaved and so he had lulled himself into a false sense of security.

While all were quietly munching away, Rouchuka's chair was pushed back and she abruptly stood up. At this point, Greta then handed her a large brown envelope which she had been concealing under the table.

"I have something to tell you all," she announced in a loud and commanding voice.

She could easily make herself heard above the murmurings and the constant chatter. Some people looked up in order to hear what she had to say while others just looked irritated at the disturbance to their digestion.

Rouchuka stepped forward and handed Gerry the brown envelope which Greta had been guarding and, at the same time, she announced to all present her future plans.

"In this envelope which I have just handed to Gerry, he will find my resignation from Vendetta Ice."

The idle chatter instantly died away and there was a stunned silence in the room which had never occurred before in the history of Vendetta. The bodyguards immediately ushered the non-essential sycophants out of the room.

Gerry nearly choked himself on a mouthful of lobster and camembert. Gerry also screamed at her but she appeared to be unmoved by his exhibition. He certainly had shown more emotion in this moment than he had ever done in the whole of his life. Isabel Franklin would have been amazed.

Rocker laughed heartily thinking that Rouchuka was joking even though he did not understand her humour.

Bluey and Kicker felt only admiration and perhaps a little envy for their colleague.

"You can't do this," exclaimed Max – eventually being the one to break the stunned silence.

"That envelope contains my legal papers together with a cheque for my fee for terminating my contract."

Gerry then came to life and strode across the room as if he were about to hit Rouchuka but he was persuasively restrained by Hal and Henry who had jumped to their feet. The bodyguard team also went on red alert in case things got nasty and Gerry needed a firm restraining hand and a disarming presence.

John tried to reason with Gerry but Vendetta's business manager looked as if he were on the point of having a heart attack at the news. Instead he collapsed in tears and sank to the floor.

Rocker rushed over to Rouchuka, leaving Gerry to the others, and pleaded with her on his knees to rescind her intention. He had never acted this way before with any woman let alone the hitherto ineffectual Rouchuka.

But she was adamant, having given the matter abundant thought, and so she would not budge under any pressure, bribes, threats or other inducements. She claimed that she wished to pursue a different line of business and that nothing would deflect her from this course of action.

Rocker had always had a keen interest in keeping the band afloat but his efforts were useless. He too wanted to punch her lights out but he was, in fact, too shocked to bestir himself any further. He simply sulked.

John for once saved the day by publicly congratulating Rouchuka on her decision and he was joined almost immediately by a chorus from Bluey, Wanda, Kicker and Jenny who were delighted at this news. Greta, of course, already knew of Rouchuka's intention this evening. Janice and Henry also added their good wishes.

Gerry had to be taken up to his room and a doctor was summoned, even at this late hour, in order to attend him. The doctor merely gave him a soporific for the night which Gerry consumed greedily together with an overdose of his own sleeping pills and a bottle of whisky. He realised that there was nothing which he could do about the break-up of the band now because Rouchuka's lawyer had firmly tied up the parcel. Gerry did, however, consider suing the recalcitrant ex-member of Vendetta and he decided to seek legal advice as soon as he had sufficient energy.

Soon afterwards Rouchuka and Greta left the party which had now more or less fizzled out, although John and Henry were left in charge of shepherding out any stragglers. The apostles who had been banished from the room by the bodyguards were, of course, bribed in the futile hope of silencing them at least for the time being.

The hotel staff were naturally unhappy about having to discard so much fine food uneaten, although some of it found its way into their own fridge-freezers as a bonus.

Jenny and Kicker discussed the night's events and this gave Kicker an incentive to follow in Rouchuka's footsteps. His papers had already been prepared by his solicitor and so he simply had to throw the signed documentation into the pudding in order to leave the band behind.

Bluey and Wanda similarly spent most of the rest of the night in discussion about how relieved they both were that the band would now finally fold or, at least, that they had an open door through which to escape at last.

Once she had returned to her room, Rouchuka spoke on the phone to a waiting Roussel who expressed his admiration of her night's achievement and stated that he hoped to see her again very shortly. Rouchuka now had no reason at all not to accede to his request and so she promised to get a flight back to France with Greta as soon as possible.

When Rouchuka's head finally hit the pillow, she slept the deep sleep of the just and she dreamt of an amazing future.

Greta tucked her mistress snuggly up in bed and also looked forward to a future with less in the way of hassle and nuisance from the brat-pack. Her salary was guaranteed by Rouchuka and she, Greta, was so devoted to her mistress that she was prepared to follow her wherever she went and whatever she did in the future.

What a night, thought Greta, in her room which adjoined Rouchuka's. And what a good night's work! Greta too dreamt pleasant dreams and she had the kind of rest which she had not been able to attain for some while now.

She awoke early with a renewed optimism for the flight back to Rouchuka's chateau in southern France.

Rocker spent little time in sleep during the night because his whole world had collapsed before his very eyes in an instant. He didn't even bother to bring a bird to his room that night. Blimey!

Myra and Max sat up for most of the night in order to discuss the implications of Rouchuka actions. But they came to no viable or feasible conclusion. They both slowly got drunk before they fell asleep with all their clothes on in Myra's room. And Myra's Bo-Beep costume was ruined in the process.

The next morning, Gerry was forced to cancel the US tour forthwith and reluctantly to pay the exacting penalty which was required, although, of course, the sum would come out of Rouchuka's severance payment. Gerry also had to halt the building of the new studio in Hertfordshire in order to avoid throwing more money down the drain.

And, naturally, the press conference had to be similarly postponed, perhaps indefinitely. Gerry pleaded the group's communal indisposition on this occasion. But the press were not convinced and they started asking a few questions of the hotel staff and the attendant fans in order to sniff out the rat.

Rouchuka rose with the lark next morning and sang along with the dawn chorus because now she was as free as a bird. And even Greta joined in.

MEDICI'S SUMMATION

They were back in their love-nest in Grove Naxton Cross on Monday morning discussing the latest developments of their blossoming project. The pair were intent on verifying progress and in determining whether all the loose ends could now be tied up securely.

As the late spring weather had improved, they sat on the patio and admired the view of the garden as the second love of Barrington's life.

"Well, what's first on the agenda, madam chairwoman," jested Barrington in order to officially open the meeting of the Medici Squadron.

Calendula was sipping her hibiscus and rosehip tea with a slice of lemon and a spoonful of honey and she was contemplating their latest moves.

Barrington had found himself an iced coffee for the occasion. They were also munching happily on Barrington's homemade brandy snaps filled with orange-flavoured cream.

Before Calendula could answer, the meeting was interrupted by "*It Ain't Necessarily So*" from Barrington's phone.

"It's from Maurice," he exclaimed as he looked at the caller's identity on the display.

"Bonjour Monsieur! Ça va, mon ami?

"Ça va bien, merci!" came the reply.

And then the conversation reverted to English because Barrington had virtually exhausted his supplies of French while Maurice spoke excellent English, having been domiciled in the UK for many years.

Barrington's short time of staying in Paris had not taught him much French. When Barrington had first met Calendula at the start of their relationship, she had become the official French interpreter because Barrington had been content to leave that side of things to his cherished partner.

"I am pretty sure she's clean," announced Maurice proudly.

"We thought so and I'm glad," chimed in Calendula who could overhear the conversation because she was sitting very close to her partner. Almost on his lap, in fact.

A three-way conversation then ensued.

Maurice reported that he had got to know Rouchuka very well – at which point Calendula and Barrington exchanged glances – but that she had resigned from Vendetta because she wanted to pursue a career in musical theatre. And she wanted to distance herself from the drug-trade.

"Greta was the spy in the camp who discovered that Gerry, Myra and Max are the main culprits in the scam. And when she told Rouchuka, that finally decided her to leave at that point."

"And has she tied up the legal side?" asked the cautious Barrington.

"Indeed," returned Maurice, "she consulted a lawyer who drew up some contract-exit documents and also paid the severance money."

"Good," remarked Calendula and Barrington virtually in unison.

"And she has prepared a sworn affidavit which her lawyer can present in court when the naughties are exposed."

"Wonderful! Thank you Maurice," remarked Calendula who was genuinely glad that Rouchuka had broken away from the festering sore and that she intended to start afresh.

"Has Rouchuka got her new career started yet?" Barrington enquired.

"No, she has only contacted a couple of agents but, at the moment, she is in the chateau having a long rest."

"Good! I see," emanated from a thoughtful Calendula while Barrington was aware of his partner's mind at work.

"Do you know when she intends to begin looking for work again?" enquired Barrington.

"No idea."

"Well, we may be able to give her a helping hand when the time is right," asserted Barrington.

"That is good news but I would leave it for a couple of weeks yet, at least. She needs a rest," warned Maurice.

They chatted on about the situation and Maurice confirmed that he had not met any of the other members of Vendetta or its crew apart from the gentle Greta.

They finally discussed Maurice's own exit plan now that his work had concluded and it was decided that Roussel should find a way to disappear from Rouchuka's life. Maurice agreed to this edict with some reluctance but he realised that all good things must eventually come to an end.

"But I will be gentle," he maintained.

Calendula and Barrington wished their colleague God speed and Barrington then set about paying Maurice a nice tidy little sum for this professional services.

"I must find out from Hal the situation with the band now," stated Barrington who was galvanised into action.

He promptly rang Hal, therefore, and proceeded to seek the details of the gossip. Hal reported Rouchuka's momentous resignation at the party at the weekend which marked the end of the southern counties bash and the effect on all those present. Gerry had been escorted to his room and the brat-pack looked like death after the announcement. Rocker was a broken man. Myra and Max looked like a couple of zombies. Bluey and Kicker, conversely, seem to have gained a new lease of life.

The US tour, of course, had been cancelled as well as Gerry's precious press conference. The editing of the *Captive Audience* video, furthermore, had to be halted even though Vendetta might risk having to pay extra in order to get the raw material re-instated in the editing suite if necessary. But that was an unlikely hope. The band was finished and so who could be bothered to throw more good money after bad?

Hal was very succinct in his reporting of the devastation.

"The band will fold, I'm sure. There can be no other option for them without their queen bee," Hal predicted.

"And how are you and Janice doing?" Calendula solicitously requested.

"Well, we will both get the hell out of here obviously. And I will be sure to safeguard Janice in the process," Hal affirmed.

"Good. Thank you."

"But we will assist you as much as we can," assured Barrington before the conversation concluded with the usual promise of a financial reward.

"Things are looking good," proclaimed an optimistic Calendula, "but we must tie up the rest of the drug-scam."

"I will also give a helping hand to those we can now tick off the list," declared Barrington who then proceeded to rattle a few cages and pull a few favours.

"Are the photos ready?" asked the ever thoughtful Calendula whose mind wanted to tie up all the finer details.

"Yes, all done."

"And we've got the recordings from Hal and Jules, yes?"

"Yes, all present and correct."

"And we've got Gerry's laptop stuff, yes?"

Calendula's mind was obviously working overtime on the details.

"And how's Tom doing?" she continued.

"He's still hard at work on Madeleine."

The pun was not lost on Calendula who grinned her comprehension of the joke.

"But we don't need to do anything about our Cynthia, do we, lion cub?"

"No, buttercup, she didn't get that involved and so she's not at risk."

"Good, but could we still pull a few strings for her perhaps?"

"I'll see what I can do?"

The two smiled at their achievements.

"So all I need to do now is to contact Winston and expose the scam."

"And collect the money, of course," added Calendula.

Barrington then proceeded to complete his administrative work. He, therefore, contacted a few agents, assembled his dossier of evidence, collated his papers and made copies of all the evidence. Jules' website hacking of Home Spun also proved useful in this respect. And then finally, of course, Barrington kissed his beloved Calendula.

Not only was Vendetta in for a roasting but the Medici Squadron also had to stitch up the recalcitrant Reggie. Barrington thus rang Tom in order to check on progress and then made an appointment for a meet-up with Andrew Ormerod in the near future.

PART 5
FONDANT ICING

JOHN'S ACCOLADE

John had been the first at the party who had openly congratulated Rouchuka on her decision to quit. John was, therefore, despised by Gerry and the brat-pack but lauded by everyone else.

John was seriously overjoyed that Rouchuka had made the break and that she was now free to pursue a career which would be more in keeping with her talents and her aspirations. He had kissed her at the party as his token of this sentiment and he had publicly wished her the best of luck. And she had reciprocated accordingly with her best wishes for his future success.

John realised, of course, that Rouchuka had been extremely brave in facing the mafia head on and he applauded her courage in doing so. John also secretly smirked at the distress of those who had, in the past, either tried to push Rouchuka around or had despised her for being a semi-recluse and a killjoy. He had, of course, always admired and respected Rouchuka in every way both on and off the stage. But now she could truly come into her own.

Janice and John had conducted a lengthy conference shortly after Rouchuka's announcement in order to plan their own future. Because the US tour had, of necessity, been cancelled, Janice had realised that she would now be out of a job. John had also felt inclined to merely sweep up the immediate debris from the southern tour and then clear out himself.

John was, fortunately for him, contracted for each project and, therefore, with the US tour cancelled, his contract was automatically rescinded with a retainer fee which he could keep because he had, in principle, been let down by his current employer. So once John's duties for the southern tour were completed, he would essentially be a free man. Yippee! But, just to observe protocol, John formally handed his resignation letter to Gerry at the official end of the southern tour with a copy to Mr Moneybags Henry.

Gerry was, unfortunately, in no state to comment on John's desertion. So John simply carried on finishing the latest project and generally hanging around in order to hear any further gossip but he was really doing nothing constructive for the remainder of his time with Vendetta.

The wind-up operation following the latest tour, of course, was a dismal affair. No one relished this work in normal circumstances but, because of the state of affairs within the band, the job was even more tedious. Vendetta, of course, could not stay on at the Sea Front hotel in Newquay because their booking period had expired. John hence rolled up his sleeves, kicked a few arses and threatened the deflated Gerry in order to get the stuff packed up and loaded into the transport vehicles.

Rouchuka and Greta had left early that morning but they had left all their things in order and so there was nothing for John and his team to tidy up in this particular neck of the woods.

Rocker had simply checked out of the hotel saying that he was going off on his own somewhere and that he did not, therefore, need a lift back into London in the minibus which John drove. No one knew of Rocker's whereabouts but they all supposed that he was retreating to his parents swanky home on the south coast. Perhaps he was going to become the recluse now? No chance, sunshine! But, of course, Rocker had left some detritus which John was forced to dispose of, although his stuff was surprisingly well organised for a change.

At last the vans were loaded with all the paraphernalia from the show and the backstage team then set off for the offices of Colossus Enterprises plc in east London. John dearly wanted to travel with the backstage party but, in fact, he found himself driving the minibus with the remnants of Vendetta and a few of the crew as usual. But this was a small price for John to pay while he still remained in the employ of the band.

John, however, realised that this trip back to London did actually have its consolation because the remainder of the brat-pack looked gloomy for a change and thus they said very little. Bluey and Wanda, together with Kicker and Jenny, however, were lively and spirited throughout the journey. John found this contrasting situation all very amusing as a reversal of the usual situation.

Bluey and Kicker both sang all the way home to London as was traditional but the stony-faced Myra and Max remained silent and sulky as well as being devastatingly hung over. Max tried to shut the rest of the team up a couple of times but he failed miserably and eventually he gave up the unequal struggle.

When John had dropped off all concerned at one of the two points in south London from which he had originally collected them, he then bid everyone a sincere farewell. By now all the members of Vendetta had realised that John's spirit would not be around for much longer.

Jenny and Wanda both urged John to keep in touch and their soon-to-be-former stage manager agreed with alacrity. Bluey and Kicker gave him genuine man-hugs which said all that needed to be said as far as John was concerned and he appreciated this gesture.

Myra and Max did thank John for the lift home but otherwise they just trundled off together with a pair of long faces. John thought that the two would probably stay in London in an attempt to assuage their gloom. But he really no longer cared and, in any case, it was not his concern anyway.

Wanda and Bluey then set off for their home in the suburbs while Jenny and Kicker made for their house in Norfolk for the forthcoming holiday.

John had toyed with the idea of driving the minibus back to the east London office so that he could pick up his things and leave the place tidy generally before he officially departed. But, after some deliberation, John decided against the upheaval and inconvenience after such a long stretch on the road.

If Colossus Enterprises wanted John to have his personal effects, such as they were, then someone could contact him at which point he might well tell the caller to dump it all. A few bags of sweets, a penknife and a ballpoint pen he could afford to lose. And the train fare back home would certainly not be worth it. Besides he wanted to be shot of Vendetta Ice for good sooner rather than later.

John thus gave the keys of the minibus to another member of the backstage crew who had travelled back to London with him. John thus decided that his ex-colleague could now drive the bus back to east London for the final stage of its journey.

So John was at last carefree and laughing all the way to the bank. He could get temporary work almost anywhere which would tide him over until he managed to get a proper job. He also, of course, had the income from his rented property or, if all else failed, he could live with his parents for a while until he got on his feet again.

John then made his way home to his one-bedroom rented flat in Purley near Croydon in south London.

The immediate first step was for John to make a few noises about his impending unemployment position. John subsequently rang a few theatrical agencies the next morning, spoke to a few friends in the industry and pulled a few strings. He now had an impressive career resumé and so he believed that work would soon be forthcoming.

John's outstretched feelers eventually came up trumps for him in that a local theatre contacted him in order to ask if he would be willing to do some temporary contract work as an assistant stage manager. John jumped at the chance, even though it meant taking a cut in salary. He looked forward to working in this theatre as his means of washing Vendetta Ice out of his soul. Because the theatre was local, furthermore, travelling costs were minimal in that John could walk to work each evening which helped him to manage on his reduced salary.

John also felt that a less pressurised job right now was exactly what he needed because it would be relatively hassle-free. And probably, with travelling repertory companies who speedily came and went, he would not really have time to become untangled with difficult personalities and be obliged to cope with nightly temper tantrums.

From this vantage point, John could now search for the job of his dreams as stage manager in a London theatre. Things seemed to be working out well for our John then. Good for you!

NICHOLAS' PENETRATION

This entanglement was a completely difference experience for Madeleine. She was not used to having such an attentive lover. Indeed Madeleine had not had much in the way of lovers at all in her entire life. She had, in younger days, had a few odd boyfriends but nothing of a passionate nature. It could be said that this Nicholas Benson bloke had awakened her to what she had been missing all these years.

They lay in bed this weekend in each other's arms while he caressed her lips and nuzzled into her cheek. Madeleine could not really cope with all this waste of time which had now become an integral part of her life it seemed. Why am I not up and doing the housework and catching up with the ironing? Guilty feelings crowded into Madeleine's mind.

Then Nicholas spoke.

"I think we ought to discuss your job again."

"Oh, that old chestnut," she countered.

"You will have to walk out, you know. You can't afford to work for a crook. It could reflect badly on you."

"But I have no concrete proof," she protested. "It's only my suspicions. And perhaps I'm being unjust to Reggie? Who knows?"

"Why don't we get some proof then?" suggested her partner.

Madeleine looked exasperated. We have gone through this hoop many time before, she thought.

"And how the hell can I get proof?"

Nicholas sat up and looked ready for business.

"Look, the guy has papers, documents. Yes? Evidence!"

"Well, yes, I suppose so. Obviously."

"Well, then we can get proof."

"What?"

"Where does he keep his papers? In his desk? In a safe? Where?"

"You're not suggesting that I steal his papers or crack open his safe? Surely not?"

Madeleine was shocked to the roots of her hair by this suggestion.

"Well, not you specifically?"

"The police, maybe?"

"I have a better way," announced Nicholas enigmatically.

"What?"

Then Nicholas elucidated for Madeleine's benefit. She instantly rejected the scheme out of hand. So Nicholas had to apply more reasoning and persuasion.

"If Reggie gets caught red handed, then you will be implicated at best or find yourself in jail at worst. Either way your life will be ruined."

Madeleine found this a very persuasive argument but she didn't see what she could do about the situation other than resign.

"Certainly resign but, before you do so, let me collect some evidence on your behalf," asserted Nicholas with a degree of determination, "that will dump him in it and let you completely off the hook."

Madeleine found these statements very curious and so she made further enquiries of Nicholas. She, consequently, discovered that Nicholas had already worked out a plan. The debate between the two continued with Madeleine showing reluctance to the scheme while Nicholas continued to press home his advantage.

The next weekend, therefore, saw Nicholas and Madeleine entering the premises of the Benefice Charity Trust with Madeleine's office keys. Madeleine then showed her lover where she worked and where the Chief Executive's office was situated. Nicholas made straight for Reggie's domain.

Nicholas seemed adept at unlocking locked drawers and filing cabinets. Madeleine was amazed to discover that he possessed this talent together with a bunch of all-purpose skeleton keys. Nicholas proceeded to take photographs of all the documentation to hand which would incriminate

Reggie. Madeleine stood by watching with her eyes popping out of her head like the organ stops on the grand five-manual organ in Westminster Abbey.

"Have you done this sort of thing before?" she asked indignantly.

"Yes," he replied nonchalantly.

Madeleine gasped and felt that she ought to have previously acquired more information about her new lover. But it's too late now, duckykins!

When Nicholas looked at Reggie's safe, however, he frowned and murmured in a defeated manner. But then, after a bit more prodding and tapping here and there, he made a telephone call.

"Who are you ringing?" cried a disconcerted Madeleine.

"A friend."

Nicholas had a brief conversation with his friend, the purport of which Madeleine did not comprehend.

"Now all we have to do is wait," announced Nicholas.

When Madeleine asked what they were waiting for and who Nicholas had called, unfortunately, she did not receive a satisfactory reply. Within minutes, however, they both heard a light tap on the outer door and Nicholas hastened to answer it. Madeleine thought she would expire at this unexpected turn of events but, when someone called Foxy entered the premises and kissed her hand, she relented.

"It won't take me a second, Miss Madeleine," proclaimed the chivalrous gentleman in front of her.

And Foxy was as good as his word. He cracked the safe open in minutes, took some photographs and then downloaded the contents of Reggie's desktop computer on to a USB memory stock.

"That'll do the trick, Miss Madeleine. Don't you worry no longer, Miss. Foxy'll look after yer all right."

And when he kissed her hand again, she melted like snow in midsummer in the Sahara.

Nicholas looked very satisfied with the course of events when he thanked Foxy and bid him a hearty farewell as he rapidly left the scene.

"We have all we need now, sweetest love. This lot can go straight down to the cop shop."

And then they left. But Madeleine was now really convinced that she needed to leave her job with all possible speed.

Madeleine subsequently tendered her resignation from the Benefice Charity Trust first thing on Monday morning and she earnestly hoped that Reggie would not notice that his precious papers had been in any way disturbed over the weekend.

Unbeknown to Madeleine, Nicholas and Foxy met up the next day in order to compare notes and to prepare their material for presentation to Barrington Flint. Both Nicholas, alias Tom Dryden, and Foxy, really Harry Ferguson, celebrated their triumph and the anticipated financial rewards which they would both receive from this little deal.

"I wasn't sure whether we needed a safe-cracker at first. So thank you for standing by," concluded Madeleine's lover.

"I'm always ready at hand," replied Foxy.

Madeleine felt, however, that she had been tricked somewhat by Nicholas who had managed with her help to enter the offices of the Benefice Charity Trust. And, which was worse, he had invited an accomplice along with him unannounced. Her ardour for Nicholas thence began to wane and Madeleine returned to keeping her home tidy, doing the usual washing-and-ironing routine at the weekends and making regular meals for herself and the freezer.

Madeleine felt a bit happier in her secure and known world and so she had very little incentive to derail it again in future. She vowed that never again would she succumb to the advances of any casual stranger who pestered her for a date. She missed Nicholas a tiny little bit but not enough to pick up the phone ever again. Having plucked the thorn from her flesh, Madeleine then lived happily ever after.

As Madeleine had a considerable amount of unused holiday time for the current year, working out her notice took only a matter of weeks before she was a free agent again. With Madeleine's experience and qualifications, of course, she soon found alternative and congenial employment elsewhere. But this time she did not want any association with a charity. Once bitten, twice shy became Madeleine's motto for the future.

Strangely enough, Nicholas did not make any further attempts to contact Madeleine and so she concluded that he was simply a fly-by-night and, therefore, he was worth no further consideration.

JANICE'S SALVATION

After the gear from the tour had been packed up, Janice managed to get a lift with the backstage crew in one of the vans going back to London where she could stay with a friend. The bedsit in which Janice had stayed previously had, of course, been let to someone else by now.

Janice didn't know what the future held for her. She was sure that she wanted to continue her career in the theatrical world or in film production but she really had no idea how to go about acquiring another job.

Hal had suggested that Janice contact a few theatrical agencies who specialised in backstage staff and he had given her some leads which she decided she could follow up as soon as time permitted. John had also given Janice the names of some of his contacts. And so there was a lot of work ahead for Janice to do in order to get back on to a money-earning platform.

As an immediate precaution, Janice quickly secured for herself a job in a local supermarket where she checked stock and stacked the shelves with produce overnight. This then meant that Janice was free in the daytime in order to chase leads, to contact agencies and to generally do what was required for finding a regular job which suited her.

Stage Right, a theatrical agency which specialised in backstage crew, was one of Janice's first ports of call. She had telephoned the agency midweek and she had made an appointment to see Mandy Philpott who was one of the company's representatives.

Janice explained about her degree in Technical Theatre Studies which she had recently completed, although Mandy felt that this was a minimum qualification for her chosen profession. On the other hand, when Janice mentioned that she had just completed a contract for one of Vendetta Ice's tours, Mandy then sat up and took a very different attitude.

So then Janice began the thankless footslog of going for interviews for jobs which Mandy had assured her would suit her admirably when, in reality, they never did.

After Janice had exhausted her supply of suggestions from Mandy to no avail, she decided to answer a number of advertisements in various professional magazines and trade journals. Janice then once again started her round of theatres and other venues which might offer her scope for work and valuable experience.

At about the time when Janice was beginning to flag from stacking shelves and checking stock, not to mention the disheartening prospect of never ever finding suitable work, Janice found that her guardian angel had been toiling at the overtime on her behalf.

Janice had answered an advertisement in *The Backstager* magazine for the post of an assistant stage manager in a provincial theatre for which she was granted an interview. Janice did not hold out any high hopes of securing such a position but it seemed interesting from the job description which she had received from the theatre and it was not that far out of London.

Janice liked the idea of working in a large provincial theatre which was not too far from the capital and so she looked forward to her interview on the following day. Janice, consequently, made sure of an early night before setting out for the out-of-town location.

The Coxwain Theatre was quite large and attracted some well-known touring companies to its stage as well as those companies who were launching their production prior to transferring to London theatreland. The Coxwain hosted a variety of genres from light opera to grand opera and from comedy to high drama and devastating tragedy. Janice believed that this span would give her much scope and interest and that she would, in consequence, greatly widen her experience.

Bella Hardcastle, the theatre's resident manager and entrepreneur, was a striking woman whom no one could ignore and who was ebullient to the point of being infectious. Janice liked her as soon as they met.

Bella bounced with enthusiasm when she met Janice who felt that her prospective employer was a far cry from the brat-pack of Vendetta. Bella asked the usual set of questions which theatre managers ask when they are looking for staff and Janice asked a similar set of questions which she would be expected to pose in the circumstances.

Apparently Janice would be required to work five or six nights a week on average and to alternate with a colleague on the existing team. Janice would be employed exclusively for a set number of performances for a given show but she would be asked occasionally to fill in for her alternate number if he were, say, unwell or unable to attend the theatre for any reason. This precaution was formulated on the show-must-go-on principle. Bella stressed, of course, that Janice would be paid extra if she did any overtime by way of filling in for her colleague. Janice found this a novel idea which was not at all an unwelcome prospect. Obviously work in the theatre would be far more rewarding than running errands for the brat-pack.

Janice was certainly interested in this job and it had definitely been worth the effort of obtaining a good night's sleep, getting up early and making the journey out of London. Bella, in her turn, was very impressed with the fact that Janice's previous contract had been with a world-famous pop group on tour shortly after she had left university.

Janice and Bella then entered into lengthy discussion about the theatre as a place of work. The Coxwain Theatre's manager was thorough in giving Janice details of the history of the theatre and of the way in which she, Bella, had built up its reputation and given it a degree of standing in the theatrical profession.

Next Janice was taken on a tour of the theatre itself through both front of house and behind the scenes where her work would be concentrated. Janice was impressed with the standard of the equipment available for lighting and effects, the storage facilities for scenery and costumes and the green room rehearsal areas. Janice certainly wanted this job if it were ever offered to her. Please, God!

Bella, similarly, seemed interested in her interviewee and she lost no time in telling her so and in inviting her back to meet her prospective colleagues in the backstage crew at a second interview. Later in the week, therefore, Janice travelled to the Coxwain Theatre yet again in order to meet two of the resident stage managers and most of the rest of the backstage team.

Janice was offered the job on the spot with a salary which was a vast improvement on her previous slave-wage. And there was the added benefit that she was permanently employed and would not simply be on a contract which would expire when a tour reached its conclusion. Janice, therefore, decided that the demise of Vendetta Ice had been a blessing in disguise.

When she left the theatre, Janice instantly set about finding accommodation for herself while working at the Coxwain Theatre. She found a small bedsit in no time at all with a lovely landlady whom Bella knew and had recommended.

Once she had found her bedsit, Janice dreamt only of contentment and job satisfaction. She would see the glory of the footlights without ever stepping on to the stage while an audience was in residence which suited her just fine. By the end of the week, Janice was ensconced in her new abode and on the following week she started work in a place which did not mess her about and with a wonderful new team.

Obviously Janice missed working with John and his friends but she knew that life had to move on. She had fallen on her feet and she did not look back. Good old Janice! Bless her little cotton socks!

JENNY'S ECSTASY

Jenny felt herself supported by a force which was strong and yet soft, supple, pliable and malleable. A force both within herself and yet outside her being. Jenny felt herself subtly moving. Or rather she was being gently moved as opposed to moving herself. It was as if she were softly swaying in the breeze in an aimless fashion. But she felt herself held and supported somehow.

Jenny could also hear music in the distance. Oh, not the raucous strains of Vendetta. God, no! This was heaven-sent music with an orchestra sweetly playing sotto voce (in a quiet voice, to you) in the background. Not drums and guitars and flashing lights and a strong beat. But with violins or was it a harp she heard? A flute perhaps? Some exotic percussion instruments maybe? A triangle and some tiny tinkling bells? A singing bowl or two? Who knows? But it was beautiful and gentle and sweet music to Jenny's ears.

Then Jenny heard someone singing, although it was not an earthly voice but that of an angel perhaps? High pitched but not strident. Silvery and sweet yet not sentimental. Jenny wondered at her experiences. Perhaps I have died and gone to heaven?

Then she felt a warm body beside her whose skin was rugged and hairy and who groaned intermittently in his sleep. Consciousness dawned for Jenny who had awoken into the real world. Although Jenny soon realised that the ecstasy of her dream of dying and going to heaven was, in fact, true. Eureka!

Jenny had died and gone to heaven on earth but here was her dearest Kicker still lying beside her. Actually he wasn't Kicker Sax anymore. He was just plain Timothy Aitken living on the Norfolk Broads and she loved him dearly and he loved her too.

Jenny had been on cloud nine ever since Rouchuka had resigned with such aplomb on such a momentous occasion. When Rouchuka had so dramatically walked out, she had unknowingly rendered a great service to that famous quartet consisting of Kicker, Jenny, Bluey and Wanda. Rouchuka had transformed the lives of these four so profoundly and so irrevocably that she had rendered them all a service for which they would thank her for the rest of their days and from the bottom of their hearts.

But it seemed to Jenny at that moment and, indeed, for ever more, that Rouchuka's greatest benefit had been bestowed on her. After Rouchuka's show-down, for instance, Kicker had immediately gone into overdrive and he had contacted his lawyer. Kicker had previously signed and returned his exit papers at the commencement of the southern tour and his lawyer was just patiently waiting for the nod from Kicker in order to despatch the documentation to the appropriate recipient at the appropriate time.

After a brief conversation, therefore, Kicker's lawyer agreed to send the necessary legal papers directly to Henry as the executive producer for Colossus Enterprises. Kicker had already spoken to Henry in order to inform him that he too was determined to resign formally and that he would be sending the relevant documentation to Henry in due course. Kicker, of course, did not want to confront Gerry who, in any case, was indisposed as a result of Rouchuka's bombshell.

Henry had seemed pleased when Kicker told him that he was on the point of formally resigning from Vendetta and he thus he instructed Kicker to despatch the papers addressed to him in person at the London office.

Henry finally asked genially about Kicker's future plans and he wished him every success. They even drank a toast together with the remains of the champers from the never-to-be-forgotten after-show party.

Jenny and Kicker were now safely home in their haven on the Norfolk Broads where they could rest after their ordeal with Vendetta. And, as far as one could tell, Vendetta no longer really existed.

The Norfolk Broads is a unique UK National Park consisting of a multiplicity of navigable waterways which stretch for some 200 kilometres skirting enchanting landscapes, peaceful marshlands and picturesque towns and villages. Kicker and Jenny's abode, indeed, was more easily accessible by boat than by car. And, in many instances, their own riverboat was the mode of transport of choice for the couple when in residence.

Unlike the brat-pack, Jenny and Kicker did not have an army of servants who pandered to their every whim and so the two had to refresh the place themselves on arrival, although Jenny did summon the assistance of a few of the locals who were more than willing to help their famous neighbours. They also stocked up well on provisions because Jenny and Kicker intended to stick around in Norfolk for some time to come.

Jenny and Kicker now became tourists for a few days in order to relax and enjoy their new carefree life. They visited their favourite haunts, such as Wroxham Barns, Whitlingham Country Park and the Bure Valley Railway, as well as some of the more secret byways and nature trails which were largely undiscovered by the tourist trade.

"I think I'll ring Bluey," Kicker suggested one morning at breakfast, "and see if he wants to come and stay for a while. You OK with that?

"Good idea and then you can discuss the future."

Jenny was, in fact, glad that Kicker was again thinking about his music because she knew that he could not live without it, although she hoped that in future Kicker's musical expression might take the form of an outlet quite different from his previous involvement with a high-profile band.

Bluey arrived soon but Wanda did not accompany him, much to the astonishment of Jenny and Kicker who thought they were both joined at the hip. Apparently Wanda wanted to become her own woman and to earn her own keep in future. Bluey, of course, had given her some money with which to get started and Wanda had then wandered off to find herself a job.

"Good for her," remarked Jenny who had realised Wanda's need for independence and she definitely admired her courage in breaking away from the fold. Jenny knew that Wanda felt insecure all the while her livelihood was tied up with Vendetta Ice's fortunes and so Jenny could understand implicitly why Wanda had needed to make the break which Rouchuka had inadvertently brought about.

Jenny now left the boys to their jamming session and their discussion about the future and she simply provided meals and drinks whenever necessary.

Kicker and Bluey debated the way in which they could carve out a future together. Both musicians were now determined to make a go of it together because they needed music as their life's work even though they did not need the money, the fame or the hassle of showbiz life.

The first step was for Bluey to officially resign from Vendetta which he set in motion through the same lawyer with whom Kicker had dealt. Following a Zoom meeting with the lawyer, therefore, Bluey received some papers to sign and to return via courier in order to legally sew up that aspect of his working life.

The boys also agreed that, if they got themselves a shrewd manager, they could form a small group with the addition of a front man or woman who could usually be easily found from among the ranks of the highly talented unemployed. And their new manager would almost certainly sort out this aspect of their business.

So the decision was made, a few agents were accordingly contacted and finally one was employed in the service of Timothy Aitken (formerly Kicker Sax) and Pete Jenkins (formerly Bluey). Bluey, of course, was utterly sick to the back teeth with being Bluey and so he dropped his stage-name like a hot brick.

They also required a change of name for the new ensemble. So the saxophonist and the percussionist assigned themselves the arduous yet exciting task of naming their new baby. They both had agreed, of course, that they should drop their former professional names because of the unpleasant associations but, unfortunately, they could not immediately think of a suitable title for their new venture.

"It will come to us one day," prophesied Timothy who had now officially relinquished the name Kicker.

Pete Jenkins, formerly Bluey, agreed. And Timothy secretly believed that if Pete were allowed to choose whether or not he adopted a stage-name, then he might not come across as boring to others.

The light-bulb moment came in a flash when Jenny announced excitedly that everyone should be thinking of a name for her forthcoming offspring.

Hence the three of them had to have a conference in order to drum up a name for the two new babies.

Timothy instantly went into hysterics and raptures over the fact that his beloved Jenny was now going to make him a father. He was the happiest man on earth and the most attentive and caring father-to-be on the planet.

And Jenny was ecstatic at the prospect of starting a family which would grow in time far away from the crazy world of showbiz.

Rouchuka obviously had no idea what damage she had unleashed into the world when she stood up at Vendetta Ice's last social gathering. Rouchuka, we love you! You've made us all so happy!

WINSTON'S REWARD

Following his fruitful and productive meeting last evening with Barrington Flint, Winston Blakefield scurried back into his office in Powton Street in the heart of magazine-land the next morning.

Now he would, at last, make his name in the world, he believed. Winston accordingly rang for his chief assistant journalist. Winston did not have a large team of writers but his second-in-command was worth six others of a mediocre standard. Kyle Ebury was much in Winston's favour.

Kyle was aristocratic and, therefore, could buy or bribe his way in anywhere. He had a physique which charmed the ladies and a scintillating personality generally. He had a gargantuan load of grey matter in his skull and he utilised it to great effect in his chosen profession. Kyle had a serious academic background but he was not at all averse to rolling up his sleeves and mucking in with mundane copy. Kyle was also an accomplished wit and he used this talent to great effect in his writing. He relished taking the piss. In short, Kyle was a genius whom Winston valued more than his own life. Winston would have sold his grandmother in order to retain Kyle as his sidekick.

Kyle breezed into Winston's office with a convivial smile and a jibe about the rubbish weather just now. Even more gratifying was the fact that Kyle brought in with him some coffee and classy biscuits for both of them. Winston, of course, lamented the demise of the tea-lady but Kyle made a very creditable substitute. Winston was grateful for this early morning snack because he had skipped breakfast in his haste to get into the office and to start work immediately. This morning he was hell bent on assembling and cataloguing the massive amount of material which Barrington had sold him last night.

"I've got the scoop of the century," announced Winston proudly and eagerly, long before Kyle had even sat down.

"Oh, yes? Queen treads in horse mature on Horse Guards Parade again?" retorted the jester.

"No, even better than that!"

"I'm all ears."

"Vendetta Ice!" asserted Winston as if Kyle would know instantly what this meant.

"No, don't tell me. A new variety of ice cream sundae. Recipe created by a young and upcoming Mafia super chef. Got it!"

"Be serious and feast your eyes on this little lot, sunshine."

And so Kyle obeyed. The two journalists trawled through the documentation, listened to the recordings and looked at the collection of glossy photographs. And then they looked in wonderment at each other.

"Fucking hell. Quite a horde we have here, then," concluded Kyle who by now was hooked, "and we've got the scoop of the century, as you say!"

"Let's get writing together and then we will need to hand this little lot over to the fuzz. Or, at least, send it as an anonymous donor."

"An anonymous donor who also sent it to us?"

"Yes, and we will soon get a recording of Isabel Franklin's interview with Vendetta's manager, Gerry Paxton. So we can use that in due season a bit later."

"Never heard of her. Where does she work then?"

"No one's ever heard of her. She was just a plant who managed to convince our Gerry that she was a freelancer."

"Smart lady. What's her number? I could give her the benefit of my extensive experience. And a bit of help with journalism as well," was Kyle attitude.

The two journos then worked their socks off for the rest of the day knowing that the copy deadline of tomorrow lunchtime for this week's edition of *Public Enquiry* was looming.

"Have you run all this past the old man?" asked Kyle.

"Already got the go-ahead for six pages."

"I like it more and more."

Eventually their task was completed and both men read each other's copy. Winston had assumed the public outrage angle while Kyle had marshalled a detailed summary of the facts – particularly the transportation routes which had been adopted by the traffickers.

When *Public Enquiry* was next published the articles which were penned by Winston and Kyle were startling and numerous and sales increased exponentially. Winston then simply waited for the inevitable accolade to arrive from the old man. And he was not disappointed. Well done, matey!

The front page spread of *Public Enquiry* proclaimed the scandal with 196-point type as the headline. Winston's opening article was somewhat low-key but it delivered the goods.

Drug-Dealers in Vendetta Ice

News has just been received by Public Enquiry of some scandalous and deplorable drug-dealing within the recently disbanded pop group Vendetta Ice.

Although the culprits cannot be named because of sub judice restrictions, reliable sources have informed Public Enquiry that it is believed that some members of the so-called brat-pack within Vendetta Ice and its business manager may be implicated.

The police are currently searching nationwide for certain members of Vendetta Ice in order to assist them with their enquiries. The public, therefore, are asked to be watchful but not to approach anyone suspicious because they may be armed and dangerous.

Sources close to the investigation inform us that the drugs were apparently shipped across the globe from the Caribbean to Asia and Europe by a circuitous route before reaching London. A network of couriers and distributors have been in operation for some months at least and the authorities in question have currently rounded up these individuals who have been identified but, as yet, cannot be named.

Further news will be reported in Public Enquiry to readers when specifics have been clarified.

Winston Blakefield
Editor-in-Chief

A follow-up article then spelled out some of the details of the drug-traffic routes and Winston and Kyle were brave enough to include some photographs. Publish and be damned was the *Public Enquiry* motto obviously.

Drug-Currency Changes Hands

Our correspondents and associates in eastern Asia have tracked down the drug-transport route which the illegal substances have taken across Asia and Europe in connection with the alleged drug-trafficking by certain members of the pop group Vendetta Ice.

The hot merchandise has been carried by a series of trucks, farm vehicles and even donkeys in the band's endeavour to disguise their nefarious dabbling in the heroine trade. Sources close to Vendetta Ice have also revealed to Public Enquiry exclusive details of route-maps and money laundering bank transactions which have shifted millions across the globe in order to finance this elicit trade.

It is generally felt that those involved in the trafficking did not need the money and so it appears to be a mystery as to why these dealings should have been an attraction to those involved. The public are understandably outraged that those in the public eye, who are worshipped by millions of fans worldwide, should stoop to such deplorable depths.

Police are still seeking to question the ringleaders who seem to have gone underground at present.

Kyle Ebury
Public Affairs Correspondent

A subsequent series of articles showed copies of the route-map with additional photographs and other documentary evidence. The legal eagles had given all the copy a cursory once-over but the magazine was still probably taking a few risks. But what the hell? It sold copies, didn't it?

Ex-members of Vendetta were also hounded by Winston and his colleagues but predictably no one was available for comment.

A few more splashes across the pages of *Public Enquiry* also documented the career and antics of the recalcitrant band. Rocker was portrayed as the sex-addict, Myra was shown as the cross-dresser and Max was depicted as the game-for-anything money-grabbing bastard. Gerry's career was also explicated but this did not, so far, contain much in the way of juicy scandal unfortunately.

Rouchuka, Bluey and Kicker were treated kindly and sympathy was sought from the public for the tragedy which had been wrought on these three upright citizens by their ex-colleagues.

Henry and John were similarly pitied. Commiserations and good wishes were sent from *Public Enquiry* in order ensure that the reputations, and hence the employment prospects, for these two were not sullied.

It had been a condition of Winston's agreement with Barrington that the innocent parties should not be castigated and sunk with the ship. And as Barrington was a useful contact whom Winston did not want to lose at any price, he had no choice but to comply with these demands.

The next issue of *Public Enquiry* was expectantly awaited by the buying public and newsagents were forced to increase their orders for next week's magazine.

Winston was delighted and so was the old man. Winston expected a reward from this and he eventually got it in the form of nationwide recognition for his services to journalism.

Kyle benefited also from the scoop which gave him fodder for jokes for some time to come. Kyle, however, was not particularly interested in monetary reward because he had aristocratic capital enough behind him. But he just liked the fun of the chase and this factor was all the reward which Kyle sought.

HENRY'S TRANSFORMATION

Once the unwelcomed news of Vendetta's demise and the drug-smuggling had hit the press, Henry was on full alert. He had suspected all along that Gerry and the brat-pack were up to no good but his suspicions had not previously been proven to his satisfaction. Now someone else had done the digging and the news had been disseminated worldwide.

Henry's immediate problem, however, was to make his own swift escape unscathed. And he spent a sleepless night in making his plans.

Henry got to the east end offices of Colossus Enterprises plc next morning in record time. Only Donna was about when he arrived and a few of the administrative staff but nobody else of much consequence.

Henry went straight to his office and cleared his desk but, at the same time, he contacted the company's accountancy firm and officially contracted them to take over full responsibility for the administration of Colossus Enterprises plc. Henry, therefore, ordered a large taxi into which he loaded the office accounts, contractual documentation, various resignations and other items which would be of assistance to the administrators.

Henry had obviously taken a lesson from the gutsy Rouchuka who had simply walked out when she had had enough. And he now proposed to do likewise but without any egg on his face.

When Donna looked enquiringly at Henry, he explained that much of the company's formal business affairs now needed to be handled elsewhere. He also told Donna that he would be leaving Colossus Enterprises and he advised her to take a similar course. Donna, however, was bemused by Henry's advice but she was still uncertain what action to take.

After Henry had left, however, some of the members of Vendetta Ice, freshly returned from their southern tour, came into the building and made straight for Gerry's office where they remained entrenched.

Donna was puzzled by these actions because she had not yet heard the scandal. She seldom read gossip magazines and, in any case, she was not prone to listening to chin-wagging anyway. And so she remained at her post.

It was not until Rocker Blaize crashed into the building and shouted his head off that she decided to leave the premises.

Henry was officially a director of Colossus Enterprises and so he merely had to resign his commission from the setup. Henry, therefore, made an appointment with his private lawyer in order to get this side of his affairs in motion. Henry thus made his way to his lawyer's office almost immediately after leaving the accountancy firm in order to ensure that his action in leaving the sinking ship would not be misconstrued. Henry's lawyer then needed to check what procedures were necessary for his resignation as a director, such as a term of notice or an early-retirement penalty clause.

And Henry also wanted to ensure that he was not implicated in the scandal which would surely consign Vendetta Ice to the annals of history. The lawyer's advice was, in essence, pretty sound and so Henry felt relatively safe with a sworn declaration of his innocence.

Henry then decided that he needed a good rest after his fracas with bloody Vendetta Ice and so he took himself off to the Canary Islands for what he considered to be a well-earned vacation. He basked in the sun, he climbed up Mount Teide in Tenerife, he frequented several lively bars and restaurants and he thought long and hard about his life.

Henry had bags of experience, a substantial bank balance and a reasonably healthy borrowing capacity. And so the obvious conclusion at which Henry arrived shortly was that he ought to run his own company. Once Henry had hit upon the idea, his thoughts gushed out at such a vast rate of knots that he could hardly keep up with his own mind.

When Henry returned to the UK, therefore, he set about the task of searching for suitable premises and eventually he found an old warehouse in docklands where he decided he could launch his own theatre company once the premises had been suitably converted. Over the course of the next several months, therefore, Henry poured a lump of money into the Sissingford Theatre project.

The warehouse was converted to a high standard by a local building company who specialised in theatrical makeovers. The Sissingford Theatre, consequently, was equipped with state-of-the-art stage facilities, equipment and lighting. The theatre was designed in order to provide a proscenium-arch stage with spacious wings and flies as well as adequate rehearsal facilities.

The audience were also well catered for with a smart box office in addition to an online booking facility. A restaurant for pre-show and post-show diners was provided together with a cafe which served light bites before each evening's performance. And, of course, a fully equipped catering section served both the restaurant and the cafe more than adequately. There was also a bar on both floors which was designed to cater for thirsty audiences.

The auditorium held 750 seats in two tiers which put the Sissingford Theatre of a par with some of the smaller London venues even though it did not compete with most of the London greats.

Once the conversion of the building was well under way and definitely on schedule, Henry's next move was, of course, to hire some staff.

Henry then put his accountant's hat on and he did some lateral thinking. The answer was staring him in the face as obvious and he did not fail to miss it. That single thought then prompted Henry to make a few phone calls and to arrange a pub meal.

From that auspicious pub meal then a number of people's lives were changed irrevocably for the better. In the fullness of time, when the Sissingford Theatre had eventually been completed, therefore, John Dawson joined the Sissingford Theatre Company plc as the full-time stage manager with his two assistants, Janice Evans and Wanda Beck. John had now attained his dream of working in a London theatre as the head honcho and Janice and Wanda had, at last, come home roost.

Janice had, of course, been sad to leave the Coxwain Theatre but she had gained valuable experience there and she was now ready to start again with a new venture which would embody all the excitement of adventure as a step into an unknown new world. Janice felt that she had come back to be among trusted friends with whom she could build a future.

Wanda was delighted to be earning her own living as an individual in her own right and not one who was dependent on her big brother. She used some of the money which her brother Pete had given her in order to acquire a small flat near to the Sissingford Theatre. And it seemed logical and sensible then for Wanda to acquire a lodger in order to help her to pay the mortgage. Janice naturally fitted the bill because the two friends worked well together both at home and at work.

In time Janice, Wanda and John were all afforded the honour of officially being appointed by Henry as directors of the Sissingford Theatre Company plc once the ship was sailing at full steam ahead and it was successfully navigating the high seas.

Janice found her work so stimulating and well paid that, in time, she was able to afford to purchase a small flat of her own and to acquire a mortgage rather than having to pay rent to Wanda. Janice and Wanda still, of course, remained close friends both at work and at play.

Janice never again worked for the Medici Squadron because she did not need the money or the distraction these days.

Henry had also asked Hal if he would like to join the company but, regretfully, Hal was now employed full-time touring the globe with a high-profile opera singer who had the world at her feet and thus needed a retinue appropriate for her station in life.

ROCKER'S APOPLEXY

"So what've you been up to then, Rocker, you naughty boy?" called a bloke from across the street.

Rocker looked bewildered.

"Read *Public Enquiry* recently?" jeered another.

Rocker was still perplexed as the catcalls and the heckling continued non-stop from various directions in the neighbourhood while he was out walking his parents' dog one morning. Rocker tried to quicken his pace but he only found that the barracking got louder and more ruffians joined the Pied Piper's throng. He, therefore, decided that the bleeding dog would have to be content with a short walk this morning as Rocker beat a hasty retreat back to his parents' home in Dorset on the south coast.

Rocker did not, however, dare to go to the newsagent in order to bring the *Public Enquiry* magazine back into the house in case his parents saw the news to which the jeering public had been referring. He was not sure what he was being accused of but he assumed that it would be very bad. The press furore following the band's breakup had surely died down by now? He surmised, therefore, that the fuss would be connected in some way to his sex-life. How sadly mistaken can you get?

Rocker hence skittered up to his room and rang his brother Jonathan in order to beg him to send a copy of *Public Enquiry* over to him by courier. When Jonathan seemed reluctant to become Rocker's servant, Rocker was forced to offer him a monetary incentive before he could get his own way. And even then Jonathan bargained for the highest price. The bastard!

When *Private Eye* arrived and its contents were read and reread from cover to cover by the completely gob-smacked and terrified Rocker, he decided to spend loads more money. Accordingly he hired a helicopter to take him to Colossus Enterprises in London post-haste.

Rocker crashed through the reception area like a man-eating tiger and, ignoring Donna's protests, he charged like a demented bull up to Gerry's office blandishing a well-thumbed copy of *Public Enquiry*. Rocker's fury mounted with every step which he took up the wrought-iron staircase. Here he found Gerry, Myra and Max camping out in the hope of not being discovered by the paparazzi who had not yet alighted from their own helicopters for the occasion.

Rocker's anger erupted at the sight of the drug-gang together hiding like skunks in a cave.

First Rocker grabbed Myra by the lapels and flung him to the ground with some choice language.

"I warned you that your drugs would kill us all, you fucking cunt!" he scream at Myra.

Myra shrugged with what dignity he could retain from the incident and then he started snivelling as if he had been beaten to death. Myra was, in fact, lucky that Rocker hadn't killed him. How had Rocker managed to control his temper? No one knew.

Having trounced Myra, Rocker turned to Gerry.

"And you're the bleeding ringleader, you fucking bastard," he continued addressing Gerry.

Gerry began to protest in a suave manner but he was interrupted by Rocker's rage.

"You tried to fob me off when I rang you from St Lucia," yelled the virtually insane Rocker.

Gerry made shushing noises and hand signals in an attempt to calm Rocker and to keep their secrets from the rest of the staff in the building. But his attempt failed. And when Gerry tried to smooth-talk Rocker, he received a stiff sock on the jaw for his insolence.

Gerry could not always pacify his victims and, on this occasion, he certainly had miscalculated his adversary. The indignity of being floored merely added to Gerry's existing indisposition and he did not have the strength either to argue any further or to fight back. He just picked himself up off the floor minus his self-possession plus an aching jaw. Rocker also, of course, hoped that Myra and Gerry would not sue him for grievous bodily harm.

Max cowered when Rocker turned to him and Rocker merely called him, "A miserable, spineless prick!" for good measure and then stormed back down to the reception area and to an astounded Donna who had probably heard every word. But Rocker was unrepentant.

"Get the hell out of here, Donna," he commanded. "Vendetta is in deep shit and the press will be hammering down the doors at any minute now. You'll be retained on full pay, of course. Don't worry but just go."

Donna, on this occasion, did as she had been instructed and Rocker thanked her. Rocker could actually be polite to women when he felt like it obviously. Donna, in fact, had some shopping to do and so she took the opportunity with grateful thanks. Rocker also ordered the rest of the staff to leave in their own interests for the same reason. But he did not divulge any gory details because they could all read that for themselves now.

Rocker then rejoined his helicopter and retreated back to his parents' home. Rocker was, of course, terrified that his parents would hear about the *Public Enquiry* article and then not believe him when he protested that he had had nothing whatsoever to do with the drug-dealing escapades.

When they did hear the news, Rocker's parents scarcely believed their son's protestations of innocence and this news evidently cemented their opinion of Jonathan as their favourite and most successful son. After all, pop stars were all the same, they maintained.

Rocker was so livid with his faithless and useless specimens of parenthood that he wanted to kill them and that bloody Jonathan too with his bare hands – along with Gerry and the other brat-pack worms.

Rocker walked out of his parents' home in disgust at their mistrust of him and he never made contact with them ever again. He managed, however, to find a cottage for rental in which he elected to hide for a while until either the paparazzi or the police caught up with him. Oh, how are the mighty fallen?

He coped with ordering food to be delivered but he was not able to hire any crumpet to feed his libido adequately enough. This was probably the worst kind of deprivation for Rocker. And, of course, he couldn't even stand the thought of taking any drugs, even if they had been accessible.

So Rocker waited for the axe to fall.

When the press did eventually locate him, of course, he was not available for comment. Rocker was hence under house-arrest with the press camping outside in the garden so that when the police did eventually arrive to take him away for questioning, Rocker was actually quite relieved at the prospect of a change of scenery. The change of scene, however, was not really to Rocker's liking when it came down to it. But now he had no choice.

Rocker had, unfortunately, spent a lot of time ranting and he had only contacted his lawyer at the last moment. Paul Dunwoody was in court regretfully and so he could not be contacted directly. Or so Rocker was informed by Jill, Paul's secretary. As Rocker had tried to chat her up a few times before now, he doubted the veracity of her statement but he was not actually in a position to question it or to make any strong-arm demands. So Rocker had no choice but to wait until Paul answered his plea and rang him back while he sat in a rather uncomfortable police custody cell.

When news of Rocker's detention hit the press, Jonathan and his parents held a council of war at which they assumed the role of judge and jury who unanimously found Rocker guilty.

He was then summarily sentence to execution at dawn on the following day for his sins against his family in particular and against humanity in general. His parents then decided to sell the Dorset house in order to get away from its reminder of their son. And so that they could return to their little corner shop up north.

VENDETTA'S DENOUEMENT

Myra, Max and Gerry were walled up in Gerry's office for several days before the police raided the joint in the early morning with all guns and truncheons blazing.

The trio had managed to persuade Donna to order in a supply of take-away food which they lived on for a while but the contents of the fridge were beginning to dwindle and, consequently, starvation was threatening. But now Donna and the rest of the office staff were long gone because Rocker had seen to that minor detail.

They had all managed to have a shower on the premises but they still wore the same clothes day and night. So Gerry's office was not the most flavoursome of places just at the moment. But at least they had the run of the place now that all the rats had left the sinking ship. Their movements were, nevertheless, severely restricted because of the hovering press deputation immediately outside.

The three, however, did nothing but row and threaten each other mercilessly but they did not actually come to blows. Gerry, for instance, remonstrated with Myra for involving Rocker in St Lucia in the first place. Myra, in retaliation, blamed Gerry for only recruiting him into the drug-clan in order to get at his money.

"You only wanted me for my money, darling," spat Myra at Gerry.

"That's the only thing you're good for, you pansy."

Max broke up the potential skirmish by telling the two warring factions that they had to keep calm and that it was important for them all to maintain a united front.

Myra then turned on Max and accused him of being so money-minded that he had lost his sense of reason and that factor in the equation had corrupted them all. Max did not put up a defence over this single fact which was patently true.

"Let's all be reasonable and think about the problem calmly and logically," interposed Gerry who was beginning to sober up a bit.

Gerry then suggested that they begin by contacting the company's lawyer. He had hoped to be able to sue Rouchuka for her untimely resignation but now Gerry had more important things on which to consult the legal eagles.

Both Myra and Max agreed that this suggestion of Gerry's was a pragmatic solution to their current dilemma.

"We could all talk to Derek over a video link as we cannot leave the premises," maintained the sagacious Gerry.

The trio, however, were not exactly well connected at this point in time.

They had taken the land line phone off the hook because so many nosey journalists had been constantly ringing. Gerry's own mobile phone needed a charger but, regretfully, he could not find the gizmo.

"Help me search for my charger, you two," Gerry demanded.

"Why have you lost it, you idiot?" proclaimed Myra who was then told in no uncertain terms to shut it.

Max complied with Gerry's request to institute a search but Myra seemed reluctant for some reason.

When Max tried his own phone, he found that there was no signal. Bloody hell, it gets worse!

Myra also tried to get a signal on his mobile but, because the phone needed a top-up, this was not an option. Myra then proceeded to hack into the office computer in the hope of being able to contact his network supplier.

But the telephone route finally had to be abandoned.

The three men in a boat without a paddle, however, managed to get an email through to Derek Shipton-Green of Pryor, Humbert and Grainger, Vendetta's corporate lawyer.

Derek, of course, readily agreed to represent the three musketeers because he appreciated the lucrative business and the notoriety which such an exposure would bring him and his firm. But Derek was forced to warn his clients that the degree of mounting evidence, which was apparently held by the press, would condemn the three of them outright when it was handed over to the authorities.

Derek also advised his clients to give themselves up because remaining in hiding would not be the long-term solution to their dilemma. Because both a change of clothing and a decent meal were calling each one of the trio, they seemed inclined to agree with Derek but, in practice, they actually did nothing in order to bring the situation about. Getting through the press cordon hovering outside would have been an ordeal in itself which none of the three wanted to face.

Having had a sneaky look out of the window, Max declared that they were already condemned by the assembled press contingent who were camped outside their offices and had been there now for some days. Max, the money-addict, speculated about how much the local hotels and guesthouses, not to mention the restaurants and pubs, might be earning from their misfortune.

The situation, however, resolved itself organically for the trinity because the law managed to track them down unaided. Robert Peeler's brigade had heard of the press gathering outside the offices of Colossus Enterprises plc and they had become very suspicious.

The authorities had, moreover, received an anonymous tip-off from a person claiming that he knew where the culprits were hiding and the police had acted on this communication promptly. But they did not reveal this nugget of information to the three men who were asked to assist them with their enquiries.

All three panicked when they were taken in for questioning. Unfortunately, because of all the panic and the bickering which had taken place, the three would-be criminals had not actually had a chance to get their stories to coincide. And then each of the three were separated and taken off in different cars in order to ensure that they could no longer confer. Poor buggers!

ROUCHUKA'S EXONERATION

Once Rouchuka had formally distanced herself from ever working with Vendetta Ice again, she planned to leave almost immediately in order to head for France and to return to the adorable Roussel.

Before Rouchuka and Greta had even contemplated ordering breakfast, however, she was accosted with a camel-string of well-wishers to her hotel room which considerably halted her departure.

Rouchuka was visited first by Kicker and Jenny who were profuse in their admiration for her, wholeheartedly congratulated her on her freedom and then wished her the best for the future. The party was soon joined by Bluey and Wanda who joined in the chorus at full throttle.

Plans were also made for a reunion at some point in the future but no dates could, as yet, be set by the six friends.

John, and later Henry, appeared for the same refrain of good wishes for Rouchuka's future. Both expressed their gratitude at having met and worked with Rouchuka. John and Henry also adumbrated how much they admired her talent and her professionalism both of which they had had the privilege to observe at close quarters. The two somewhat tearful men then took their leave of Rouchuka and Greta with many promises to keep in touch.

Rouchuka and Greta caught a chartered flight to Montpellier Airport and then took a taxi straight to the chateau. As Greta had telephoned ahead to announce their impending arrival, the villagers and the vineyard workers were all out in force in order to greet their esteemed mistress and her companion in ultra-polite French style. All the estate workers took turns in greeting the pair.

Rouchuka noticed, however, that Roussel remained somewhat in the background and he only approached her when summoned. Although Roussel's eyes betrayed their delight at the site of Rouchuka, she detected a slight reticence and even an embarrassment at their meeting again in France. Rouchuka, however, appreciated that Roussel might feel this way because ostensibly she was still his employer. He may not, therefore, have felt comfortable in her presence in front of his fellow workers, she reasoned.

Some of the men took the luggage into the chateau and Rouchuka and Greta followed. Rouchuka was a little disappointed, however, to notice that Roussel did not. He simply returned to his work in the vineyard with a shy smile and a discreet nod. This situation could be difficult, conceded Rouchuka. But I am sure that I can sort it out soon.

The next morning early, Rouchuka decided to take a tour of her vineyard and the viniculture plant. She walked through the vineyards and she sampled some of the grapes herself. They certainly tasted delicious and so she assumed they would make good wine. Currently some of the early grapes were being harvested and so much activity was in evidence.

In the fermenting plant, Rouchuka watched the crushing, pressing, clarification and fermentation processes with interest but with little technical knowledge. She had, of course, had the whole viniculture process explained to her in detail previously and so now she was just merely observing and checking up.

Another shed which Rouchuka visited conducted the wine ageing and bottling processes and, of course, this was the place where the addition of the chateau's own decorative label was affixed to the bottles.

Rouchuka seemed satisfied with what she had seen and the books of account which she had inspected regularly bore testament to her assumption. Roussel, however, seemed hell bent on avoiding her during her tour of the premises and this fact worried Rouchuka even more.

The next morning, however, life took a different turn for Rouchuka and her concerns about Roussel, therefore, flew out of her mind.

An official car drew up outside the chateau and an official-looking official alighted and made his way towards her door. The man spoke only broken English and so Rouchuka was forced to ask for Roussel to come to the chateau in order to act as a translator.

Apparently Monsieur Pierre Rimoux was a detective inspector who represented the French police. Detective Inspector Rimoux invited Rouchuka to accompany him to the local commissariat (police station, to you) in order to answer some questions about Vendetta's drug-capers.

Rouchuka was naturally alarmed but Roussel assured her that Inspector Rimoux was merely looking for evidence and that she was not suspected of any crime. Rouchuka was apparently to speak with an English detective inspector over a video link at the commissariat. She would not need a lawyer present according to Inspector Rimoux but she did take the precaution of asking Roussel to come with her.

Inspector Rimoux conducted Rouchuka to a private room on arrival at the French police station where the video link was set up. Here Rouchuka met Detective Inspector Tony Croonacre and Detective Sergeant Dimity Myers from Scotland Yard who were conducting the enquiry into the alleged drug-trafficking charge for which Gerry, Myra and Max were currently being detained in custody.

Tony Croonacre was scrupulously polite to Rouchuka and he was even bordering on being obsequious. Tony was obviously a pop music fan who was slightly in awe of Rouchuka's status within the culture but, Rouchuka noted, Dimity, fortunately, did not suffer in this somewhat deferential manner. Girl power!

Tony felt convinced, in fact, that Rouchuka was not a part of the dastardly drug-plot even though he did not actually specify this belief categorically to his interviewee. But, nonetheless, Rouchuka's fears were allayed by Tony's general attitude and politeness.

Tony's line of questioning focused on any evidence which Rouchuka might be able to provide which would either substantiate or negate the data which he already had to hand. Rouchuka realised that Tony did already have a considerable body of evidence in order to his support case. And her questioning was, therefore, a means of verifying existing information. Rouchuka, for instance, was asked whether she was aware of the fact that Gerry, Myra and Max were prone to conducting late-night meetings in the hotels in which Vendetta had stayed while on tour. Rouchuka confirmed that such meetings had taken place but, of course, she had no idea whatever of what might have been discussed.

Rouchuka also confirmed that drugs were an integral part of the brat-pack's raison d'être. She added, of course, that she had never felt the need to take any drugs herself and Tony hastened to assure her that her conduct was not in question. Apparently a number of other members of Vendetta's crew had already informed Tony of Rouchuka's innocence and the fact that generally she was a recluse when not on a stage.

Tony also asked Rouchuka whether she had any knowledge or suspicion of the drug-trade or drug-dealing activities within Vendetta and she replied that rumours were constantly flying around but that she seldom took notice of such gossip.

Dimity Myers then checked some dates and times with Rouchuka with regard to various tours at home and abroad which Vendetta Ice had undertaken and Rouchuka was able to verify these dates and times satisfactorily.

Rouchuka was then asked to dictate a short statement to Dimity which she would be asked to sign in due course and which would be submitted as evidence when the case against Gerry and company came to court. This statement, Tony told her, would be typed up and brought to the chateau by Inspector Rimoux when it was ready for her signature. Rouchuka assented willingly.

Tony concluded his questioning by thanking Rouchuka profusely and then asking her if she would be willing to be called as a witness in court if necessary. Rouchuka consented even though she did not feel that she had much to contribute to the prosecution.

"I hope that I will not need to disturb you again, Miss Chantry. But, if I need to, I will contact you directly myself."

More polite thanks and good wishes were exchanged between interviewer and interviewee.

Inspector Rimoux then volunteered to arrange for a car which would drive Rouchuka and Roussel back to the chateau.

Rouchuka invited Roussel into the chateau for a mid-morning coffee when they arrived back at the chateau and he felt obliged to accept. Not to beat about the bush, Rouchuka immediately accused Roussel of avoiding her.

"Sweet Rouchuka, you must understand that I did wrong in making love to you in England. Please forgive me for over-stepping myself, will you? I did wrong. I know and I am so sorry."

"Roussel, you did not do wrong. I wanted you," she protested earnestly.

But Roussel still hung his head in shame.

"I should not have come to England and not have been to sleep with you. I am so sorry."

"But Roussel . . ."

"I cannot see a future for our relationship. I am sorry. Please forgive me. I respect you very much. And it will never happen again."

Rouchuka burst into tears of anguish when her reasoning obviously failed to convince her erstwhile lover. She could not reconcile the poignancy of Roussel's lovemaking with his claim that he was somehow bad.

"I must leave here because I have been very bad and I take advantage of a lovely lady."

Rouchuka still could not believe her ears but she realised that it was no use trying to dissuade him from his intentions. She, therefore, had no alternative but to accept his resignation from the vineyard and its viniculture project and so allow him to take his leave.

Roussel left the vineyard almost immediately and he was considered by all to be a great loss to the wine-making project.

His fellow workers, of course, had an inkling of why Roussel was leaving so abruptly but they merely exchanged glances rather than indulging in gossip-mongering about their esteemed overlady.

Rouchuka cried herself to sleep that night but at a deep level she understood that the two were really worlds apart and that this early separation was, in fact, for the best in the long run. Roussel's departure did not, however, deter her from her wish to make her residence here in France permanently.

Roussel returned to the UK and to his usual fly-by-night existence once more. But there was just a scintilla of sadness in his breast as he left such a beautiful lady behind in his own homeland.

Medici's retribution

Calendula and Barrington had hired the Fiesta Princeling for the occasion because they wanted to reap their rewards in style. The Fiesta Princeling was an Indian restaurant in the heart of Mayfair.

The management had reserved one of their largest rooms for the event and the restaurant's chefs had flexed their culinary muscles for the drop-in buffet lunch.

The spread consisted of a hot jalfrezi beef curry for the most resilient of the guests, a medium-strength chicken bhuna for the less adventurous and a vegetable biryani for those who were either vegetarians or who had a delicate digestion or both. The usual assortment of accoutrements accompanied these delicacies, such pilau rice, dahl, curried vegetables, naans, poppadoms, samosas, raita and, of course, mango chutney.

Barrington pinched a samosa and a poppadom or two before the guests arrived but Calendula was too excited to eat.

The invitation to the buffet stated that guests could arrive at any time between 12 noon and 3 pm. Calendula hoped that they would not all come at once. The waiters were, however, on stand-by in order to replenish supplies of food as they were consumed. The Medici Squadron duo were anticipating a full house and they had catered accordingly and, as it later turned out, they were not disappointed.

The first to arrive was Tom Peel, followed swiftly by Bill Brewer, Jan Stewer, Peter Gurney, Peter Davy, Dan'l Whiddon, Harry Hawke and, finally, of course, old uncle Tom Cobley and all. The Fiesta Princeling restaurant soon, indeed, resembled Widdecombe Fair. Winston Blakefield also put in an appearance but he left Kyle back at the ranch in case he should be tempted to flirt with the delectable Calendula.

All guests were greeted with handshakes and man-hugs for the men and hugs and kisses for the women present.

When a sufficient number of guests had arrived and feasted both their eyes and their bellies on the nutritious fayre, Barrington called the meeting to order.

"I suppose you are wondering why I have gathered you all here today?" Barrington commenced.

The assembled company greeted him with a volley of jibes and some outrageous guesses at which their hosts merely grinned.

"I am here to donate some goodies to you in exchange for the usual remuneration, of course."

The party knew of Barrington's trade and had dealt successfully with him on numerous occasions in the past. The guests included both representatives of the gutter press and the glossy magazines as well as a few familiar faces from the more respectable newspapers.

Barrington outlined what he had on offer to the amazement of his audience.

"We have for you today, ladies and gentlemen, a recorded interview with one Gerry Paxton, late of Vendetta Ice."

A gasp went round the room and murmurs of appreciation were also distinctly heard.

"You will hear both of us on the recording but, of course, my Calendula actually conducted the interview while I simply took the pictures."

Calendula nodded in order to acknowledge the smiles and the thumbs-up signs from the gathering.

Barrington continued his spiel.

"The photographs of Gerry's bathroom may provide you with evidence which you might find a tad useful," he continued enigmatically.

"Any sex poses?" asked one of the group.

"Nah! Even better than sex."

"Anything about the recent scandal?" asked another.

"See for yourself. The evidence is patently obvious."

"We will," was the rejoinder from several.

"And we also have a recording of Calendula's lunch with the head of the brat-pack."

The listeners were incredulous.

"You mean she actually managed to have lunch with our Gerry?"

"Sure did," replied Calendula who was fascinated to watch the antics of the audience, "but I drew the line at getting into bed with him."

A guffaw of laughter and unprintable comments went round the room like wildfire.

"You will hear her voice, of course, both during the interview and while at lunch but Gerry thinks she's called Isabel."

Again laughter rang out around the room.

The waiters and management of the Fiesta Princeling could not, fortunately, understand what was going on. But they did realise that their traditional food was much appreciated and was being devoured avidly by the guests.

After Barrington's announcement, the cohort of journalists were anxious to get away in order to digest both their meal and their booty. For the smokers in the room, of course, there was an even greater urgency to get out of the restaurant in order to be able to light up.

One of the last to leave, and yet the first to arrive, was Barrington's old friend Ronald Turner of the Guardian Media Group which incorporated both The Guardian and The Observer. Ronald was delighted to have been invited to the delicious lunch and to received his share of the gossip.

Calendula, Barrington and Ronald caught up on each other's respective news. Calendula asked after Ronald's wife and she sent her love by return to Dotty. She then left the boys alone so that they could chatter and reminisce.

Now that Calendula's appetite had been restored because the excitement had died down, and all except Ronald had gone home, she helped herself with eagerness to what was left of the Indian buffet lunch.

While Calendula settled the restaurant bill with some of the used notes which the Medici Squadron had received for their efforts, Barrington and Ronald chatted about the previous time when Ronald had received Barrington's favour. They spoke of the time when they had both helped to expose certain members of the government who had been up to naughties at the expense of the electorate. Happy days!

A new government was now in power and Ronald wondered how long it would be before the Medici Squadron would dish some dirt on the latest bunch.

Ronald and Barrington then discussed the situation with regard to the Vendetta Ice scandal. The prosecution of Gerry, Myra and Max was now going ahead and the triumvirate were in custody. The rest of the clan had been cleared of any wrongdoing, Barrington was pleased to confirm. Both Rouchuka and Kicker's sworn affidavits were of help in this respect.

Barrington was able to give details of the late-night meetings of Gerry, Myra and Max and to explain to Ronald the way in which the drugs made their way across Asia and Europe. He also mentioned that recordings had been made in St Lucia and downloads had been taken from Gerry's computer but Ronald was not that interested to report on the finer details of the scandal because his principal concern was the misconduct of political animals rather than celebrities.

After Ronald had departed, Calendula and Barrington now had the job of ordering a taxi and then loading into it the hordes of money which they had earned this lunchtime from the press contingent.

ROUCHUKA'S REINCARNATION

Greta was concerned for her mistress who had retired to bed early that night. She also noticed that Rouchuka had experienced some disappointment when Roussel had left the vineyard.

Greta had wondered about Rouchuka's relationship with Roussel who had come over to the UK to see her pop music swansong in Newquay. She deduced that their relationship was a little more than friendship when Rouchuka had dinner with Roussel after the show.

Greta had planned to return to the UK in order to visit her parents while Rouchuka was taking a long enforced rest following her severance from Vendetta Ice. But, it seemed, that she, Greta, might be needed in France for a while longer and so she remained uncomplaining.

Rouchuka was, indeed, dismal for a while but, after a few days, she decided to muck in with the workers. She thus joined the grape-harvesting team and she gained great satisfaction from this open-air employment.

Rouchuka, however, soon realised that she inhibited her workers from really enjoying themselves in the vineyard while gathering the grapes. So she elected to retire from the scene in order to allow the pickers to relish their work because they were then free to have uninhibited fun with constant jokes and laughs. And, as a result, the harvest got completed in record time.

Rouchuka then confined herself to the chateau for a while and contented herself with some simple tasks, some home-cooking with local produce and the supervision of the final stages of the restoration work.

She also told the faithful Greta that she could, if she wished, visit her family with all expenses paid but Greta chose to stay for a while. Greta was now on Rouchuka's payroll as her full-time companion, of course.

One afternoon, however, Rouchuka's rest on the patio in the garden after lunch was interrupted by a phone call from London.

"Could I please speak to Rouchuka, that is Harriet Chantry?" asked a polite English voice.

"Speaking," came Rouchuka's reply.

"My name is Conrad Baldwin," the caller announced.

Rouchuka kerbed her instinct to reply that she had never heard of him and she wondered whether he might be attempting to sell her something. Then she realised that she recognised the name from the archives of her memory but could neither place him nor could she put a face to the name. But how did he get my number?

"Your number has been given to me by a few members of the orchestra with whom you did some recording recently," Conrad explained.

I see, thought Rouchuka. That explains it. I wonder what he wants?

"I am a director who specialises in musicals," he continued, "and I understand from the musicians I spoke to that you would consider switching to musical theatre."

At last, Rouchuka recalled his name and who he was. Rouchuka held her breath as she speculated about what might come next. Could it possibly be? Will this be my lucky break?

"Because I am currently casting for *Les Miserables*."

Rouchuka wanted to scream but she resisted the temptation.

"Really," was all that she could muster in reply.

"Would you be interested, by any chance, in doing Éponine Thénardier for me?"

Rouchuka wanted to scream even louder but still she resisted the attraction.

"Would you be able to come to the theatre in London. I am currently working at the Wyndfrome Theatre in Covent Garden. Do you know it at all? Would you be able to drop in to meet me sometime?"

"Yes to both your questions," she replied but, at the same time, she warned her caller that she was currently in France and that she would need time in order to arrange a flight.

The two chatted for some considerable while more about the show, the performance dates, Conrad's vision for the musical and the role of the tragic Éponine in *Les Miserables*. Rouchuka listened attentively and she took due note of all information imparted.

Conrad promptly sent Rouchuka an electronic link to the music score together with a rehearsal schedule. The two also made a tentative date for their meeting and Rouchuka said that she would confirm this appointment once her flights had been booked. Their conversation then concluded.

Now Rouchuka screamed aloud and Greta came running in with concern. When Rouchuka told Greta the news they hugged with joy for many minutes.

Rouchuka explained about the musical and how pleased she was to be starting her new career. Greta was delighted now that her mistress was beginning to come back to life again and that she, Greta, could return to her home in the UK.

Rouchuka's next step was to book flights for herself and Greta, to download the music score and to race around to a local répétiteur with whom she had worked before in the district in order to learn the part at least well enough for an audition.

At the informal audition, Rouchuka sang Éponine's principal number, *On My Own*, while Conrad accompanied her on the Yamaha grand piano. The song, she felt, really suited her voice and Conrad was delighted when she accepted the part. Rouchuka now signed yet another contract but this time her contractual obligation was underpinned by sound judgment.

The musical *Les Mis* is based on the original novel of *Les Miserable* written by Victor Hugo and published in 1862.

Éponine is the tragic heroine who dies for her love. Not unlike Rouchuka herself, Éponine is a resourceful streetwise girl who falls hopelessly in love with the young Marius Pontmercy who spurns her love in favour of another. Éponine is then tragically killed by the revolutionaries in the 1832 French Rebellion when delivering an important letter to the hero, Jean Valjean. Éponine, of course, is caught in the cross-fire while Rouchuka herself fortunately manages to escape and to survive to live another day.

During rehearsals of *Les Mis*, Rouchuka met the talented and good-looking Quentin Kilroy, who was playing the role of Jean Valjean, and the two of them became great friends. During the course of the run of the show their friendship blossomed into something more than friendship and Rouchuka found herself forgetting her erstwhile lover Roussel.

Rouchuka and Quentin later turned their fun-and-games relationship into something more serious and long-term. The press, who were continually hovering for any whiff of scandal, of course, spent a great deal of time trying to detect a loophole in the relationship. But they failed. Poor buggers!

Les Mis ran to packed houses for several years and it launched Rouchuka on her new career in musical theatre. She loved every second in her new habitat and she never regretted her switch into this genre.

From the launching platform of *Les Mis*, she went from success to success throughout most of the repertoire of musical theatre and light opera and she was certainly a happier bunny for it. Love her!

VENDETTA'S INCULPATION

Detective Inspector Tony Croonacre and Detective Sergeant Dimity Myers did the rounds of the wider Vendetta company so as to interview possible witnesses and to take witness statements as they had done for Harriet Chantry, alias Rouchuka, in France.

An impressive collection of statements, therefore, had been assembled from Pete Jenkins (Bluey), Timothy Aitken (Kicker Sax), Wanda Beck and Jenny Lander as the band's closest associates.

John Dawson and Henry Sissingford were also among those who had been contacted by Tony and Dimity in order to obtain further evidence and to check whether these key figures might have been involved in any way.

The full backstage crew, both permanent and temporary, the bodyguard team and the office staff in London had similarly been interviewed and asked to make a statement.

Hal Caxton proved to be an important witness from the bodyguard team but his evidence was clearly only really hearsay unfortunately. But Tony and Dimity decided, however, to keep Hal's statement at the top of their pile just in case. Hal agreed in principle to appear as a witness, if necessary, when the trial came to court.

All the individuals connected with Vendetta Ice, including Hal Caxton, were cleared of any wrongdoing beyond reproach.

The staff of the hotels in which the band had stayed on their UK tours were also contacted and interviewed by Tony and Dimity. Cynthia Pringle who had brought some room-service items to Myra's room at the Hotel Splendora in the north had been a key witness to one of the clandestine meetings between Myra and Gerry. But again there was little corroborative evidence in support of her claims. Tony, nonetheless, asked Cynthia if she would be prepared to give evidence in court and she willingly consented.

The catchment net, of course, was cast even wider afield than merely the UK because leads had to be followed up across the cosmos. Tony's opposite numbers in various outposts in South America, Asia and Europe were hence detailed to round up the known suspects and to bring them in for questioning. Some of this overseas horde was eventually brought to book and the convictions gained assisted Tony and Dimity to clamp a few others in irons in the UK.

Our Sidney Hackett in St Lucia got hauled in for a grilling by the police force and the customs officials out there as did Rowan Boyd-Fuller. Despite a lot of squirming and false alibis, Sid was eventually nailed by evidence from Myra who shopped him unwittingly during the UK investigation and, fortuitously for the law, Myra's evidence was admissible in the Caribbean.

Rowan Boyd-Fuller, strangely enough, managed to evade prosecution by pleading ignorance. But then the law cannot always managed to get its pigeons brought bang to rights. Perhaps Rowan had been punished enough by life already not to need any extra bashing now from the fuzz?

Pisquito and Ichiro in South Korea were approached by the local constabulary and both were heavily bribed so that they would reveal information about Nipisos somebody-or-other who was eventually identified as a key player in the game.

A similar pattern of cracking down on the ringleaders in Asia and Europe commenced and the results, when they finally materialised, were commendable. There were, consequently, many celebratory drink-ups for police forces across the globe when the drug-ring was eventually broken up and successfully prosecuted.

The international press contingent, of course, made everyone's life an utter misery on whatever side of the criminal fence the victims sat. The police were hounded for inefficiency and sloth while the criminals were castigated for their insensitivity to the suffering of others, their money-grabbing proclivities and their wicked personalities. It was the same pattern the world over.

Gerry, Myra and Max who were by now safely in custody were spared a hammering by the world press. But none of them saw this as an advantage.

The court proceedings at last began.

Gerry Paxton, Nigel Dulse (Myra) and Robert Pollard (King Max) stood before the beak – and, of course, the world's press – at the Central Criminal court in London.

All three were glared at by a High Court Judge whom the defendants were obliged to address as "My Lord". This was the only occasion on which the three had ever genuflected to a high-up personage in their life.

All three initially submitted a plea of not guilty to the court, despite forceful legal advice to the contrary, and so a jury had to be selected and sworn in for the highly publicised trial.

Derek Shipton-Green of Pryor, Humbert and Grainger, as the solicitor acting for the triumvirate, was, of course, in court and so was the overpaid barrister-at-law, Sir Hilary Norbert-Livingstone, who was representing them. Obviously the party had a Rumpole-of-the-Bailey-type barrister by their side for the trial in order to mitigate some of the shock.

The body of evidence against the three musketeers, it transpired, was overwhelming. Unbeknown to the trio, the press had passed on information to the authorities from an anonymous source and this evidence stacked up on investigation.

The evidence which was presented in court consisted both of documentary information and recorded data. The court heard the contents of audio recordings and watched video files which had documented the secret meetings between Gerry, Myra and Max. A certified and verified copy of Gerry's laptop computer was also presented and considered by both judge and jury. Photographs of drug-dealing and trafficking individuals who were transacting business were also put forward and these named villains were cited as proven network-contacts whom Gerry had recruited.

Sir Hilary, the Defence Counsel, of course, questioned both Harold (Hal) Caxton and Cynthia Pringle as prosecution witnesses. But they really did not give much evidence of any substance. They merely testified to the fact that a meeting had taken place between Gerry and Myra at the Hotel Splendora. Well, a cat a can look at a king!

The defendants regarded Hal's testimony as a sheer betrayal even though he did not seem to offer much in the way of concrete evidence which, incidentally, Sir Hilary summarily scorned.

When Max saw Cynthia, he believed that he vaguely remembered her from the northern tour but he was not really sure.

And, finally, a whole haystack of witness statements was shuffled through.

The Crown Prosecution Service was confident of its success in this case and history has now proved that their foresight was correct.

All three had really no option but to change their plea to guilty in these circumstances and in the thrust of such incriminating evidence. The faces of the twelve good men and true on the jury also prompted the change of plea.

Initially Myra had truculently maintained that he intended to retain his plea of not guilty in court to the end of his days and he steadfastly ignored his lawyer's advice in this respect. Max, however, gave Myra a good clip round the ear and told him not to be such a silly tart and so Myra eventually relented in the nick of time (pun intended).

The jury would probably have taken all of ten seconds to reach their verdict but with the change of plea, the jury was dismissed. The surly judge then lost no time in pronouncing sentence on the prisoners. He castigated the triumvirate, furthermore, for wasting police time and court time and so they got an extra biff on their sentence.

All three were condemned to life imprisonment with a recommendation from the judge that each would serve a minimum of sixteen years because there were no mitigating factors. Some present in court were sorry that the judge did not put on a black cap and sentence all three to be taken to a place of execution. But some ardent fans were devastated.

ANDREW'S TROPHY

Maureen took herself off to the powder room at which point Andrew came to life.

"Well, what's in this case, then?"

"We can't discuss it here, obviously. Too public."

"You're up to your old tricks again, aren't you? Evasion with a capital E."

Barrington's expression was impassive.

"For God's sake, tell me the gist of this stuff, at least? You can do that, surely."

Andrew was now getting desperate but his friend remained unmoved as usual.

"Just in outline, perhaps?" Andrew pleaded.

"I've already told you," protested Barrington.

Andrew tried another tack.

"Calendula, I appeal to you. Can you give me an inkling of what's in this case at my feet, please? There's not much time left."

"I bet when you were a kid, you kept pestering your Mum to open your Christmas presents before Christmas," came Calendula's non-involvement reply.

"I might have known you'd side with him."

Barrington then saw Maureen returning and so he began to speak.

"All right, I'll tell you, Andrew. Er . . . Well, no, I can't now."

Maureen sat down again. Andrew scowled at Barrington but he had to concede defeat.

The two couples were dining in the Linden Tree – a glamorous restaurant in Kensington. Calendula and Barrington had decided to take their friends out to dinner rather than suffer Maureen's cooking. Maureen, of course, had shown the usual level of embarrassment at not being able to entertain them in own her home because of her lack of culinary expertise. But Calendula had brushed her protests aside and she said that it would make a change for them to dine out.

Both Calendula and Barrington, of course, really suspected that Maureen and Andrew often dined out in order to get a decent meal once in a while even though Andrew was on a punishing health-kick diet. Barrington felt sympathy for his friend Andrew and so he decided to give him a break from the purgatory of healthy food and fitness.

The appetisers consisted of coquilles St Jacques, which was chosen by both the girls, a seafood chowder for Barrington while Andrew, the health-freak, opted for a cold cucumber and avocado soup. Yuk!

The main course comprised a lamb and dahl casserole for Calendula, a Moroccan beef stew for Barrington, a lasagne for Maureen and some turkey kebabs for Andrew. Maureen had been adventurous in choosing the coquilles St Jacques for her starter but she drew the line at lasagne for her main course and no one commented.

The meal was accompanied by a few bottles of prosecco and red merlot, which the restaurant claimed has been specially imported for their establishment, and finally some brandy and liqueurs to finish off the evening.

Andrew, however, could not wait to get back home in order to open the pandora's box which Barrington had given him and which had sat beneath their table taunting him for the entire evening.

Once home, Andrew tore up the stairs to his home office, ignoring Maureen's enquiries about where he was going, and he proceeded to open the box.

To his delight, Andrew found a dossier on Reginald Trevelyan which was completely and utterly incriminating. Just the stuff which Andrew could sink his teeth into and which would ensure his annual bonus again this year. He knew Barrington was an annoying tease but this little lot was well worth it.

Andrew, there and then, set about collating the material and formulating in his mind the way in which he could expose Reggie in one of the next editions of *The Times*. There was a general news page on to which Andrew's copy could conveniently fit.

Andrew was so alive with excitement even at this time of night that his writing skills were honed to perfection in composing his copy ready for publication in no time at all.

And so, to this end, Andrew called his direct line manager the next morning in order to ensure that space would be reserved for his scoop when it could be released. Andrew's immediate superior was delighted with the news item which he felt would pep up the newspaper's profile quite a bit.

A taster article, the first of many, subsequently, appeared in *The Times* newspaper at the earliest possible opportunity when it was safe for Andrew to reveal his knowledge to the readers of the newspaper.

Benefice Charity Trust Breaks Trust

Reginald Trevelyan, the Chief Executive of the Benefice Charity Trust, has been accused of underhand dealings in connection with his administrative responsibilities.

Mr Trevelyan is believed to have been operating a financial scam for some time now which has involved forming companies which then apply for the Charity's own funds. Mr Trevelyan's modus operandi has allegedly been to create a series of bogus companies, apply for funds from his own charity and then fold the companies in question having pocketed the trust's money and kept quiet about the occurrence.

Sources close to The Times have unearthed this skulduggery which is now in the hands of the official prosecuting authorities.

Apparently Mr Trevelyan has also operated for a number of years and his latest bogus organisation is cited as Home Spun plc, a company purporting to sell designer-label natural wool garments made in Scotland and the Isles. Home Spun's website has been investigated and it transpires that no business has ever been conducted. The company is registered solely to Mr Trevelyan but it appears to have no employees.

Andrew Ormerod
Political Affairs Editor

A subsequent article in the following day's edition of *The Times* was also penned by Andrew in which he exposed the fact that Reggie had been active in the money laundering industry by working for King Max of Vendetta Ice.

Benefice Charity Money Laundering

Following our report yesterday of the elicit financial activities of Reginald Trevelyan, the Chief Executive of the Benefice Charity Trust, it has come to our notice that Mr Trevelyan has also been instrumental in money laundering activity on behalf of others.

Mr Trevelyan has now been named in connection with the illicit drug-dealing affair for which the pop group Vendetta Ice are currently being prosecuted.

It seems that there is a connection between Reginal Trevelyan and Mr Robert Pollard, known professionally as King Max, of the disgraced music band Vendetta Ice.

Sources close to the Vendetta Ice investigation have notified The Times that Mr Pollard employed Reginald Trevelyan to undertake money laundering on his behalf in order to disguise the proceeds of the drug-trafficking business.

Neither Mr Pollard nor Mr Trevelyan have been available for comment but The Times will continue to bring its readers up-to-date news on this important development in this scandalous cause célèbre which has shocked the world and its financial markets.

Andrew Ormerod
Political Affairs Editor

The news obviously continued in this vein for days to come and Andrew was delighted with his discoveries as well as the praise which he received from his newspaper's top management.

REGGIE'S COMEUPPANCE

Reggie was quite sorry when Madeleine handed in her notice because she had found a better job. Reggie did not really pine for the loss of Madeleine herself but he did worry about the accumulating pile of administrative work which had resulted from her absence. Reggie had, of course, employed a temporary secretary but she did not seem to know her way around the office as Madeleine once did.

Apart from the paper mountain of filing in the office and the fact that he could not find the petty cash tin, however, Reggie was, in essence, very pleased with himself these days.

He had formed yet another make-believe company and this one was quite a large concern and, therefore, Reggie would be justified in applying for a large grant from the Benefice Charity Trust. Reggie had created a website, had devised a portfolio of data about the company's aims and, of course, had written up an impressive set of accounts for the trust's consideration. All was in order and had been carefully put together by Reggie with his insider knowledge so as to impress the trust's Board of Governors.

Hence Reggie confidently believed that he was on to another winner. When the Board of Governors convened in order to consider the latest crop of applications, therefore, Reggie felt quite sure that he would soon be reaping the profits of his labours.

Long before the news of Reggie's misdeeds hit the public domain, Reggie was back in his office in order to chair a meeting of the Board of

Governors. He sat at the helm with a degree of aplomb as if he were an omnipotent being who perched on high and looked down on the cosmos and approved of what he saw. The governors debated every case carefully and then gave each applicant either the thumbs-up sign or the thumbs-down dismissal according to their considered opinion.

While the board meeting was in progress, however, an urgent knock came on the boardroom door and a nervous temporary secretary entered hastily in a dither.

"What do you want?" asked Reggie testily.

"Well, Mr Trevelyan . . ."

But the secretary was not allowed to finish her sentence.

"This meeting cannot be interrupted. Please wait until we have finished," asserted Reggie by way of not giving the secretary even a chance to state her case.

"But, Mr Trevelyan . . ."

Before the secretary could continue, however, the boardroom door was flung open and Detective Inspector Tony Croonacre and Detective Sergeant Myers stood before the distinguished company.

Reggie began to remonstrate at this unprecedented interruption by these strangers but he was stopped in his tracks when Tony Croonacre waved a warrant for his arrest in Reggie's face together with a search warrant for the premises.

Now all hell was let loose. Anita Banks, Lionel McNaughton and Philip Cowan, Reggie's fellow board members, all rose to their feet in unison as if commanded by an external force.

"What is the meaning of this?" demanded Philip.

"What right have you to come in here and disturb us while we are in conference?" asked Anita.

"What authority do you have to barge into a private meeting?" requested Lionel.

Donald Patterson of Patterson Promotions, an honorary member of the Board of Governors, however, elected neither to comment nor to question the authority of the police because he was not at all surprised that old Reggie might have been a naughty boy. Donald, of course, had had his suspicions of Reggie for some time now but he did not know the nature of Reggie's criminality.

Tony silenced the room by stating his business categorically to the infuriated governors and by reciting the famous words of caution when arresting a would-be felon about not having to say anything. When Tony got to the bit about "Anything you do say may be given in evidence," Donald resisted the temptation to say "knickers", thinking that it might harm Reggie's defence.

Reggie was thus charged with offences relating to concealing the origin of illegally-obtained money and with passing funds through a complex process of foreign banking transactions (money laundering, to you). And he was unceremoniously frogmarched off the premises in handcuffs while his fellow board members collapsed in hopeless despair.

Anita burst into tears of frustration. Philip threw the pile of applications for grants on to the floor in a temper. Lionel simply sat still and stared out of the window transfixed by shock. No one could believe that Reggie was a criminal. But was there no smoke without fire?

Donald then claimed that he had urgent business to which he should attend and he left the premises promptly. He also planned to resign from the Board of Governors on his return to the office so that no imputation could be attributed to him. It's called covering your back, you know.

The temporary secretary, furthermore, could not get away from the office quick enough so that she could return to her employment agency and demand another job forthwith. She wanted to distance herself from any scandal obviously. But would she sell her story to the press perhaps? Don't even think about it, sunshine.

Back at the cop shop, Reggie was interrogated by Tony and Dimity during which time Reggie discovered that the fuzz had quite a tidy little body of evidence with which to substantiate their claims and they certainly had enough with which to condemn Reggie outright. Tony, for instance, had photographic evidence of the contents of Reggie's safe, a record of the innards of his desktop computer and documentary evidence in support of his website scams with specific reference to Home Spun plc. That anonymous copper's nark was at it again!

Tony's search team also regurgitated much which would hang Reggie several times over and his house was additionally inspected with a fine-tooth comb within a few hours. Tony, moreover, had confiscated Reggie's office computer which was now in the hands of the technical whizz-kids. After the wizards had given Reggie's computer the once over, of course, they uncovered his numerous charity scams and that made for a very interesting discovery. Tony and Dimity chuckled heartily over a lunchtime drink while Reggie was languishing in his detention cell.

Reggie's bank accounts across the world were, furthermore, unlocked and his taxation documentation too was eagerly prized open. The accounts of the Benefice Charity Trust were similarly scrutinised with a microscope by a couple of number-crunching smart arses.

When all this evidence was thrown at him, Reggie was sensible enough to admit to his wrongdoing even though he did not actually regret any of it.

Apparently Robert Pollard, formerly King Max of the discredited Vendetta Ice band, had revealed Reggie's involvement in the money laundering business in connection with the drug-dealing racket. And this had set the police authorities hot on his trail. What a bastard you are Max, thought Reggie.

Max's kosher accountants, Prentice, Klevier and Degottle, were also questioned in depth about Reggie's activities but, fortunately for Reggie, they had nothing interesting to reveal which might further incriminate him.

Reggie was thus shortly up before the beak at the Central Criminal Court and he was duly sentenced to ten years to be served at her majesty's pleasure not only for his money laundering activities but also for his numerous charity scams.

The press, of course, as ever hot on the heels of all criminals, with *The Times* at the forefront, feasted for many days on Reggie's demise while the Medici Squadron enjoyed the fruits of their labours as press informants.

When Madeleine read of Reggie's arrest, charge and sentencing, she quaked in her boots. She realised that she should have gone to the police a long time ago with her suspicions, although she was glad that her former employer had eventually been run to earth while she was working elsewhere.

Reggie languished in clink for many years to come but he made a few friends along the way. He was, however, able to buy favours by instructing his fellow inmates about the ways in which dirty money could be placed in legitimate financial institutions, layered by a series of smart book-keeping practices and, finally, integrated into legitimate bank or building society accounts from which it could be withdrawn with impunity. Reggie also taught his fellow criminals about ways in which they could restructure their ill-gotten gains by breaking up vast sums into smaller units and then spreading the load across into several much smaller accounts.

Reggie wondered, in fact, whether being a teacher of criminals would not be an excellent way for him to earn money in future after he had been released from bondage. This plan, however, backfired for Reggie because his criminal-tuition vocation was detected by the prison warders and so Reggie found himself with an extended sentence once the news had reached the prison governor's ear.

VENDETTA'S INCARCERATION

So the troika of Gerry Paxton, Nigel Dulse and Robert Pollard eventually went down to the dungeons of hell.

They were sadly watched by Harriet Chantry and Greta, who had flown in from a weekend in France for the occasion, but Rouchuka was not sure whether this action was in order to show solidarity for her ex-colleagues, to gloat at their humiliation or to celebrate their final demise. But she gave nothing away with any of her facial expressions.

Rouchuka and Greta sat with their friends Timothy Aitken and his pregnant wife-to-be, Jenny Lander, and Pete Jenkins with his half-sister Wanda Beck. All wore a serious expression but they still felt that they needed to be present for this occasion. The group of friends, of course, had to fight off the paparazzi and for this task they had hired a full security guard contingent just like old times.

John Dawson and Henry Sissingford, however, elected not to be present at the trial but they had asked Wanda to keep them posted which she did efficiently.

After the conclusion of the trial, lunch was on the agenda for the unit in order to catch up on each other's news. There was, of course, an acute sadness about the occasion because it was not one which could be celebrated formally, although there was a positive sense of relief now that the whole sordid charade was over.

All present contemplated their own freedom both in terms of their personal liberty as well as their release from the bondage of being contracted to the group which had formerly been known as Vendetta Ice.

Harriet, still professionally known as Rouchuka, reported on her success in and enjoyment of her role in *Les Miserables*. Everyone was agreed that this career change was the best thing ever for Rouchuka.

Kicker and Jenny handed the assembled company invitations to their wedding which was due to take place in a few weeks. And Jenny and the proud father-to-be spoke about baby things, such as prenatal classes, hypnobirthing and ultrasound scans, and cooed continually.

Wanda reported on her work for the Sissingford Theatre and the success of the venture. Rouchuka was very interested in following the progress of this venture because she had been asked by Henry to open the theatre project officially at a press conference before the opening night. Not another press conference surely? Why was the world so zealous about holding numerous press conferences yet so loathe to talk to the press at all other times?

Rouchuka also added that she hoped to take some of the cast of *Les Mis* to the Sissingford Theatre for a special guest appearance as her further contribution to Henry's excellent project.

John, although not present at the trial itself, elected to join the group of friends for lunch and all were delighted to see him again. He too added to the news about the Sissingford Theatre and he brought Janice and Henry's good wishes.

Detective Inspector Tony Croonacre and Detective Sergeant Dimity Myers, who had been in court sitting in the section allotted to the Crown Prosecution Service lawyers, also celebrated the outcome of the trial and indulged in a round or two of self-congratulation despite the fact that someone else had done all the spade work for this particular case.

Hal and Cynthia had a quick drink before Cynthia had to return to her work at the Hotel Splendora up north and Hal had to fly back to his high-profile opera singer who was strutting her stuff currently at the Sydney Opera House.

Cynthia reported that she had been officially offered the job of Catering Manager at the Hotel Splendora. She would be taking up her new post in the autumn because Kevin Clayburn, the present incumbent, had decided to retire a few months earlier than originally planned. Had a few string been pulled for Cynthia here perhaps?

Hal, of course, remembered Kevin from his time with Vendetta on their northern tour. Hal then spoke of his new job for the opera singer and it seemed that he was gaining more job-satisfaction with this luminary than he had ever done with the brat-pack at Vendetta.

The beleaguered Rocker Blaize had deliberately absented himself from the court hearing because he was currently on probation himself for aiding and abetting the culprits and, therefore, he wanted to keep out of the public eye. He generally kept a low profile these days since the scandal had erupted. Rocker had been prosecuted by the legal beavers but he had skilfully managed to escape with only a crippling fine and a probationary term because he did a cunning deal with the police by ratting on his ex-colleagues. And he thought himself bloody lucky in consequence.

Rocker's drug-taking and womanising had now diminished considerably because he did not want to court any further trouble and his probation officer had recommended that he take a course of counselling. At last plain Dave Wellington had been introduced to this new word.

After his probationary term and his counselling experience, Dave Wellington dropped the Rocker Blaize handle, gave up the glitzy showbiz life completely and returned to live permanently in Castle Lucia with Marie and Léon.

Marie and Léon agreed, albeit with some reservations, to the arrangement for the sake of the remuneration and their tied residence. They did, however, managed to negotiate with their master that their dog Timeo could have a greater freedom in the grounds of Castle Lucia in future and this sweetened the pill of having Dave permanently on their doorstep and under their feet.

Léon was slightly sorry that Dave did not do so many drugs and women these days because it meant that he, Léon, would lose his commission from negotiating the supply. But, hey ho! You can't win 'em all!

The guilty parties at the trial were sent to different confinement institutions across the UK wherein the depths of hell are reached. No luncheon parties for these guys!

Gerry's notoriety had been well publicised in the worldwide press and so his reputation proceeded him to jail. Gerry continued to be a drug-baron in his new abode as well as the arch wheeler-dealer within the confine. In many respects, Gerry made quite a considerable profit out of being incarcerated and he certainly increased his knowledge and aptitude for crime. After all, when you mix with hardened criminals, some of it will rub off.

Initially Gerry had been incensed over the fact that what he had said to that bloody Isabel Franklin woman had reached so many shores. His words had also been highly embellished and unrecognisably distorted in the process. Gerry did not, furthermore, relish having his innermost thoughts exposed to the news-reading public. Gerry had expected to be praised for his success but, conversely, he was maligned by the journalist. Gerry did not even consider tracing this unknown Isabel because he reckoned that he was in enough shit already. Once in clink, however, Gerry benefited from his publicised misdeeds because he was now infamous in the criminal fraternity.

When Gerry's time was up, he was then well qualified to carry on his bad deeds and to make even more money which he would not live long enough to spend.

Myra had a whale of time because his sexual services were well sought after and he was able to charge large sums for the pleasure. Because Myra was allowed to bring his guitar into prison, he was, moreover, much in demand as an entertainer. Myra wondered what other crimes he could commit so that he could get back inside, after his release, in order to rejoin his new lifelong friends.

Max, however, found the experience not to his liking really and he rapidly dived down into a state of deep clinical depression which eventually meant that he had to be transferred to a psychiatric institution, the staff of which would care for his mental state and would ensure that he remained alive. Here Max managed to get through life more successfully but he would have liked to have ended it all if possible. Poor fellow!

Another person who was not present at the trial was Reggie Trevelyan who was himself in custody thanks to the confessions of his erstwhile partner in crime Bob Pollard. Reggie, however, followed the trial of the century on the television in his prison cell and he found the event quite amusing and enlightening for some reason.

MEDICI'S CELEBRATION

It had become a tradition now for Calendula and Barrington to celebrate their triumphs with all their friends. And they usually held their celebration in their villa in southern France.

Calendula and Barrington had purchased their small country house as a tax-dodge which no one who mattered in authority knew about. It had been rather run down when they had first purchased it and so the tumbledown dwelling had not creamed off too much of their accumulated savings.

The villa had only three bedrooms and it consisted of a two-storey building. An estate agent would probably describe the villa as a bijoux residence. The small entrance hall led the visitor to a small lounge as well as to a kitchen-diner and a downstairs loo. Upstairs three bedrooms and a bathroom completed the layout.

All rooms were of a neutral decor and a uniformity which resembled French rural culture together with some exposed brickwork and other authentic original features. A log-burner graced the lounge and oil-fired central heating had been installed. Mains drainage was a luxury which was not afforded this property but, at least, the septic tank worked tolerably well.

The residence, however, had an extensive amount of ground attached to it and so it made sense for the party to be held outdoors. The weather fortunately in mid-summer was kind to the owners of the villa and their guests.

Barrington elected himself as the head chef for the occasion while Calendula, the professional artist, was in charge of the decorative arrangements.

Calendula had made some ornamental bunting and an array of streamers for the occasion with a floral theme. She hung her adornments on the trees and on the marquee which the couple had hired for the event in order to keep everything dry if the weather should turn nasty.

Calendula had also provided table-tents for each guest so that everyone knew where to sit when the meal was served. Calendula's table-tents exhibited her calligraphic expertise and they helped all the guests to identify each other. The names on the table-tent place setting were for Maisie Clifton, Maurice Moreau, Jules Axminster, Vince Craven, Hal Caxton, Cynthia Pringle, Janice Evans, Tom Dryden, Foxy Ferguson and, finally, Gemma Gallagher.

There was a hiatus once everything was ready and before any of the guests had actually arrived during which time Calendula and Barrington had to kick their heels while patiently waiting for the jollity to commence.

"So, what shall we talk about, primrose?" requested Barrington as he caressed his beloved partner.

"Our next assignment, perhaps? Or the previous one even, lovebug?"

"The exposure of James Fetherington surely must be done and dusted by now?" replied Barrington referring to last's year project when the politician had been the target of Calendula's highly efficient seduction routine.

"Well, we could take a look at the present government, for instance."

"I have not heard anything untoward on the grapevine."

"Oh, just give it time."

The lovers then proceeded to discuss their latest success but this conversation was interrupted by some voices which sought entry into their garden. Calendula and Barrington now hurried to greet the first of their guests and these newcomers were swiftly followed by the rest of the invitees.

Pre-dinner drinks were served by a number of girls from the village who usually officiated on these occasions and helped Barrington with the washing-up and the clearing-up on the following morning. This team loved these events just as much as their hosts because they were well-paid, well-fed and genuinely appreciated by their employers.

Once everyone had arrived and all the guests had had a chance to be introduced to those whom they did not yet know, Barrington sounded the gong for supper to commence. The invited guests then feasted their eyes and their appetites on the delicious food which had been lovingly prepared by their host.

The sumptuous fayre consisted of five courses.

The first course comprised escargot à la maison Flint, for those who were adventurous enough to be able to stomach the idea of land snails, and duck liver paté, for those who were not. Barrington had lightly fried the escargots in butter with lashings of garlic, lemon and parsley.

The main courses were a variant of coq au vin made with a local vino and a crown roast of rare lamb cutlets. A quiche Lorraine was also thrown into the pudding for good measure.

Next a salad niçoise, a salade verte and a salade Lyonnaise, together with some baguettes made by the local baker, were presented in order to cleanse the palate in the French tradition.

Barrington then prepared a cheese board platter which consisted of a blue Fourme d'Ambert, a Beaufort, a Comté as well as some Roquefort. The French bread also came into its own again during this course.

The desert course comprised a soufflé au chocolat and a dish of oranges drenched in Grand Marnier with coffee to follow.

Some bottles of white Alsace riesling and muscadelle for the first course were followed by a red Côte Chalonnaise and a Grenache as a fitting accompaniment for the rest of the meal.

A good time was had by all and many anecdotes were related of the adventures which had taken place during the project.

Maisie, for instance boasted in jest about having slept with the notorious Rocker Blaize while Maurice spoke affectionately of the lovely Rouchuka.

Cynthia also amused the assembled company by relating the way in which she had skilfully evaded Max's advances while still keeping him cleverly dangling on a string.

Jules and Vince, moreover, spoke of their escapades in Asia and Europe and all those present roared with laughter at their antics and the scrapes out of which they managed to extricate themselves by a hair's breadth.

Hal and Janice next told of their near-misses in the hotel at Newquay when planting Jules' listening devices. Janice then asked the invitees to the party if anyone would be interested in relieving her of her impressive collection of detective fiction.

And Gemma related her seduction of Rowan who had somehow managed to steer clear of conviction.

Tom and Foxy, finally, recalled their invasion of Reggie's premises in order to collect their evidence.

Calendula and Barrington, of course, were the only ones who were party to the complete picture from the bird's eye view perspective.

Once the evening had wound up, Calendula and Barrington relaxed in the small hours of the morning. The guests had all returned to their local accommodation. And all the helpers were dismissed with a "see you in the morning" farewell reminder.

"So what shall we do now?" asked the head chef.

"Might it not be time for a shower, poppet?" replied the set designer.

Barrington gave a broad smile in order to signify his consent and his pleasure at the prospect. The couple somehow always managed to find the energy for high jinks at the end of a long and arduous day. Blimey! How long would they be able to keep this tradition going, do you think?

THE HEEL OF ACHILLES

The Heel of Achilles is the first novel in the Medici Squadron series which traces the antics of Calendula Fortescue-Bligh and Barrington Flint of the Medici Squadron.

The lascivious and mendacious politician James Fetherington believes that he can successfully keep his double-dealing securely under wraps when he teams up with Secretary of State Gregory Tranter. James, however, soon falls prey to the insidious and convoluted manoeuvres of Calendula Fortescue-Bligh and Barrington Flint of the Medici Squadron who mischievously worm their way into his psyche.

SPARRING PARTNERS

Sparring Partners is the third novel in the Medici Squadron series which traces the antics of Calendula Fortescue-Bligh and Barrington Flint of the Medici Squadron.

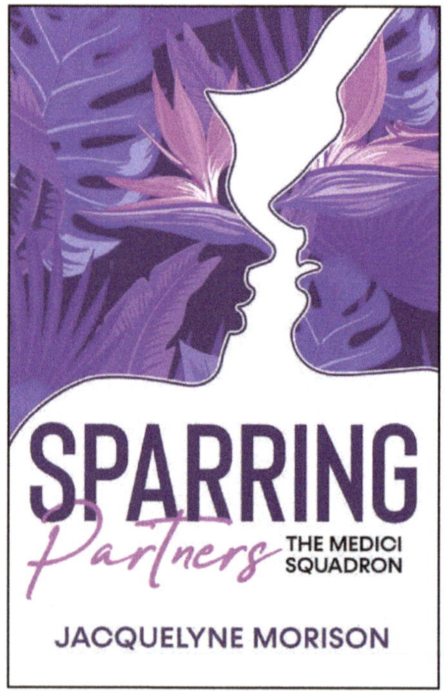

Lucinda Ketterworth is a self-made entrepreneur who runs the hugely successful Squirrels Bank Hall, a health retreat, which attracts shoals of the idle rich. Lucy also offers an additional service for her guests in order to accommodate their needs fully. Members of the Medici Squadron, headed by Calendula Fortescue-Bligh and Barrington Flint, however, decide to unearth Lucy's salacious extramural activity with a view to exposing her duplicity